A DYING FALL

Clive Egleton

This title first published in Great Britain 2004 by
SEVERN HOUSE PUBLISHERS LTD of
9–15 High Street, Sutton, Surrey SM1 1DF.
First published in 1974 in Great Britain by Hodder and Stoughton
under the title *The October Plot.*
This title first published in the USA 2004 by
SEVERN HOUSE PUBLISHERS INC of
595 Madison Avenue, New York, N.Y. 10022.

British Library Cataloguing in Publication Data

Egleton,   Clive,   1927-
    A dying fall
    1.   Hitler, Adolf, 1889-1945 - Assassination attempts - Fiction
    2.   World War, 1939-1945 Secret service - Fiction
    3.   Suspense fiction
    I.   Title
    823.9'14 [F]

    ISBN 0-7278-6131-X

Printed and bound in Great Britain by
MPG Books Ltd., Bodmin, Cornwall.

A DYING FALL

Recent Titles by Clive Egleton from Severn House

NEVER SURRENDER

THE SKORZENY PROJECT

A SPY'S RANSOM

This book is for David and Sheila
with my true admiration

'Of course it was a long shot but even now with the benefit of hindsight, I still think it was worth the gamble because it was the last opportunity we had to end the war in Europe that year. Although we were forced to rely heavily on Major-General Gerhardt of the Panzer Grenadier Division Ludendorf, whose contacts in the German Resistance appeared to enjoy some kind of special immunity from the Gestapo, I never completely trusted that man and to be honest, if Ashby had not been in command, I doubt very much if I would have volunteered. At first it seemed to me that either Gerhardt was just another crackpot like Hess who'd come before him, or else he was trying to save his own skin after the débâcle of the July Bomb Plot.

Ashby, however, was the one person who had unswerving faith in the enterprise and the strength of purpose to see it through when it seemed that every hand was turned against us. In my view, he was just about the most under-rated man in the entire British Army, and whatever his faults, there is no escaping the fact that under his leader-ship we nearly brought it off and re-drew the map of Europe.'

An extract taken from a copy of the After Action Report sub-mitted to the Office of Strategic Services which was given to the author by Major John Ottaway (Retd.) US Army, who was attached to Force 272 for Operation Leopard—the intended assassination of Martin Bormann in the Hall of Peace, Münster, Westphalia on Saturday, 14th October, 1944.

BERLIN

Thursday, 20th July, 1944

'Caesar has his Brutus—Charles the First, his Cromwell
—and George the Third ("Treason", cried the Speaker)
... may profit by their example. If this be treason, make
the most if it.'

PATRICK HENRY IN A SPEECH IN THE VIRGINIA
CONVENTION, 1765.

I

THE CITY SWELTERED in the July heatwave, and in the distance Jurgens thought he could hear the rumble of an approaching storm. From his vantage point on the roof of the Bendler Block he could see the massive Flak Tower in the grounds of the Berlin Zoo which, like a giant sugar cube, rose to a height of forty-five metres to dominate the skyline. There were five similar towers in the Humboldthain and Friedrichshain Districts all of which had been constructed between 1941 and 1942, but at this moment in time, they were only of passing interest.

Since twelve minutes past four that afternoon the city should have been in a state of unrest, but in the Tiergarten people were just strolling home from work, and when he looked towards Wilhelmstrasse some fifteen hundred metres to the north-east, there was no sign of any activity around the Reich Chancellery or the Foreign Office. He was crouching on the roof of the Reserve Army Headquarters, the hub and nerve centre of the revolt, and the only soldiers in evidence were the sentries on the main gate. The army should have been pouring into the city from every direction to seal off the Government quarter, to arrest Goebbels and to seize the radio station, but instead they were quietly skulking in their barracks because no one would believe that Hitler was dead.

Stauffenberg had taken a bomb into the Führer Headquarters at Rastenburg, had seen it go off and when he'd said that it was impossible for anyone to survive a blast of that magnitude, his word had been good enough for Hasso Jurgens, but not, it seemed, for Major-General Paul Heinrich Gerhardt. When he'd learned that Jurgens, in response to codeword 'Operation Valkyrie', had set off along Route 96 with a hundred and thirty men drawn from the headquarters staff of the Panzer Grenadier Division Ludendorf, he'd telephoned OKH Headquarters at Zossen and arranged for the small column to be turned back thirty-two kilometres to the south of the city.

Jurgens had come on alone because he thought he owed it to Stauffenberg, Beck, Quirnheim and the other conspirators, but for all the good he was doing, he might just as well have stayed at home. The scene in the Chief of Staff's office had depressed him immeasurably because, at a time when action was required, there was Colonel-General Beck engaged in a futile debate with Fromm, the commander of the Reserve Army, and Fromm had been trying to persuade the old man to commit suicide because he'd heard from Keitel at Rastenburg that the Führer was still alive. They ought to have shot Fromm, but instead they'd placed him under arrest and then, as if anxious not to seem unduly harsh, they'd sent down to the mess for a cold tray and a bottle of wine so that he shouldn't go hungry. It was, thought Jurgens, a damn funny way to run a revolution.

He glanced in the direction of Prinz Albrechtstrasse where the Gestapo Headquarters was situated and wondered how much longer it would be before there was some reaction from that quarter. Sooner or later they would wake up to the fact that something very odd was going on in the Bendlerstrasse and then there would be all hell to pay. Perhaps they already knew but were reluctant to make a move against the conspirators because they feared a head-on clash with the army. Well, Jurgens had news for them—they'd find any number of allies inside the Bendler Block who were only too keen to do their duty for Führer and Fatherland. He'd heard them talking in the corridor on the third floor on his way up to the roof and he knew damn well that they wouldn't lift a finger to help Stauffenberg. And remembering this, Jurgens began to feel isolated and cut off and he wished he knew what was happening. He was prepared to bet that Stauffenberg was still on the telephone making one last vain effort to persuade the reluctant Generals to act, but they never would. They'd sworn an oath of personal loyalty to the Führer in August 1934 and they were afraid to go back on it. Unable to bear the suspense any longer, Jurgens suddenly left his post on the roof and went back inside the building.

The staff officers were still lounging about in the corridor on the third floor but now they seemed more excited, and an officious Major in the intelligence branch was attempting to organise a search of the building. As Jurgens came towards the group, he stepped forward and accosted him.

'Did you hear the news flash on the Deutschlandsender a few minutes ago, Colonel?' he said.

'No, I didn't,' Jurgens said abruptly.

'There was a bomb attempt on the Führer but fortunately he sustained no more than a few slight burns and bruises. I knew damn well there was something funny going on. I've just been talking to the Signal Corps Lieutenant in charge of the communication centre and he tells me that he's had to deal with a flood of signals.'

'What's so unusual about that?'

'They were addressed to Paris, Vienna, Athens and Brussels and the originator is supposed to be Field-Marshal Erwin von Witzleben.'

'Yes?'

'Well, don't you find that odd, Colonel? Fromm commands the Reserve Army, not Witzleben.'

'I see. Have you spoken to Colonel Stauffenberg about this?'

'I can't get near him.' The Major eyed Jurgens suspiciously. 'May I ask what you're doing here, Colonel?'

'I'm here on behalf of my commander. He wanted to know why the Panzer Grenadier Division Ludendorf is being starved of replacements, but I can't find a single officer in the Personnel Branch.' He frowned and then said coldly, 'I fancy they're too busy gossiping elsewhere.'

'We have reason to believe that there is a conspiracy against the Führer...'

'And what do you propose to do about it, Major——?'

'Steiner, sir. I'm about to organise a search party.'

'Oh, yes?'

'But we're unarmed.'

Jurgens tapped the pistol holster on his hip. 'But I'm not,' he said. 'While I make a reconnaissance of the second floor, I suggest you try to obtain some arms and ammunition from the Town Commandant.' He pushed Steiner to one side and walked on. His heart was thumping wildly.

A small crowd had gathered in Stauffenberg's office now and among the newcomers Jurgens recognised the figure of Witzleben. Apart from lecturing Beck and pointing out how badly the whole affair had been mismanaged, the Field-Marshal wasn't contributing a great deal towards the success of the enterprise. It suddenly came home to Jurgens that he was watching the death throes of the conspiracy and the urge to run was irresistible.

He walked down to the main entrance, strolled past the guards and entered the forecourt. He could see the Kubelwagen parked between an Opel 'Blitz' and a Wanderer saloon but there was no sign of his driver, and then he remembered that he'd told the Ukrainian auxiliary to wait in the canteen, and although momentarily he toyed with the idea of going back inside to fetch him, he eventually decided against it. The need to get well clear of the Bendler Block was uppermost in his mind and he set off at a brisk pace towards the Tiergartenstrasse.

Any thought of rejoining his unit was out of the question because inevitably someone at Zossen would remember Gerhardt's frantic telephone call and the Gestapo would run a check on him. If he was to survive, he'd have to go into hiding and, as the first step in that direction, he would have to get rid of his uniform. In all Berlin he knew only one person who might be prepared to help him. His sister, married to a doctor, had a house in Falterweg on the edge of the Grunewald Forest.

As he turned into the Potsdamer Platz, the leading elements of the Berlin Guard battalion passed him going in the opposite direction towards the Bendlerstrasse. Quickening his stride, he walked into the station and, in an attempt to cover his tracks, bought a ticket to Nicollassee which was one stop beyond his chosen destination. He took the S Bahn up to Friedrichstrasse, changed on to the Potsdam line and then left the train at Grunewald to walk the rest of the way to the house in Falterweg.

He'd almost reached it when it occurred to him that he'd

14

overlooked one vital factor. When his father had died in the summer of '41, Jurgens, who was a bachelor, had nominated his sister as his next of kin and her address was listed in his personal record card. In retrospect, Zossen had been the critical point because if he'd then turned back with the rest of the column, he might just have got away with it, but in choosing to go on alone, he'd tipped his hand. If he was lucky it might take the Gestapo a few hours to reach the conclusion that he'd been involved in the conspiracy, but this in no way altered the fact that sooner or later they would check out his next of kin. Although in his own mind he was absolutely certain that the most savage reprisals would be taken against anyone who even unwittingly helped him now, it still required a conscious effort of will-power to walk on past Falterweg and enter the Grunewald.

He moved deep into the forest and then turning off the ride, he found a quiet spot which would suit his purpose. As if in a trance, he loosened the flap on his pistol holster and withdrew the 9mm Luger automatic. It was a weapon that his father had carried in the First World War and in presenting it to his son, he could never have foreseen the use to which it would eventually be put. Jurgens looked at it, hesitated and then snapped the toggle action back to send the round sliding into the breech. It was a precision-made weapon and even after the passage of years, its mechanism functioned perfectly.

At ten minutes past nine on the evening of the 20th July, 1944, Hasso Jurgens opened his mouth and thrusting the barrel upwards into the roof, squeezed the trigger. Travelling on an inclined plane of fifty-five degrees, the bullet in exiting removed a large fragment of his skull and spattered the bushes behind him with particles of bone and brain tissue.

In choosing to die by his own hand, he had inadvertently pointed an accusing finger at Gerhardt and set in motion a train of events which, taken collectively, would have a profound effect on the final outcome of the war.

Friday, 15th September to
Sunday, 8th October, 1944

'All the business of war, and indeed all the business of life is to endeavour to find out what you don't know by what you do; that's what I called "guessing what was the other side of the hill".'

ARTHUR WELLESLEY, DUKE OF WELLINGTON, 1769–1852

2

DORTMUND STATION WAS operational again but only just. As he stepped down from the train and looked up, Kastner could see the pale September sky through the twisted girders of the roof above the platform. A haze of brick dust hanging in the air produced a false overcast and blurred the definition of each object in sight. The rubble was stacked in untidy mounds in the centre of the island and, as he walked towards the exit, particles of broken glass crunched under his shoes. In passing, he noticed a derelict 4–6–2 locomotive abandoned in a siding while some two hundred metres beyond this, the down lines were a tangle of corkscrewed rails and gaping craters.

Wollweber was waiting for him outside the station with a 1939 Mercedes limousine. He was a short, corpulent, middle-aged man who seemed to think that it was obligatory for a member of the SD to wear a black trenchcoat and dark Homburg even on a warm day such as this. His watery eyes blinked in recognition behind the gold-rimmed glasses and a tentative smile etched itself on his rounded face.

'I hope you had a good journey, Herr Kastner?' he said politely.

Kastner opened the door, tossed his briefcase on to the back seat and got inside the car. 'You know very well that the train was two hours behind schedule,' he said curtly, 'so let's not waste time making polite conversation.' He closed the door in Wollweber's face and then waited impatiently for the older man to join him.

If Wollweber was offended he took great care not to show it. He had it on good authority that Kastner was highly thought of by Reichsführer Heinrich Himmler and by General of the SS Ernst Kaltenbrunner, head of the Reich Security main office, and in his view, it was politic not to antagonise a man who had such influential and powerful friends. Wollweber eased his bulky figure into the car, closed the door and started the engine. Looking over his shoulder, he reversed out of the parking space.

Kastner said, 'I assume the body has already been disinterred and examined?'

'We took action immediately we received your instructions over the teleprinter link.'

'And?'

'We are unable to ascertain the identity of the air-raid victim but it certainly isn't Major-General Gerhardt.'

'You're quite sure of that?'

'We examined the body most carefully and there was no sign of an old tattoo scar. Do you wish to see for yourself, Herr Kastner?'

'No,' said Kastner, 'we'll drive straight to Iserlohn. I want to have a talk with the so-called widow. She has some explaining to do.'

The car bumped over the potholes in the cobbled road and then swerved wildly as the offside front wheel momentarily slid into the tramline. The Hauptbahnstrasse no longer existed; it was merely a highway cutting through acres of rubble, but here and there a fire-blackened shell of an apartment building remained and on the walls the fading chalk marks told their own story—Number 48, ten dead in the cellar, Number 126, eight dead in the cellar, query one still alive? Sometimes it was simpler to pour in quick lime than to dig out the bodies, and in the industrial cities it was not unusual to see an array of postcards displayed outside the newsagents from relatives seeking news of another's survival.

The scene depressed him, and Kastner, suddenly feeling in need of a cigarette, took out a packet of Lucky Strike and lit one. He had developed a liking for American cigarettes and, although he had an almost unlimited supply provided by a friend in the Luftwaffe who confiscated them from prisoners of war under interrogation, he saw no good reason why he should offer one to Wollweber.

Wollweber said, 'The whole of the Ruhr has had a bad time of it.'

'It isn't any picnic in Berlin either but we learn to live with it.'

'We all do,' Wollweber said hastily, 'because in the end we know that victory will finally be ours.'

He glanced surreptitiously at Kastner to see if there was any reaction, but the face of the man sitting next to him was devoid of expression. Wollweber was more than a little afraid of him and with good reason.

Kastner was not human; it was said that he rarely needed more than four hours sleep in twenty-four and that when others dropped in their tracks from sheer exhaustion, he was still fresh and alert. He was acknowledged to be the best interrogator in the Reichs-Sicherheits-Hauptamt and this was partially attributable to the experience he had gained in the Criminal Police from 1931 until he transferred to the SD in 1937. He was an ardent Party member, who owed much of his early advancement to Reinhard Heydrich, but when the latter was assassinated in Prague by Jan Kubis and Joseph Gabchick with the help of the Czech Resistance Movement, he had proved himself to be clever and able enough not to need a patron. At thirty-seven, he was the personification of the mythical blond Aryan created by Goebbels but rarely seen in the flesh. He was also a ruthless killer.

Wollweber said, 'The pre-alert was issued just a few minutes before I left the office.'

'Oh, yes?'

'I expect it will be the Americans again. It beats me how they can keep on coming in daylight when the Luftwaffe is knocking them out of the sky.'

'Are you doubting the claims made by our pilots?'

He was not sure whether Kastner was pulling his leg or not, but Wollweber wasn't taking a chance on it. 'Of course not,' he said quickly.

Kastner opened the side window and flicked the cigarette out into the gutter. 'Naturally,' he said, 'I assume you've interrogated the mortuary attendant?'

The question, coming when it did, almost caught Wollweber off guard. It hadn't occurred to him to interrogate the attendant but he wasn't going to admit it.

'We've had one session with him but I plan to have another shortly. I believe he could tell us a great deal more about Frau Gerhardt than he has disclosed so far.'

'Instead of gossiping with the man,' Kastner said bitingly, 'ask him how the identity papers belonging to a Wehrmacht General came to be found on the body in the first place. And understand this, I want the answer by the time I get back to Berlin tonight.'

Wollweber licked his lips. 'I'll get on to it as soon as we've finished our business in Iserlohn,' he said nervously.

The sirens started to wail as they reached the outskirts of Dortmund and, above the noise of the car, the faint but distinctive crack of the 88mm flak guns could be heard, and later, when they were on a parallel course, Wollweber saw the myriads of white cotton balls which marked the burst of each shell hanging limply in the sky in the far distance.

'Looks as if Düsseldorf is getting it,' he said anxiously. There was no reply and, taking the hint, Wollweber lapsed into silence.

No bomb had yet fallen on Iserlohn. The trams still clanked through the cobbled streets, the market was still held twice a week on the Schillerplatz and, apart from a scarcity of goods on display in the shop windows and the usual propaganda notices outside the post office, there was little tangible evidence of the war. The town had had its share of evacuees from Essen, Dortmund and Düsseldorf and there was a Flak Unit in the barracks on the outskirts, but somehow these strangers did not greatly affect the lives of the inhabitants.

Langestrasse was one of a number of streets which ran out of the market place and climbed the steep hill dominating that particular section of the town. There were a number of small shops and shabby-looking flats at the lower end of this street, but farther up, the apartment buildings gave way to detached houses of individual character. In comparison with those on the crest, Number 77 Langestrasse was a comparatively modest house for a man of Gerhardt's standing.

Kastner said, 'Are you sure this is the right place?'

'I did check the address with the post office earlier this morning.'

'That's what I call foresight.'

'Should I come with you?'

'No,' said Kastner, 'you can wait outside.'

He left the car, walked briskly up the front path and rang the bell. The photograph they had on file in the Amt IV did not do justice to the woman who answered the door, for the camera had given her a tight-lipped expression which made her seem plain and uninteresting. She was wearing a navy-blue suit over a white silk blouse, low-heeled shoes and silk stockings, all of which Kastner thought must have been acquired in Paris at some time or other. The long brown hair softened the angular face, and in his opinion, she appeared much younger than thirty-five.

Kastner said, 'Frau Christabel Gerhardt?'

The woman nodded.

Kastner held out his identity card. 'I'm from RSHA, Berlin,' he said. He waited to see if there would be any reaction, but although the brown eyes were watchful, she was quite calm. 'I'm here on official business. May I come in?'

'Please do,' she said quietly. She stepped to one side, and as he entered the tiled hall, she closed the door behind him. Kastner followed her into the lounge and sat down in an armchair facing her across the width of the room. Silver-framed portraits of her children and of Gerhardt in army uniform were carefully arranged on top of a large writing desk, and on each window ledge there was a row of potted plants. Through the half-drawn curtains in the alcove he could just see the heavy furniture in the dining room.

'Where are the children?' Kastner said abruptly.

'At school.' She glanced at her wristwatch and then added, 'But they should be home shortly.'

She was much too calm for his liking and he sensed that he would have to apply a great deal of pressure before she caved in. No doubt Christabel Gerhardt had mentally prepared herself to face the fact that eventually she would be questioned by the Gestapo and had tried to anticipate the line her interrogator would take.

Kastner said, 'We're trying to locate your husband, Frau Gerhardt.'

'You must know he's dead,' she said quietly. 'He was killed in an air raid.'

'And you identified the body?'

23

'Yes—it was a horrible experience. He was terribly mutilated.'

Kastner took out a packet of cigarettes. 'Do you mind if I smoke?' he said.

'Not at all.'

He held out the packet towards her. 'Would you care for one? They're American.'

'I don't, thank you.'

Kastner lit the cigarette and inhaled. 'It must have been very harrowing for you,' he said softly, 'no head, no legs—imagine being confronted with such a sight.'

'I tried not to look and there was no need to really because they had found his wallet and papers, and when they drew back the sheet and I noticed the wedding ring I'd given him on his finger, I knew it had to be Paul.'

'And when was the last time you'd seen him alive?'

'He came home on leave on the Wednesday and then left for Dortmund on the afternoon of Friday the 18th of August.'

'And subsequently, on the 28th of August, his body was dug out from beneath the ruins of the Kaiserhof Hotel?'

'Yes, it was a great shock.'

Kastner smiled thinly. 'I don't want to distress you,' he said, 'but I just want to clear my mind on a few points.'

'Of course, I understand.'

'Do you know what kind of place the Kaiserhof is?'

'Yes,' she said reluctantly, 'the police informed me that it was a favourite haunt of the local prostitutes.'

'And because he'd been with another woman, you allowed him to be buried in Dortmund?'

'He'd left me,' she said flatly.

'Well, Frau Gerhardt, don't grieve too much about it,' Kastner said drily, 'your husband's still alive and well and in hiding somewhere. We matched the body against his medical documents and certain tattoo scars were missing.'

'I don't believe it!' She thought she had struck the right note of incredulity but Kastner was not impressed.

'You know, I think you're a very good actress, Frau Gerhardt, but I'm not being taken in. Your husband had to die because he was involved in the July Bomb Plot.'

'You know that's completely untrue.'

'He sent an armed detachment into Berlin on the afternoon of the 20th of July with orders to . . .'

'You have the wrong man, Herr Kastner,' she said calmly. 'Lieutenant-Colonel Jurgens, acting entirely on his own authority, mobilised one company and set off for Berlin. As soon as my husband heard about it, he arranged for the column to be turned back at Zossen.'

'Because he developed cold feet.'

'My husband was awarded the Knight's Cross for bravery,' she said angrily. 'He certainly wouldn't run away from a man like you.'

'He saw Stauffenberg frequently.'

'Naturally. Stauffenberg was Fromm's Chief of Staff so he could hardly avoid meeting him.'

Kastner rose from his chair, walked across the room and leaned over Christabel Gerhardt. Reaching past her, he stubbed out his cigarette. 'He was involved, and you helped him to disappear, and I want to know where I can find him.'

'He was not involved, I did not help him to disappear and I certainly don't know where he is now. And furthermore, Herr Kastner,' she said quietly, 'I'm not interested in his whereabouts. There was another woman.'

'Whose name is?'

'If I knew that, I'd tell you.'

She was hard, much harder than he had expected and he admired her for it, but despite her outward composure, her eyes were dilated with apprehension. Given a little time to think things over, she would begin to sweat, and he could afford to wait.

'I hope,' he said harshly, 'I hope for your sake that he wasn't involved in the Bendlerstrasse conspiracy. Perhaps you recall the case of old Field-Marshal Witzleben? He was tried on the 8th of August and two hours later we hanged him at Plotzensee from a butcher's hook on a short length of piano wire. He was naked when he died and he was hung up like a side of beef.' He smiled icily. 'As a matter of fact, we filmed the executions on the orders of the Führer. Did you know that?'

'No,' she said huskily, I didn't.'

'Perhaps I will arrange a private viewing of the film for you—after all, it could happen to you.'

She swallowed hard and he could see that it required all of

her strength of will to stay calm. 'Before you make any further accusations,' she said, 'you ought to know that two days before my husband came on leave, he had a long and private talk with Reichsführer Himmler.'

For a few brief moments he was completely thrown off his stride as he tried to weigh the implications which lay behind that assertion. Where Himmler was concerned you could never be sure.

'Really?' Kastner said quietly. 'Should that impress me? After all, Reichsführer Himmler replaced Fromm as C-in-C of the Reserve Army at midnight on the 20th of July and it's only natural that he should wish to meet his Divisional Commanders.'

'I thought you ought to know, that's all.'

Kastner stepped back. 'I shall call on you again,' he said, 'and until then your movements will be confined to the environs of Iserlohn, and of course you will inform us immediately should your husband or any of his friends attempt to get in touch with you. Do I make myself clear?'

'Perfectly.'

'Goodbye for now then, Frau Gerhardt.'

His footsteps echoed in the hall, the door slammed behind him and presently she heard the car start up and drive off, but it was some minutes before her heart stopped thumping. Before he went away, Paul had warned her that something like this would happen but because they had had so little time to prepare a fool-proof cover story, it had been worse than she had expected. Kastner was toying with her like a cat with a mouse, and she knew that from now on the telephone would be tapped, her letters would be intercepted and opened before they were delivered, and she would be under constant surveillance.

On the afternoon of Tuesday, 22nd August, 1944, a sales representative of the Uddenholm Steel Corporation left Hamburg on the through train for Helsingör. His papers, which were in order, were checked at Puttgarten and then again before he boarded the ferry to Sweden. As soon as he landed at Hälsingborg, he caught the first train to Stockholm where he presented himself at the British Embassy claiming that he was Major-General Paul Heinrich Gerhardt, holder of the

26

Knight's Cross and formerly commander of the Panzer Grenadier Division Ludendorf, but now acting as an emissary of the German Underground.

On Saturday, 26th August, he was flown to England in the bomb bay of an unmarked RAF Mosquito and subsequently was taken by car from Middleton St George to Aylesbury Prison where he was held in solitary confinement for a week before being transferred to Abercorn House for interrogation in depth.

In his desire to gain the trust and eventually the co-operation of the Allied Intelligence officers who were questioning him, Gerhardt willingly disclosed details of the order of battle, state of training and general morale of the various formations in the Reserve Army, and in so doing, earned their contempt. And as a result, it began to dawn on Gerhardt that no one was interested in hearing why he had chosen to come to England, which was a pity, because he had a plan to end the war.

On Friday, 15th September, convinced that they had squeezed him dry, the Allied interrogators turned Gerhardt over to Lieutenant-Colonel Michael Ashby, head of the German Section.

3

EVEN THOUGH THE window was barred, it did not restrict the view of the rolling English countryside which stretched before Gerhardt as far as the eye could see. Oak, elm and beech tree dotted the landscape in haphazard fashion, in keeping, it seemed, with the irregular shape and size of each field. To the professional eye it was good tank country except that the sharply undulating nature of the ground coupled with a number of false crests would restrict the field of fire of any Panther equipped with the long 75mm gun and in consequence the armour would tend to move cautiously. But, in truth, the Panzer Divisions had lost their dash and élan long before they were up-gunned with the 75 and 88mm, and of what use were the Panthers and King Tigers if the crews were incapable of maintaining them? Nowadays mechanical failure accounted for almost half the total tank losses, but three years ago it had been a different story.

Gerhardt had been with Guderian's Panzer Group then, spearheading Von Bock's thrust into central Russia, and nothing had stopped them. From Brest Litovsk to Smolensk, motoring on their tracks, they'd gone through the Soviet armies like a knife through butter, but in the end the cup had been snatched from their lips. The road to Moscow lay open but instead they had found themselves back-tracking some four hundred miles to complete the destruction of Budyenny's forces trapped in the Kiev encirclement. They'd all but worn out the tracks on their Mark IIIs and IVs but, by God, they'd achieved something no other army had or ever would.

The mirror above the washbasin reflected the mixture of pride and arrogance in his lean face and Gerhardt was suddenly disturbed, for such an attitude would not make an ally of Ashby. Tact and honesty and perhaps diffidence were required and all he had to offer was bravery. This meeting could be the most important event in his life, and if he were successful, the effects could be far reaching.

A Bedford fifteen hundredweight came down the long narrow drive and drew up outside the house and a tall officer in battledress stepped out. Looking down from above, Gerhardt saw that he was a Lieutenant-Colonel and knew instinctively that this must be Ashby. He was a little disappointed that his visitor had not arrived in a staff car, for in his opinion, a man who arrived in a Bedford truck obviously did not have much influence. He noticed also that Ashby walked with a slight limp and he wondered if this was the result of a war wound.

Gerhardt checked his appearance in the mirror, ran a comb through the sleek black hair and then nervously adjusted his tie. He'd arrived from Sweden wearing a well-tailored suit but, for reasons of their own, his interrogators had confiscated it and issued him with a brown pinstripe which, fitting badly, hung loosely on his slight frame and made him look ridiculous. In his anxiety to create a favourable impression, he first arranged the upright chairs so that they would be facing one another across the trestle table and then he straightened the lightweight blanket which covered its surface. Gerhardt, who had expected his visitor to knock, was surprised when Ashby walked into the room unannounced.

He was hardly an inspiring military figure and he seemed indifferent to his appearance. No effort had been made to face the lapels on the utility battledress blouse which was of a slightly different shade from the trousers. Although his face reflected the pallor of a man used to working in an office there was no hint of flabbiness about his body, but the set of his mouth indicated a certain disenchantment with life. Until he removed his cap, Gerhardt had thought that they were roughly the same age, but the shock of fair hair suddenly made him look younger and he guessed, correctly as it happened, that Ashby was about thirty-five.

He smiled almost shyly and said, 'My name is Ashby. Won't you please sit down, General.'

Gerhardt refrained from bowing and Ashby gave no sign that he wished to shake hands with him. 'I'm pleased you were able to spare the time to come and see me,' Gerhardt said formally.

The smile vanished immediately. 'I was ordered to—some people are of the opinion that my section is under-employed, General.' Ashby took a cigarette out of a crumpled pack and lit it and then leaned back in his chair.

A complete rundown on this particular General had given him an insight into Gerhardt's background and character. This was a man who, as the son of a minor government official, owed much of his advancement in the army to the National Socialist Party. He was known to be ambitious and ruthless, and even though he'd tried to conceal it, being a prisoner of war had done little to blunt an arrogant nature. Gerhardt saw himself as an emissary for the German Underground and evidently he expected to be treated as a willing ally. Ashby thought that it would do no harm if he reinforced a growing suspicion that the British Government attached little importance to what Gerhardt had to offer.

'Tell me,' said Ashby, 'have you had an interesting war?'

'I've fought in Poland, France and Russia.'

'By any standard, I've had a very quiet one. I went to Norway in 1940 with 24 Brigade because someone thought that my knowledge of German would come in useful. Since we failed to take any prisoners, I was diverted to Harstad where for five weeks I guarded a supply dump with a scratch force of gunners until we were evacuated on the 8th of June. My battle experience was seeing a few Heinkel IIIs bombing Narvik in the distance.'

There was, in fact, a good deal more to Ashby than he had chosen to reveal. By May 1941, he had established a network of safe houses which stretched right across Europe from Madrid to Karlsruhe. Known as the Express Way, this route was a means of inserting and extracting intelligence agents, and it remained in operation until it was finally closed down in February 1942, by which time the quality of the information being fed back had led Ashby to conclude that it must have been blown some time in November 1941. The leak was eventually traced to Raoul Garcia, a jeweller in Madrid who, in return for a numbered bank account in Zürich, had become a double agent. This man, supposedly a Socialist who had fought for the Republican Government in the Spanish Civil War, had been responsible for delivering at least four agents into the hands of the Gestapo.

On 10th February, 1942, Ashby had arrived in Madrid via the KLM flight to Lisbon from Prestwick and subsequently kept watch on Garcia's apartment in the Avenue José Antonio. Three nights later, he broke into the flat, surprised Garcia with his Gestapo contact and, in killing them both, was obliged to make his escape through the bedroom window. The apartment was on the second floor and, as a result of landing heavily, he had fractured his right ankle. Since he couldn't afford to miss his flight, medical attention had had to wait until he reached Lisbon. The incident had almost caused a diplomatic row and had offended not only the Foreign Office but also his opposite numbers in the Special Operations Executive who ran the Iberian desk.

'And then you were assigned to the German Section?'

'Who told you that?' Ashby said quickly.

'One of the officers who questioned me shortly after I arrived here at Abercorn House.'

'Major Dryland?'

'I think that was his name.'

'I bet he didn't tell you the half of it. Do you know what I've been doing for the last four years? Sitting on my backside in a comfortable office in St Albans engaged in the vital task of screening the German Nationals we interned at the beginning of the war in order to see if some of them might be released.'

'What is the point of telling me all this?'

Ashby said, 'The whole point, General, is that my section is a bit of a laughing stock, and I can't think of anyone in authority who would pay much attention to me.'

'I tried to interest your colleagues in my plan.'

'Oh, yes?'

'They found it amusing.'

'I can imagine that.'

Gerhardt smiled faintly. 'Suppose you and I share the joke, Colonel?'

Ashby stubbed out his cigarette. 'Why not?' he said. 'I've got nothing better to do.'

Gerhardt propped his elbows on the table and pressed the tips of his fingers together while he carefully weighed each word before he spoke. He needed to fire Ashby's enthusiasm without being too obvious and this was not going to be easy.

'Hitler apart,' he said with emphasis, 'who would you say was the next most powerful man in Germany today?'

'Himmler?'

'It's Bormann. He controls the Nazi Party machine and as deputy leader, he is constantly at Hitler's side. His influence is enormous and he is a compulsive intriguer. Men such as Goering, Himmler and Goebbels both fear and hate him because he now virtually runs Germany from behind the scenes, and without him, I think the whole power structure would collapse. I doubt if Hitler, who since July has gradually deteriorated and is now a very sick man, could hold the edifice together without his help.'

Ashby said, 'I have a feeling that this is where we come to the funny part. According to Dryland, if we help you to kill Bormann the Home Front collapses, the German Underground comes out into the open and we get a clear run into Berlin while you lot hold off the Russians. That's about the gist of it, isn't it?'

'It's a little more subtle than that.'

'I would certainly hope so, because you'd either have to be very naïve or impossibly arrogant if you think you can make a deal with us at this stage of the war.' Ashby pointed at the window. 'Out there,' he said, 'are millions of people who look upon Stalin with something approaching affection and think the Red Army is bloody marvellous, and they would never stand for it, if for one moment, they thought we were, in some way, about to stab the Russians in the back.'

'Major Dryland has obviously distorted everything I said to him,' Gerhardt said bitterly.

'Oh, he ridiculed your idea all right but I doubt if it suffered much distortion.'

The atmosphere was strained and Gerhardt knew that he was in danger of antagonising Ashby to the point where there would be open hostility between them. He needed to convince this man that his motives were not suspect and obviously his initial approach had been wrong.

'If I told you that I had been opposed to Hitler from the

outset I would be lying.'

'Now at least you're being honest.'

'This also is honest,' said Gerhardt. 'I knew that the war was lost after Stalingrad but I did nothing about it because I was content to follow orders. I had first-hand evidence of the massacre of Jews in the Babyi-Yar ravine just outside Kiev in 1943 but, apart from making a verbal protest to my Divisional Commander I avoided taking any positive steps.'

'And then you changed your mind?'

'Yes.'

'Why?'

'Because Stauffenberg proved to me that I was not alone.'

'After this war is over,' Ashby said quietly, 'there will be a settling of accounts. In coming over to us now, General, some people will think that you are merely trying to save your own skin.'

'I think it probable that my wife has already been arrested and is now being questioned by the Gestapo. If anything should happen to her, I don't think I would wish to go on living.'

'I believe you.'

For the second time that afternoon, Gerhardt smiled hesitantly. 'I hope you will also believe that if you do accept my plan it may, just may, help to end the war.'

Ashby could see that Gerhardt was on the point of allowing his enthusiasm to cloud his judgment.

'You weren't so modest when you tried it out on Dryland.'

'I may have over-estimated its possibilities, but this much I do know—if we can lead people to believe that Bormann was killed on the express orders of Himmler, we shall succeed in turning the Nazi Party machine against its own security service. I doubt if even our docile Field-Marshals could idly stand aside and do nothing in such a situation.'

He could see from the expression on the other man's face that the idea was beginning to take hold and although this was what he wanted, Gerhardt was at a loss to know why and how it had happened.

'You know,' Ashby said thoughtfully, 'if we could pull this off, it really would be something.'

Gerhardt smiled. 'I think there is little doubt that it would have a profound effect. I imagine your people will wish to know how much support a team of infiltrators can expect to get inside Germany?'

'You can bet on that,' said Ashby, 'and I'll need a lot of data to convince them that it's a feasible proposition.'

The man was in a pitiful state. Both cheekbones showed extensive bruising and the eyes had closed to narrow slits; the right arm, bent at the elbow, had been so badly dislocated that bone and tendons protruded through the broken flesh. No longer able to walk because the soles of his feet had been flayed with a bamboo cane, he had to be carried into the room and placed in a chair. His name was Johannes Lehr, and his pre-war experience with a small firm of building contractors had led him to being drafted into a Civil Defence Technisch-Nothilfe Battalion based on Minden. Until his arrest, Lehr had been in command of a rescue squad and during the month of August 1944 when the air raids on the Ruhr had reached a new and horrific peak, his Teno battalion had been called in to assist the local authorities in faraway Essen, Gelsenkirchen and Dortmund. It was his misfortune to be in charge of the team which had brought out the dead from beneath the ruins of the Kaiserhof.

Wollweber closed the file on his desk and then looked up to face the prisoner. 'I should congratulate you,' he said acidly, 'you were on to a very good racket while it lasted. In times like these, I can think of quite a number of people who might wish to disappear officially. Tell me, how much were you paid to find the body of General Gerhardt?'

Lehr moved his lips with difficulty. 'I wasn't,' he said thickly.

'You seem to forget that less than forty-eight hours ago, the mortuary attendant from Dortmund picked you out on an identity parade held in your battalion barracks. Must I also remind you that in his sworn statement this man declares that he saw you place a ring on the finger of one of the unidentified victims laid out in the mortuary, and that when he questioned you about it, you paid him the sum of three hundred Reichsmark to forget the incident.'

'He's lying to protect himself.'

'But we searched your bunk in the barracks and under the floorboards we found a tin box containing eight thousand,

34

seven hundred and sixty-eight Reichsmark. I suppose you'll be telling me next that this sum represents your life savings.'

'I've told you before,' Lehr said obstinately, 'I don't know anything about a tin box; if you found one, it must have been planted there.'

'Presumably by an enemy of yours?'

'Possibly.'

A smirk appeared on Wollweber's face. 'Oh, come now, you must do better than that.' The plump soft fingers drummed the desk. 'Why persist with this stupid story when every man in your team has confessed that they are in on your various little rackets? We know for a fact that you have been fencing looted property through Erhard Thierback's junk shop on Bismarkstrasse!'

'I'm not saying anything.'

'With the evidence we already have in our possession, we could have you tried and executed if we so wished. Of course, I'm not saying that I can get you off, but five years wouldn't be so bad, would it? I mean, it's better than dangling on the end of a rope? And all I want is the name of the man who asked you to arrange Gerhardt's death.'

Lehr was approaching his fiftieth birthday and he had no illusions left. He was a dour, stolid Westphalian and although he gave the impression of being the converse, he was not slow on the uptake. Not for one minute did he believe that Wollweber would keep his word, but in helping the Gestapo, his life would be prolonged for a few days or even weeks if he was lucky and, viewed objectively, there really was no alternative.

He said, 'I don't know his name but I can describe him.'

'Try not to be vague,' Wollweber said harshly, 'because it won't help you.'

'I only met him the once.'

'Let's hope you have an excellent memory then.'

'It was on a Sunday, about five weeks ago in Minden. He came up to me in the Ratskeller while I was having a drink and we made the contract.'

'Just like that?'

'Why not? Erhard Thierback had made all the preliminary arrangements.'

'Perhaps Thierback can give me his name.'

'He makes a point of never asking for names.'

'So?'

'So this man's about sixty, maybe older, well dressed but his suit was a little shiny. He's a small man, thin face, white hair and I thought he might be a professor or a lawyer or something like that. I also think he lives locally.'

'Why?'

'Thierback said he seemed to know his way around the city.'

Wollweber sighed. 'You know,' he said smoothly, 'I don't think you're helping us at all.'

'There's more—he kept his right hand tucked inside his jacket pocket while he was talking to me and I got the idea that he didn't want me to see it. Anyway, when he came to leave, he forgot all about it as he pushed the door open. He's missing one, maybe two fingers and he holds it like a claw as though he had arthritis.' Lehr half-closed the palm of his left hand to demonstrate what he meant. 'See, like this,' he said.

The room seemed to be getting darker and Lehr knew that if he didn't get back to his cell where he could lie down, he was going to pass out.

Wollweber said, 'Where did you collect the General's clothes?'

'Clothes?' Lehr said muzzily. 'What clothes? He gave me an envelope containing the money, a gold ring and a Wehrmacht pay book.'

'And?'

There was a roaring noise in his ears and his voice seemed to come from a great distance. 'I was told what sort of body was required.'

It was possible that he was lying but Wollweber didn't think so, for in his judgment, Lehr was not an inventive man and the description had too much of an authentic ring about it to be a mere figment of the imagination. It was, in any case, the first tangible lead that had been uncovered and it might just placate Kastner. For all their surveillance measures, the watch on the Gerhardt woman had so far proved abortive, and from his point of view there was much to be said for widening the search to include Minden. It would at least get Kastner off his back. He had Lehr taken back to the cells and then, picking up the phone, he placed a call through to Berlin.

4

DRYLAND STOPPED TO buy a copy of *The Star* from the vendor outside the London Pavilion and then, tucking the newspaper under his arm, he turned the corner into Shaftesbury Avenue and hurried towards the Trocadero where he had arranged to meet Leonard Pitts of the Ministry of Economic Warfare. Dryland was a slim, athletic-looking young man of twenty-six, and his service dress uniform, tailored by Hawkes of Savile Row, fitted him perfectly. His hat, by Herbert Johnson of Bond Street, was worn at a slightly rakish angle in the style originated by Admiral Beatty, and this impression of the jaunty, combat-experienced officer was completed by the two medal ribbons displayed above the left breast pocket. Of these, the Africa Star with First Army clasp was in a sense rather fraudulent.

Although he had been in North Africa during 1942 and the early part of '43, Dryland had spent most of his time in Algiers and only on rare occasions had he ventured forward to First Army Headquarters, but since he was on the strength of that army, he was entitled to the appropriate clasp and the fact that he did not deserve it, had not prevented him from promptly claiming the award. As he was quite blatant about it, this faint streak of dishonesty, which had always been present in his character, was looked upon as a sign of eccentricity in an otherwise personable and efficient Intelligence officer.

Like the Rainbow Corner on the opposite side of the street, the Trocadero had been a popular haunt with the Americans, but since the Normandy landings their presence in London had not been so noticeable. This apart, there had been little change, for Scotch whisky was still as scarce as ever. As he walked into the room, Dryland saw at a glance that Pitts had not yet arrived, and edging his way through the throng at the bar, he found himself a niche in the corner and ordered a small beer.

The battle for Arnhem was still dominating the headlines in the paper and in an effort to secure the Heveadorp ferry, the Polish Brigade had been dropped south of the Neder Rijn River that morning. Further down he read that the Guards and the 82nd United States Airborne Division had run into stiff opposition north of Nijmegen in their bid to link up with the British 1st Airborne which, after five days of savage fighting, was slowly being cut to pieces. Dryland put the paper to one side and looked up in time to see Pitts enter the bar.

He stood there on the threshold, a large shambling man in his late fifties, his baggy three-piece suit looking as if he had slept in it. In 1940 he had been lured away from the quiet sanctuary of Oxford to join the political warfare section in Hugh Dalton's Ministry, and having enjoyed the comfort of a somewhat cloistered existence for many years, it had been a shock to Pitts when he discovered that in London he was expected to fend for himself. A confirmed bachelor, he lived alone with two neutered Siamese cats in a mews flat off Cadogan Gardens. He had been Dryland's history tutor when the latter was up at Oxford and on occasions, he was still inclined to treat him as an undergraduate. His blank gaze swept the room until at last recognition dawned and he ambled towards Dryland with a broad smile on his face.

Dryland said, 'I'm glad you could make it, Leonard. Can I get you a drink?'

His watery eyes took in the row of bottles displayed behind the bar. 'Since one can't get a decent port these days,' he said morosely, 'I think I'll settle for a whisky.'

'I'm afraid it will have to be Irish, sir.'

Pitts favoured the barman with a disbelieving stare which had no effect whatsoever. 'In that case,' he said ponderously, 'I'd be obliged if you would drown it in ginger ale.' He turned a calculating eye on Dryland. 'Are you dining here by any chance, Tony?'

The inquiry was made in the hope that, as usual, he would not have to pay, and Dryland was getting just a little tired of Pitts's habit of sponging off him. This time he had a cast-iron excuse.

'Laura's expecting me for dinner,' he said.

'Laura?'

'Laura Cole, one of our secretaries. I met her husband in Algiers in 1942—he's an officer in the Pay Corps.'

'Pretty, is she?'

'Attractive.'

'I recall you had an eye for the girls when you were up at Oxford.'

Dryland put on a wry smile. 'I always run into problems.'

'I don't see where the problem arises if her husband is still in North Africa.'

'My problem is an Acting Lieutenant-Colonel by the name of Ashby.'

'Oh, yes?' Pitts said vaguely. 'I don't think I know him.'

'You will. He's stolen a march on the Special Operations Executive of your Ministry.'

'Really?'

'I'm not joking.'

'My dear Tony,' Pitts said grandly, 'I'm sure what you have to say is much too serious to be taken lightly. Who is this man Ashby?'

'Have you come across MI21?'

'No.'

'I'm not surprised; it's easily the most dormant intelligence department in the War Office. If you look them up in the staff list, you'll find they are known as the German Section and I'm afraid we made the error of turning Gerhardt over to them after we had finished our interrogation in depth.'

Pitts glanced about him. 'I don't think we should discuss this affair in public, Tony,' he said guardedly.

'Why not?'

'My dear boy, think of all those posters—careless talk costs lives—that sort of thing.'

'Ashby has a plan to assassinate Martin Bormann.'

'For God's sake, keep your voice down.'

'It involves active co-operation with the Nazi Party,' Dryland said softly, 'at least, Gerhardt implied as much when he

39

first broached the subject to us, but our friend Ashby has been astute enough to erase any such inference in the paper he presented to the Director of Military Operations.'

Pitts raised his eyebrows in mock surprise. 'It's got as far as that, has it?'

'He short-circuited the usual channels.'

'How?'

Dryland finished his beer and ordered another round. 'The old pals act,' he said. 'You know how these regular officers cling together—someone probably said, "Let's give old Michael Ashby his chance."'

'The War Office isn't a charitable institution, Tony, he must have impressed them.'

'He met Gerhardt for the first time last Friday and now, six days later, DMO has cleared his plan subject only to final approval by your Ministry. That's what really impresses me.'

'I'd be more impressed if you came to the point.'

'All right, Leonard—your department can veto this project and I want you to stop Ashby. Shall I tell you why?'

'Not here you won't,' Pitts said firmly. He drank the rest of his whisky hurriedly and placed the empty glass on the bar. 'We'll take a taxi back to my place, if we can find one.'

Dryland stole a glance at his wristwatch and saw that he had about forty minutes in hand before he was due to meet Laura Cole. Even allowing for the journey at both ends, he calculated that he had ample time to win over Leonard Pitts. His argument was, after all, extremely simple—the war was virtually won and now the prime consideration should be to safeguard the peace. There must be no more dissension among the Allies, for Churchill's infatuation with the Balkans had already soured Anglo-American relations, and he shuddered to think what might happen if it became known that the War Office was secretly making overtures to the German General Staff through a deadbeat Lieutenant-Colonel called Ashby.

'Very well,' said Dryland, 'let's go. I'm sure if you speak nicely to the doorman, he may be able to get us a taxi.'

'Tipping,' Pitts said loftily, 'helps to perpetuate our class system and it is an anti-social habit. I will not be a party to it.'

*

Ashby was looking for eleven men and he had come north to a camp just outside Ormskirk to find them in the ranks of the Pioneer Corps 1268 Company, a unit composed entirely of Austrian and German Nationals. A high percentage of these men had spent the early part of the war in an internment camp on the Isle of Man and were known to Ashby, whose section had vetted them before they were released. They included doctors, lawyers, writers, artisans, intellectuals, democrats, communists, socialists, conservatives and trade unionists. United only in their hatred of the Nazi Party, they were a fractious group of men who, since being released, had been employed on menial tasks for which they were totally unfitted, with the result that they had become demoralised. After a day spent in their company, he was forced to recognise that they were scarcely the ideal material for a great enterprise.

He had started with a list of thirty possibles taken from the records his section in St Albans had built up over the years, and as one by one they had appeared before him in the bare Nissen hut which had been set aside for his use, they had answered his probing questions truthfully or evasively according to their natures, so that by the end of the day Ashby had been forced to reject all but three. The names of these men— Gunther Albach, a forty-five-year-old lawyer from Berlin, Ewald Remer, a thirty-nine-year-old lecturer in political history from the University of Heidelberg and Karl Frick, a labour leader from Hamburg—leapt at him from the otherwise naked sheet of foolscap clipped to the millboard.

Of the three men, only Frick was equipped for the task he had in mind. A dedicated communist, he had gained a reputation for being a tough negotiator and long before 1933 his activities in the Hamburg shipyards had made him an enemy of the Nazi Party. He had seen the writing on the wall when Hindenburg had appointed Hitler to be his Chancellor and on the day the aged Field-Marshal had died, Frick had left Germany for good. Exiled in Paris, he contributed articles to *L'Humanité* and earned a precarious living as a writer until the Spanish Civil War broke out. German intervention in that conflict saw him become one of the first volunteers for the International Brigade. With the defeat of the Republican Government, and having twice been wounded in action,

Frick arrived in England in April 1939.

It seemed to Ashby that in failing to get the men in the numbers he required, he might just as well face the fact that the operation would inevitably be shelved. A priceless opportunity would go by default and he would have to return to his poky little office in St Albans where he would be forced to sit it out for the rest of the war. If that happened, his only consoling thought was that no one could possibly object if he took a few days leave. He rarely saw Katherine and the children who were living up in Yorkshire on her father's farm and he knew that they were gradually drifting apart. Jeffrey was just eight and Elizabeth was only six and it was scarcely surprising that he was a stranger in their eyes. In the last five years, the family had spent less than a month together.

The soldier tapped politely on the door before he entered the hut. He looked absurdly young and at a guess Ashby thought that he was still under twenty. He had an open, almost childlike face and any woman would have envied him his long black eyelashes.

He said, 'May I attend to the blackout, sir?'

'You needn't bother, I'm just about to leave.'

The soldier hovered and looked embarrassed. 'I'd like to volunteer, sir,' he said quickly.

'For what?'

'I know you've been interviewing a lot of men today and I wondered if you would consider me?'

Ashby said, 'And your name is?'

'Scholl, sir, Klaus Scholl.'

'And your age?'

'Nineteen, sir,' he said eagerly. 'There are others of my age in the company who would like to...'

'I don't suppose you even know what you're volunteering for, do you?'

'No sir, but I would like to play a bigger part in this war than I'm now doing.'

'You'd better see to the blackout.'

'Does that mean you won't consider me?'

'Did I say that?' The boy shook his head. 'Well, then,' said Ashby, 'don't jump to conclusions.'

Scholl turned away, switched on the lights, and then picking up the plywood screens, slotted them into the window frames.

'How long have you been in England, Scholl?'

'I arrived here in June 1939 with my mother and sister.' He swallowed and then said, 'You see, my mother is Jewish and my father decided to get us out of Germany while there was still time.'

'Did he come with you?'

'No sir,' Scholl said woodenly, 'he had to remain behind because he was an Inspector of the Criminal Police in Wuppertal and the authorities would not let him have a passport. We last heard from him in 1942 when my aunt in Zürich forwarded a letter he'd written to my mother saying that he'd been granted a divorce.' Anger showed in his pale green eyes. 'They had no right to make him do that.'

'Does it bother you being a kike?'

'What?'

'A yid—one of the chosen—a Jew—does it get under your skin?'

'Sir,' Scholl said loudly, 'have you got something against Jews?'

'No, I just wondered if you were sensitive about it.' Ashby smiled. 'Before I cut you off in mid-sentence, you were about to say that you knew of others who might like to be interviewed.'

'I know of one who would.'

'Yes?'

'Willie Haase—unlike me, he's a pure Austrian. His father was a close friend of Chancellor Schuschnigg, and since he was on their wanted list, he had to get out of Vienna in a hurry when the SS followed the army into Austria.'

'I think I'd like to meet him.'

'Now?'

'Yes. Don't look so worried—if he's like you, I want him.'

Scholl was too young, too sensitive and too immature but Ashby was playing the numbers game. At the back of his mind was the knowledge that no one in Whitehall had expected him to find a team of German nationals but now, with a bit of luck, he could tell them that he had Gerhardt, Albach, Remer, Frick, Scholl and Haase. With six he was halfway there, with six already committed, the Special Operations Executive might even allow him to tap their resources.

Laura Cole avoided looking at the picture frame on the dressing table whenever she brought Dryland back to the two-roomed flat in Grenville Place just off the Cromwell Road. To make love to another man in front of her husband's photograph still troubled her vaguely. On those rare occasions now when she was really pricked by her conscience, she liked to think that he was probably keeping a mistress happy somewhere in Algiers, and of course there was no getting away from the fact that he was in a much safer place.

He was exposed to very little danger in a Base Pay Office seven hundred miles from the nearest fighting, and he certainly had never seen a flying bomb trace its fiery comet across the night sky, had never held his breath when the deep-throated snarl of its jet engine suddenly cut out, counted off the seconds while it plunged towards the earth and then jumped when the warhead exploded. He didn't have to cope with ration books, clothing coupons and shortages; he didn't have to queue for buses and trains or limit himself to a bath once a week in five inches of tepid water. He didn't know what it was like to make two ounces of butter last for a week or a meat ration which was barely sufficient for one meal, but above all else, Laura Cole had convinced herself that since he was having such a marvellous time of it, he was never bored or tired or sick of the damn war.

They had pub-crawled after dinner and although she was pleasantly tight, she resented it when Dryland took the key out of her hand and opened the door.

'You don't own me,' she said belligerently.

'Of course I don't.'

'Then stop acting as if you do.'

Dryland closed the door behind him. 'Are you trying to pick a quarrel with me?' he said lightly.

'I don't like your attitude.'

'I annoy you?'

'You most certainly do.'

'In that case I wonder you can bear to work in the same office with me.'

As she placed the camel-hair coat on its hanger in the

wardrobe, she caught a glimpse of the petulant expression on his face in the full-length mirror and she felt uneasy. No one had to remind Laura Cole that she would still be working in a munitions factory in Acton but for Dryland's intervention and that if she left her reserved occupation for any reason, she would have to go wherever the Ministry of Labour directed.

She faced him with a bright smile. 'Now you're being stuffy,' she said pertly.

Dryland sat down on the bed. 'I've had a bad day.' He lay back and patted the eiderdown and then, in a persuasive tone of voice, he said, 'Come over here and be nice to me.'

Laura Cole hesitated briefly before kicking off her shoes and then she walked across the room and lay down on the bed beside him. 'What is it this time?' she said.

'A man called Ashby—he's about to upset the applecart with a plan to co-operate with the German Underground.'

'What plan?'

Dryland thought about taking her into his confidence and decided against it. 'He's hoping to arrange a separate peace,' he said. The lie was, in any case, stronger than the truth and suited his purpose better.

'He must be crazy.'

'I made the same mistake and underestimated him. Ashby may be self-effacing and devious but he's a long way from being crazy. He's hoodwinked our chief and the Department of Military Operations, and unless Pitts can block it through his Minister, his plan will receive official support and blessing.'

'And then what happens?'

He reached out and touched her shoulder-length brown hair. 'Well, I expect we shall have to lend him a hand.'

'We?'

'Ashby will have to keep in close touch with interested parties here in London and he can't very well do that from his St Albans office. I daresay we can find a corner for him and provide any secretarial support he'll require.'

'And is that where I come in?'

Dryland rolled over on to his side and brushed his lips against her mouth. 'Maybe. It would certainly be a tremendous advantage to know exactly what he has in mind.'

'So that you can put a spanner in the works?'

Dryland managed a convincing laugh. 'Good heavens,

Laura, whatever put that ridiculous idea into your head?'

He kissed her again and this time his mouth opened and her tongue found his. By any standard, she was an attractive and desirable woman and one who was easily aroused, and Dryland knew that as long as he professed to care for her, Laura Cole would be only too happy to do anything he asked of her. He placed a hand on her knee and slowly moved it up under her dress until he was able to caress the softness of her thighs above the rayon stockings.

5

TRUSCOTT'S OFFICE WAS on the ground floor of the Main Building and faced the inner, triangular-shaped courtyard which was permanently in shadow. Furnished to War Office scales and decorated in the drab style favoured by the Ministry of Works, the only touches of colour in the room came from the maze of charts, posters and graphs which covered every wall. Pride of place in this exhibition of military art had been given to an organisational chart which, by means of a family tree, reminded Truscott of the various intelligence sections for which he alone was responsible.

In relation to the other sections, MI21 was something akin to an illegitimate child, and as such, its place in the family was indicated by a dotted line. Until the Gerhardt affair had arisen, this broken line had not seemed very significant, but now Truscott had discovered that, because the chain of command was ill-defined, Ashby was able to consult the Director of Military Intelligence without reference to him. It was not an arrangement which exactly pleased Truscott, but since he had been in the chair for a bare three months and his opinion of Ashby had necessarily been formed as a result of a one-day visit to St Albans, he was reluctant to make an issue of it.

He had been posted into the appointment after commanding an armoured regiment in Italy and he had little taste for office politics. Dryland had led him to believe that Ashby was a nonentity but clearly this assessment was false. It had become quite apparent that he was a man to be reckoned with, for, in the course of one day and contrary to all expectations, he had succeeded in forming the nucleus of a team.

Truscott looked up from the report he had been studying and smiled at Ashby. 'I'm impressed,' he said. 'You obviously didn't intend to let the grass grow under your feet.'

'It might just do that if those people at the Ministry of Economic Warfare dig their toes in.'

'Why should they do that?'

'I don't know, it's just a feeling I have.'

'I think we should work on the assumption that your plan will be approved,' Truscott said firmly. 'And obviously as a start we shall have to provide you with office space in London so that you can keep in touch with everyone.'

'But I don't need an office in London, Colonel.'

Truscott ignored the interruption. 'And I propose to let you have Mrs Cole.'

'Who's she?'

A frown creased Truscott's forehead. 'Take it from me,' he said decisively, 'she's a very competent secretary who is familiar with the War Office routine. You'll find her a great help.'

'Of course you do realise that I shall be away from London for most of the time?'

'Oh?'

'You see, I've arranged to train my team at Trawsfynydd.'

'Where's that, for God's sake?'

'It's a battle camp in North Wales.' Ashby smiled tightly. 'I've got six Germans, only two of whom you could say were soldiers; the others are untrained and unfit.'

'Now that you've brought up the subject of fitness, how's that ankle of yours?'

'The limp doesn't bother me.'

Truscott lowered his eyes. 'I'm glad to hear it,' he said quietly, 'I just wanted to be reassured.'

'I'm a little out of condition from sitting behind a desk, but it won't take me long to get back into shape. Of course, when you stop to think about it, whether I'm fit enough for the job is irrelevant—I'm the only man who can possibly carry it through because no other officer in your department believes in Gerhardt.'

There was a great deal of truth in that statement. From the moment he'd arrived in England, Gerhardt, like Hess before him, had been treated as a crank. Left to himself, Truscott had to admit that in all probability he would have listened to Dryland's advice, and the plan to assassinate Bormann would have been quietly dropped. Not for the first time he wondered at Ashby's influence.

'What are we going to call this team of yours, Michael?'

The Michael came as an afterthought and it was the first time that Truscott had addressed him by his Christian name.

'I hadn't really thought about it,' he said.

'How does Force 272 strike you?'

'It sounds impressive.'

'Well, that's settled then.' Truscott picked up the folder on his desk and leafed through the report until he came to the annexure he was looking for. 'I see you're still short of five men,' he said, 'all of whom have to be specialists.'

'That's right—I was hoping you could persuade the Special Operations Executive to loan us a few.'

'I'll do my best but I can't guarantee that you'll get them.'

'Nobody could ask for more than that.'

Truscott closed the folder abruptly. The remark had left him with the feeling that somehow their positions had been reversed and he was mildly irritated. 'When do you hope to assemble your Germans?' he said coldly.

'They're on their way to Trawsfynydd now, I plan to join them this evening.'

'A bit premature, isn't it?'

'We can't afford to wait for official approval before we start training. The way things are going, within a short space of time there won't be much left of the German Resistance.'

'So what do you propose to do?'

Ashby smiled. 'We'll get the BBC to send them a message of encouragement,' he said, 'that should start the ball rolling.'

Pitts lived in squalor without apparently being aware of it. The net curtains hanging stiffly in the windows were grey with dirt; books which had been removed from the shelves at one time or another now lay discarded in chairs, on the floor and in uneven stacks on the drop-leaf table, and the pungent, foul smell in the room came from a much-used dirt box. One of the two Siamese cats was cleaning itself in front of the electric fire while the other, curled up behind Dryland on the

49

back of the armchair, appeared to be fast asleep. A saucer containing a few pieces of fish and a bowl of water lay in the hearth.

Dryland, forced to sit on the edge of his chair, was too close to Pitts for his liking. At frequent intervals a plump hand came to rest on his thigh and squeezed it affectionately.

Pitts said, 'You must understand that I did my best to stop it, but events were running in Ashby's favour.'

Dryland moved his right leg and the offending hand was swiftly withdrawn. 'What events?' he said morosely.

'My dear boy—the war—what else? Surely you must have realised that Arnhem is about to end in failure?' Pitts shook his head sadly. 'I don't know of a single official in the Ministry who now believes that the war in Europe will be over this year, so perhaps it's hardly surprising that this scheme should be received with something approaching enthusiasm.'

'The Russians won't like it.'

'The Russians, Tony, are still sitting in Poland and no Allied soldier has yet put foot on German soil except as a prisoner. Our people are now in a mood to grasp at almost any straw which might bring this dreary business to a rapid end.' He picked up his glass of port and eyed it thoughtfully. 'Mind you,' he said, 'I don't give much for his chances even though we have agreed to assist him. Most of our best men are already committed, and of those that are available I can think of at least one who is very difficult.'

'And who might that be?'

'Cowper.'

'I don't think I know him.'

'He's a Captain with an MC and bar; did very well in the Western Desert and Italy operating behind the lines; caused no end of trouble on the German wireless nets when he chipped in with false instructions. I'm told that at Alam Halfa he succeeded in changing the axis of a Panzer battalion so that our anti-tank gunners were presented with a perfect defilade shoot.'

'And that makes him a liability?'

'As far as he is concerned, the only good German is a dead one—there are no exceptions. I imagine,' Pitts said drily, 'that that will scarcely go down well with the people Ashby has recruited.' He leaned forward and placed the glass of port on the occasional table. His hand again sought out Dryland's knee and pressed it warmly. 'The Americans have also expressed an interest in the affair, Tony, and they've asked if they can attach an observer to the team while it is under training.'

'What good will that do?' Dryland said cautiously.

'Dearest boy, the State Department doesn't share our schizophrenic attitude towards the Russians because Roosevelt actually believes that he has some influence with Stalin. You don't think they will allow us to upset that special relationship, do you? At the first hint of a deal with the Wehrmacht they'll be on to the Foreign Office and the project will be killed.'

'Ashby has hoodwinked the War Office, what makes you think that he won't do the same to your pet American?'

'Because Jack Ottaway is one of the most experienced operatives in the OSS. Believe me, he's no fool.'

'Not even an intelligent man can see through a brick wall. On the surface, he's planning to assassinate Bormann, and not until the Wehrmacht opens the gates for us will the truth really be known and by then it will be too late.'

Pitts stifled a yawn. 'Time and again I've heard you say that Ashby is about to make a deal with the German High Command but there isn't a shred of evidence to support the allegation, Tony.'

'Do you think I'm a liar?' Dryland said angrily. 'I debriefed Gerhardt—remember? He tried to sell me the idea before he ever met Ashby.'

The sudden outburst startled Pitts and he recoiled instinctively. 'I'm not questioning your integrity, Tony,' he said huffily, 'I would scarcely have argued against backing the concept if for one moment I'd thought that you had been lying.'

An open rift with Pitts was the last thing Dryland wanted and offending him had been a stupid mistake. He held out the olive branch.

'I'm sorry, Leonard,' he said, 'I didn't mean to fly off the handle. It's just that I thought you and I were in agreement.'

'We are, Tony,' Pitts said earnestly, 'we are, dear boy.' The hand was back again on his thigh but in a curious way he was hardly aware of it. Pitts was smiling warmly and for some unaccountable reason Dryland experienced a feeling of relief.

'We must wait and see what happens, Tony. If you do get something definite on Ashby we can always warn our friends.'

'In the State Department?'

'If you so wish,' Pitts said softly, 'but I can think of other parties who have a vested interest.'

The River Weser was low for the time of year and the current hardly disturbed the dark waters, and in keeping with this sombreness, such was the efficiency of the blackout in Minden that the buildings on either bank looked lifeless and empty.

Four men were parked off the road in a broad expanse of meadow which flanked the river at this point, and in the moonlight it was just possible to see the Kaiser Wilhelm monument which, high up on the hillside, faced out across the Westphalian Gap at the Bismarck statue on the opposite side of the Weser. Kastner, however, was not watching the distant hills.

For Johannes Lehr, handcuffed to a uniformed policeman in the back of the car, it was not a pleasant homecoming. His face so bore the marks of Wollweber's interrogation that few of the men who'd known him when he was serving with the Teno battalion would have recognised him now. He was curious to know why they were parked by the river, but successive beatings had so broken and cowed his spirit that he was afraid to ask. He could only suppose that Kastner was watching the house which faced the river and in this he was correct.

The house, partly screened by a row of trees, belonged to Ernst Osler, at one time Doctor of Philosophy and Director of International Studies at the University of Münster. In June 1917, at the age of thirty-one. Osler was serving with the 24th Saxon Division on the Messines-Wytschaete Ridge which dominated the Ypres salient. It had been common knowledge among the soldiers of his company that the British had been tunnelling towards their positions, but they had had no conception of the scale of this enterprise. In the space of two years, the sappers of 2nd Army had driven nineteen galleries under the German positions on the ridge into which they had packed a total of one million pounds of ammonal. On the morning of the 7th June, just as they were being relieved by the 3rd Bavarian Division, these nineteen mines were exploded simultaneously. In the resultant holocaust, the better part of both divisions were decimated. Seconds later 2400 guns began to pound the survivors. Osler's company, reduced to a handful of men, was the only unit to hold its ground in the face of the enemy on that dreadful morning. By nightfall, Osler, his right hand shattered by a bullet, was the only man still on his feet. Before the month was out he had been awarded the *Pour le Mérite*.

Twenty-seven years later, the Gestapo, looking for a man with a crippled right hand had, as a matter of course, checked through the local records of all persons in receipt of a disability pension and thereby had found the man they were after.

This achievement would have satisfied most men, but not Kastner. Wanting to be absolutely sure before making his next move, he had arranged for Lehr to be sent up from Dortmund so that he could formally identify the suspect. That much was straightforward, the rest wasn't. Arresting Osler hinged on whether or not he believed that Gerhardt was just one more General running away from the shambles of the July Bomb Plot. It would be a convenient and comforting hypothesis if that was really the case, but at the back of his mind there was a nagging doubt. The attempt to conceal Gerhardt's disappearance had been clumsy but his escape from Germany had been well organised. It might be that he had stumbled upon yet another subversive group, but there was just a chance that it was something else altogether. Gerhardt, he thought, could be an emissary of some kind.

Kastner leaned forward, tapped the driver on the shoulder and said, 'You stay here while we go across to the house.'

In the darkness of his bedroom on the second floor, Osler saw the three men leave the car and move towards his house. He had been discreetly watching the car for some time with the edgy feeling that its presence was in some way connected with himself, and now suspicion had become a certainty. He noticed that the men were keeping close to one another and, as they drew closer, he recognised the short, stocky figure of Lehr who was limping badly.

Discovery was a possibility that Osler had lived with from the day Gerhardt had escaped to England, but with the passage of time he had been lulled into a sense of false security. He heard their footsteps on the tiled path and presently the doorbell rang, but although he knew that his deaf housekeeper could not hear it, he remained there in the window as if in a trance. It wasn't until they started pounding on the door that he went downstairs to meet them.

The voice was loud and arrogant. It was a voice which had struck fear into the hearts of men all over Europe these last five years for all too often it was the prelude to a long journey in a cattle truck which ended at the gas chamber. The door shook as a foot slammed against it and a crack suddenly appeared in the glass panel.

A surge of anger swept through Osler. 'All right,' he shouted, 'all right, that's enough, there's no need to break down the door, I'm coming as fast as I can.' Opening to the limit of the security chain, Osler peered through the gap. 'Who are you and what do you want?' he said.

'Police. We want to come inside.'

'You have some means of identification?'

Kastner pointed to the uniformed policeman. 'Do you think he's going to a fancy dress party?'

Osler slipped the security chain, stepped to one side to allow them to enter, and then closing the door behind them, switched on the hall lights. 'We have to be careful about the blackout,' he said primly.

'That's not the only thing you need to be careful about.' Kastner turned to Lehr. 'Is this the man?' he said sharply.

Through lips which were still swollen, Lehr said bitterly, 'Oh yes, he's the one all right. If it wasn't for him, I wouldn't be in all this trouble.'

Now that they were close to one another, his appearance shocked Osler. The face, covered in yellow bruises, was like an over-ripe melon which threatened to burst out of its skin.

Kastner said, 'I don't suppose you recognise your friend, do you, Doctor? But he knows you and that's good enough for me.' A thin smile showed briefly but there was no warmth in it. 'We have much to discuss and this is hardly the place for a serious talk.'

Osler touched his dressing-gown. 'If you can give me a few minutes,' he said, 'I'll go and change.'

'That won't be necessary.'

'Oh?'

'You have a study?'

'Why, yes.'

'Then perhaps you would lead the way?'

Osler hesitated, unsure of himself and then, recovering, said, 'Of course. Please follow me, Herr——?'

'Kastner.' He paused for maximum effect before adding, 'Of Amt IV RSHA Berlin. I expect you know about my department?'

'I'm aware of its existence,' Osler said drily. He opened the study door and ushered Kastner inside. 'Do you want your friends to remain in the hall?'

The bleak smile came back again. 'They are not my friends, Doctor. The man Lehr is a prisoner, the policeman is there to see that he doesn't run away—they're quite used to waiting in corridors.' His eyes took in the crowded bookshelves. 'You have a fine library,' he said mechanically.

'Unfortunately I find little time now to enjoy it.'

Kastner dropped into an armchair and crossed his legs. 'Naturally, your work for Foreign Minister Ribbentrop must be very demanding.' He took out a packet of Chesterfields, lit one and idly watched the thin stream of blueish smoke curl up towards the ceiling. 'You haven't closed the door properly, Doctor.'

'I'm sorry, I thought I had.'

'That was careless of you, wasn't it?'

'The lock doesn't always catch.'

'If you say so.'

Osler walked across the room and sat down behind the desk. He clasped his hands together to prevent them shaking. cleared his throat nervously and then said, 'How can I help you, Herr Kastner?'

'You are a very influential man.'

'Oh, I don't think so.'

'There's no need to be so modest, Doctor. We all know what a superb job you made of the Katyn affair, Reich Minister Goebbels was loud in his praises.'

'The murder of ten thousand Polish officers by the NKVD was a terrible crime against humanity, but I know now that compared with the actions of our Einsatz Kommandos on the Eastern Front, it was almost a misdemeanour.'

'You're very frank, but then with Martin Bormann for a friend you can afford to be.'

'I wasn't aware of that.'

'You're being coy again, Doctor. Need I remind you that in 1933 when Martin Bormann took over the management of the Führer's personal funds so thoughtfully provided by Krupp and other industrialists, he came to you for advice, and that through your Swiss friends you were able to suggest some very profitable investments? You see,' Kastner said casually, 'I know a great deal about you.' He pointed to the silver-framed photographs on Osler's desk. 'Your son Joachim, for instance, was a Stuka pilot until he was killed in an air battle off Dover in July 1940, your daughter Irmgard is a doctor practising in Leipzig, and your other son, Karl, is serving with the Flak.'

'You are well informed.'

'I try to be, but sometimes I wonder if I really am.' Kastner leaned forward in his chair. 'You puzzle me, Doctor,' he said.

'Oh?'

'I ask myself why an intelligent man such as yourself should become involved with a petty criminal such as Lehr. Surely, if your friend Gerhardt wished to disappear, you could have arranged a more subtle method? Or was somebody supposed to hush it up?'

'I don't think I understand you,' Osler said hesitantly.

'Oh, come now, we can afford to be frank with one another. I know that it has become politic for our leaders to insure themselves against certain eventualities. Why, even our Heinrich keeps a few tame Jews under his personal protection as a bargaining factor should the worst happen. You follow me?'

'I'm beginning to.'

'Gerhardt is safely in England.'

'He is?'

'We keep a very close watch on the British Embassy in Stockholm, Doctor.'

Osler said nothing, his eyes were on Kastner, searching for a sign that he was about to strike. If events followed a logical pattern, he would shortly be arrested and then it would only be a matter of time until he appeared before Judge Roland Freisler charged with treason. The newsreels had given Osler a very clear idea of the treatment he could expect to receive there. He recalled the pathetic figure of Field-Marshal Witz-leben as, hollow-cheeked and gaunt-eyed, he had stood before the People's Court, obliged to keep his hands in the pockets of his trousers because they had removed his braces, and Freisler had jeered at the Field-Marshal and asked who was this dirty old man who played with himself.

'You know what I think?' said Kastner. 'I think that maybe our Party Secretary is up to something.'

Osler stared at him. 'What did you say?' he whispered.

'On the 10th of May, 1941, Rudolf Hess took off from Augsburg in a Messerschmitt 110 and flew to Scotland, apparently hoping to negotiate a peaceful settlement of the war. At the time, we knew he had undoubtedly been influenced by his old mentor, Doctor Karl Haushofer, head of the geopolitical institute in Munich. He had also been in touch with you. It now seems likely that Martin Bormann as Hess's former secretary was also aware of his intentions. At least, that is my supposition.'

'What are you trying to say?'

'I think Bormann is using Gerhardt as a special emissary.' Kastner leaned forward and stubbed out his cigarette in the ashtray on Osler's desk. 'At any rate, Doctor,' he said softly, 'I'm inclined to believe that that may be the case and hence, I'm prepared to wait. You understand?'

'I'm afraid not.'

'I want to see what happens. If events go a certain way, I want you to remember that I did my best to protect you. In a sense, you are my investment in the future, but I should point out that I intend to cover myself against all risks. I shall have someone watching you all the time—so please, let's have no more indiscretions.' Kastner stood up. 'It's been a pleasure meeting you,' he said smoothly, 'please don't bother to get up, I can see myself out.'

'That man...'

'Who? Lehr?'

'Yes. What will happen to him?'

'Don't worry, your name won't enter into it, Doctor. Lehr has been up to his ears in any number of rackets. We'll keep him on ice in a concentration camp.'

Long after Kastner had departed, Osler was still sitting at his desk. He found it almost impossible to believe that he was still at liberty and he wondered at the mentality of a man who, presented with an open and shut case, had chosen to ignore the evidence before him because of the tenuous association which Osler had with Martin Bormann. He was unaware that Kastner's seemingly inexplicable behaviour had also been influenced by the BBC.

Earlier that night, at Ashby's request, the German language news broadcast had ended with a quotation from Goethe which translated read: Over all the mountain tops is peace.

6

MIST SHROUDED THE Welsh hills and the fine rain had soaked through the rough serge battledress, and his boots were no longer waterproof because the long, wet grass had wiped off the protective dubbin. The damp woollen socks were chafing the skin and as a result there was now a painful blister on the heel of his right foot and Ashby was aware that, with each passing mile, his limp was becoming more pronounced. He had planned this cross-country march of thirty miles with the object of sorting out the weak from the strong but, with less than half the distance covered, he was already fast approaching the limit of his endurance. Sheer will-power alone kept him going. Behind him, strung out over the best part of a quarter of a mile, a line of men followed on in single file, their shoulders bowed under the weight of the equipment they carried.

Way, way at the back, Gunther Albach, the forty-five-year-old lawyer from Berlin, was on the point of collapse. He had concealed the fact that he had been running a temperature before they'd started out on the march and now he had good cause to regret his quixotic behaviour. His body felt as if it were on fire and his legs were like ton weights which refused to move beneath him. He knew that his corpulent figure, balding head and myopic eyesight had ensured that he would always be the butt of every joke and he felt this keenly. Albach had spent the greater part of his life indoors behind a desk and when he'd been in practice, he had gained a reputation for never walking when he could ride in comfort. To add to his misery, the Lee Enfield kept slipping off his rounded shoulder and when it wasn't doing that, his rolling gait caused the rifle butt to bang painfully against his hips. Sweat trickled into his eyes and made them smart and this, coupled with the raindrops on his glasses, made it impossible for him to see the pothole until it was too late; his left foot plunged into it and there was an agonising wrench on the calf muscles as he toppled forward and lay face down in the grass. When at last he found the strength to get up again, the others were no longer in sight.

Cowper moved easily on legs that were strong and supple. In the disastrous retreat of June '42 he'd walked two hundred miles through the desert to get back to his own lines after his half-track had gone up on a mine. Compared with that experience, a march through the Welsh hills on a wet day was a mere stroll. He was twenty-five, lean, dark, fit and supremely confident, and although he was some three inches shorter than Ashby, he was conceited enough to regard himself as the bigger man in every sense. Unlike the others, he walked with head erect. No one in the Special Operations Executive had seen fit to explain precisely why he, Quilter and Stack had been loaned out but he could hazard a guess. Apart from Gerhardt and Frick, and of course Quilter and Stack who made up the rest of the British element, there wasn't a soldier among them. They had to be whipped into shape and it was clear to him that Ashby, who obviously had never heard a shot fired in anger, was not the man for this task. Something drastic would also have to be done about the leadership if this rabble, which someone with a perverted sense of humour had called Force 272, was ever to see action. It suddenly occurred to Cowper that he could always report his misgivings on this score to SOE and, in that instant, he decided to put Ashby on the rack.

At the age of forty-one, Gerhardt was still physically at the peak. Throughout his service he had made a point of keeping fit, and although he did not excel at any particular sport, he had followed, with almost religious fanaticism, a schedule of exercises which included a two-mile run before breakfast. It had not been possible to continue this routine while confined in Aylesbury Prison and at Abercorn House, but this lapse of a few weeks had made little difference to his condition. Other men might allow the physical effort of marching to so dull their minds that they thought only of when it would end, but not Gerhardt, his thoughts ranged far into the future.

If the war ended in unconditional surrender, then in all probability there would be no standing army in post-war Germany and the outlook for the officer class would be very bleak, but the situation would be entirely different if he could bring the war to an honourable conclusion. Germany then would need some kind of a para-military force if only to safeguard internal security. Survival, Gerhardt thought, was everything because even if the Bormann plot failed it would matter little so long as he was still alive. When the time came to re-build Germany, he was quite certain that the Allies would look favourably upon anyone aspiring to political leadership who was a known anti-Nazi, especially if that someone had a conservative outlook. Whatever the outcome, there was a good chance that one day he might become the Foreign Minister or better still, the Minister of the Interior. Control of the police and intelligence agencies was a secure base from which to reach out for power. In becoming the Postmaster of Freiburg, Gerhardt's father had fulfilled a life-long ambition; his son, however, aspired to greater heights.

Because he was lost in thought, it was some time before Gerhardt realised that they were circling in a westerly direction and were therefore starting on the return leg to camp.

Quickening his stride, he caught up with Ashby. 'I see we're turning for home.'

Ashby stopped and, slipping the rifle off his shoulder, sat down on a mound of earth. 'We'll take a breather,' he said, 'and give the others a chance to catch up with us.'

Gerhardt took out a packet of Players and lit one. 'It's strange,' he said.

'What is?'

'Me, dressed in British army uniform and tramping the Welsh hills.'

'You're not the only one who thinks it's a strange business, General.' There was an insolent smile on Cowper's lips. 'Or shouldn't I call you that?' he said softly.

'I don't think it's very appropriate in the circumstances, do you?'

'You have a point, one must be correct.' Cowper turned his back on Gerhardt, ostensibly to watch the rest of the team as they closed up on them. 'I see we've lost a Kraut,' he said in a flat drawl, 'that fat fellow—Apbach, is it?'

'Albach,' Ashby said coldly.

'Oh yes, Albach. I'm very bad at remembering names, Colonel.' He faced Ashby and smiled brightly. 'It's one of my failings, you know.'

'Lack of tact being another?'

Cowper looked puzzled—as an act it was almost convincing. 'Did I put my foot in it?'

'Kraut?'

'Oh, I see—well, my apologies, but it is just a nickname—you know—sauerkraut. Your people eat a lot of that stuff, don't they, General?'

Ashby glanced at his wristwatch. 'It's time we moved on,' he said curtly.

'What about Albach, don't you think someone ought to go back and look for him? He could get lost in these hills.'

'The idea is that we should march thirty miles in under eight hours.'

'Oh quite, but haven't we done more than half the distance already, Colonel?'

'So what if we have?'

'Well, I was thinking that if Mr Quilter, Sergeant Stack and myself went back the way we came, we'd cover more than thirty miles, and if we picked up Albach en route it'll save us organising a search party later.'

'In case you've forgotten, Captain Cowper, I've said this is a forced march.'

'Would it help if we got back to the camp at the same time as your party, Colonel?'

Cowper's tone of voice stopped just short of being insubordinate but Ashby was forced to concede that he had a point. If Albach didn't make it back on his own, he would have to send out a search party eventually. His authority was being challenged obliquely and he needed to reassert it and make it clear to Cowper that he was in command, but on this issue he was not in a very strong position to do so. If he dismissed Cowper's suggestion out of hand, he would be acting like the worst kind of martinet.

'All right,' said Ashby, 'you go ahead and take Mr Quilter and Sergeant Stack with you.'

Cowper nodded; the gesture seemed to indicate that, in accepting his advice, Ashby had acted wisely. 'We'll get cracking then,' he said. Turning about, he set off at a fast lope with Quilter and Stack close on his heels.

Gerhardt waited until they were out of earshot and then said, 'He means to reach camp before we do.'

'You may be right.'

'If he does, you will have made a big mistake. You should have made him come with us.'

'Did I ask your advice?'

Gerhardt flushed. 'No,' he said, 'but in the circumstances I...'

'Then please get the men on their feet,' Ashby said mildly, 'we've lost too much time as it is.'

Ottaway took one look at the bleak rain-shrouded hills and said, 'Jesus, what a dump. Are you sure this is is the right place?'

The driver, a shrivelled-looking gunner in his early forties, said, 'This is trousers all right.' His voice contained an appropriate note of gloom.

'I wanted Trawsfynydd.'

'That's what I said. The only thing you'll see around here, mate, is sheep and Land Army girls and they've been here that bloody long, you can't tell the difference between them and the sheep. Come to that, the ATS aren't much better either.'

Ottaway opened the door and stepped out of the Hillman pick-up into the driving rain. 'Well, thanks for the lift anyway,' he said.

'Don't mention it, chum.' The dead cigarette clinging to his lower lip moved up and down as he spoke. 'I expect I'll see you again some time.'

The gears grated as he shifted into first and the car leapt forward like a startled fawn when his foot slipped off the clutch. The elderly gunner, so Ottaway thought, was about the worst driver he'd ever encountered, and that was saying something.

The camp was just a collection of Nissen huts dotted about

haphazardly on the only flat piece of ground in sight, and the spider's web of cinder tracks which branched off from the main path in all directions added to the confusing maze. Ottaway checked his movement order again and then looked round for a unit signboard which would indicate precisely where in this God-forsaken hole he might find Force 272. His eyes lit on the camp post room and he moved hopefully towards it. He tried the door, found it opened and stepped inside the hut. A girl, her back towards him, was busily stoking the fire.

He had often thought that the ATS uniform had been designed by a misogynist determined to make every woman look a frump but this was one girl who had defeated that aim. Even the thick khaki stockings and the heavy lace-up shoes could not disguise the fact that her legs were very shapely, and the skirt, instead of flaring out like a bell tent, had been tailored to fit hips and thighs snugly.

'If that's you, Maggie,' she said abruptly, 'the post hasn't arrived yet.'

Ottaway cleared his throat. 'I guess I'm not Maggie.'

The girl jumped and, still clutching the shovel in her hand, she turned and faced him. 'I'm sorry, I thought it was someone else. Can I help you, sir?'

The top of her head was about on a level with his eyes and Ottaway judged that, allowing for the low heels, she was still about five eight. The bone structure of her face was perhaps a little too angular but this slight imperfection only made her seem the more attractive. The elderly gunner could be right about the Land Girls and the rest of the ATS but he obviously hadn't laid eyes on this girl.

Ottaway said, 'I'm trying to find Force 272.'

She smiled warmly. 'Would that be Colonel Ashby?'

'Yes. You know him?'

'Not very well. I've spoke to him once or twice, that's all.'

For some unaccountable reason, Ottaway was glad to hear that Ashby was only a casual acquaintance. 'I wonder if you can tell me where I can find him?'

The girl reached for a greatcoat which hung from a peg on the wall. 'I think I'd better show you the way.'

'I don't want to put you to any trouble.'

'It's no trouble, sir.'

64

Ottaway made a wry face. 'Can't we cut out the sir business? What do I call you?'

She smiled briefly as if amused. 'My name is Corporal Bradley, sir.' She walked past him and opened the door. 'Perhaps you'd like to follow me?'

'That I would,' Ottaway said under his breath.

Force 272 occupied two Nissen huts on the far side of the camp, one of which had been divided in two by a hardboard partition. One half served as an office, while the other was occupied by Sergeant Stack who slept apart from the Germans. A farmhouse, commandeered by the army in 1939, had been converted into a makeshift Officers' Mess. The attractive Corporal Bradley pointed out the office and then left him to it.

Ottaway tapped on the door and a languid voice said, 'Come in,' and then added, 'you'll have to give it a shove, it sticks in the wet.'

The advice was well meant and Ottaway took it literally. He put a lot of force behind his shoulder and stumbled into the hut. A Captain, immaculately turned out in a gaberdine suit of battledress, was perched on the edge of a table, idly swinging one leg. He seemed amused by Ottaway's undignified entrance.

'Well, well,' he said, 'if it isn't one of our gallant, American allies. What brings you here?'

'This is Force 272?'

'It is. You're not joining us, are you?'

'So my movement order says.'

'That is bad luck. My name's Cowper, what's yours?'

'Ottaway, Jack Ottaway.'

Cowper shook his hand limply. 'Looking for our intrepid Colonel?' he said.

'I've been ordered to report to a Colonel Ashby.'

'Yes—well, I'm afraid he's still not back from the march yet. I can't think what's keeping him, I've even had time to bathe and change.' Cowper slid off the table and walked over to the window. 'Where have you come from?' he said abruptly.

'London.'

'What sort of journey did you have?'

'Terrible—at least it was as far as Crewe. The train was

packed, people jammed together in the corridors like so many sardines in a tin. I gave up my seat to a woman who had two kids and a small baby. You know what?—it was so crowded she had to put the baby in the luggage rack above her head.'

'War is hell,' Cowper said mockingly.

'I haven't always been stationed in London.'

Cowper turned round and eyed the cluster of medal ribbons on the American's chest. 'No, I don't suppose you have, but then neither have I.'

'Oh?'

'Western Desert and Italy. How about you?'

Ottaway hesitated and then said, 'France.'

A heavy foot kicked the door open and a tall, mud-covered figure entered the hut. Cowper took his hands out of his pockets and, in a deliberately slow manner, stood to attention.

'We'd about given you up for lost, Colonel,' he said cheerfully, and then sensing that perhaps he had gone too far, he smoothly changed the subject. 'Oh, by the way, sir, this is Major Jack Ottaway—apparently he's joining us.'

Ashby grasped the outstretched hand and shook it firmly. 'How do you do,' he said politely. 'Have you settled in yet? Is your room all right?'

Ottaway looked embarrassed. 'I've only just arrived so I guess nobody has had time to show me around yet, Colonel.'

'We must put that right. Cowper will show you to the Mess and then, after you've unpacked, we must have a chat. See to it, will you, Miles?'

'Of course, Colonel.' Cowper paused, and as if the thought had just occurred to him and was of little consequence, he added, 'Oh, incidentally, I'm afraid we've seen the last of Albach. We took him round to the MI room and the doctor packed him off to hospital. I gather he thinks it may be pneumonia.' He glanced sideways at Ottaway. 'If you're ready, I'll take you over to the Officers' Mess.'

'There is just one thing before you leave, Major Ottaway,' Ashby said quietly.

'Yes, sir?'

'I'd like to know why you're here?'

To get this kind of welcome after a miserable journey lasting more than nine hours in crowded, dirty, slow-moving

66

trains without even a bite to eat, was for Ottaway the final straw.

'I didn't ask to come to this lousy, God-forsaken hole, Colonel, but you needed an expert on escape and evasion, and that's why you were landed with me.' He picked up his bag and walked out of the hut before Ashby had a chance to say anything.

After a few paces, Cowper fell in step beside him. 'Now perhaps you know what I meant about it being your bad luck,' he said conversationally.

In 1928, at the age of fourteen, James Ramsay Stack had enlisted as a boy soldier, leaving behind him an ugly back-to-back house in Bootle, a widowed mother, three elder brothers, two of whom had been on the dole for more than a year, one married sister and an unmarried one who was six months pregnant. For some reason which even he found hard to explain, joining the army was not just a means of escaping from a depressing background but rather the fulfilment of a childhood desire. It was a decision which he had never regretted. On that cold January day when he had reported to the depot in Bury, he found himself in the company of three other boys of the same age, two of whom had since died, one of smallpox in India before the war and the other on the beaches of Dunkirk; the third was a prisoner of the Japanese. Only Stack remained—a born survivor.

A short man of stocky build and with sandy hair, he was naturally quiet and withdrawn, and for this reason he was thought to be unfriendly. He had joined the Long Range Desert Group because that form of soldiering appealed to him, but in remaining with Special Forces he had undoubtedly forfeited promotion, a fact which did not worry him one little bit. He had chosen to learn German because, in fighting them, it seemed the logical thing to do, and much to the surprise of his then Commanding Officer, he had shown a remarkable aptitude for mastering the language. He was completely self-contained, a calm, methodical soldier whose fieldcraft and marksmanship would have done credit to any gamekeeper. Although he personally never bothered with such statistics, it was on record that in three years of active service, he had accounted for forty-six men. In so doing, Stack had been awarded the DCM and the MM and had gained a reputation for being a ruthless, unfeeling killer. Nothing could have been further from the truth. He simply did the job he had been trained to do. As he saw it, it was no part of a soldier's duty to die for his country, rather his duty to ensure that the enemy died for his.

When Stack had returned to England in April 1944, the War Office seconded him to the Special Operations Executive as a weapon training instructor and while stationed at Kirkcudbright, he'd met and become attached to a local girl. Although they had been parted for less than forty-eight hours, two letters were already on the way to her, and he had just finished composing the third. Careful and thorough in all things, he read it through before sealing it in the envelope on the back of which he had written SWALK. This finished, he then opened the door of the Nissen hut, saw that the rain had eased off and decided that he would drop it into the post box on his way to the ablutions.

The bath hut was one of the few brick structures on the camp and it contained eighteen showers arranged in two lines back to back. Stack thought that lack of privacy was one of the few drawbacks to army life and whenever possible he preferred to take a shower when he was fairly certain that no one else would be using them.

He struggled through the black-out entrance, opened the inner door, groped for the switch and turned on the dimmed lights. Somewhere a shower had been left running and he swore under his breath. To waste precious hot water when solid fuel was in such short supply was not only careless but criminal. The noise seemed to be coming from the row of showers on his left and he went to investigate. It was then he noticed the pair of naked feet sticking out of a cubicle at the far end of the hut.

Remer was unconscious and lay in a corner on his back, his head supported by the dividing walls. The stream of water from the sprinkler above was playing on to his chest and although it ran down his stomach and thighs in tiny rivulets, traces of lathered soap still remained in his groin and in the pubic hair. There was also a slight graze on his chin and his breathing was laboured and heavy.

Stack turned off the shower and, lifting Remer out into the

passageway, he saw that blood was still oozing from a gash on the back of the German's head. Judging from the nature and size of the wound he thought it likely that the skull had been fractured. Remer could have slipped on the greasy duckboard and struck his head against the regulator, but on the evidence available, Stack thought it doubtful. Clearly he needed more than rudimentary first aid and, pausing only to cover the naked body with his towel, Stack left the shower room and ran towards the Medical Centre.

Within the space of twelve hours, Force 272 had just suffered its second casualty.

7

THE SAUCER WAS chipped and the cup, which was of a different pattern, had a crack stretching from the lip halfway to the base. Both should have been discarded long ago but in these days of almost universal shortage, crockery was not an easy item to replace. Pitts added two saccharin tablets and while he waited for them to slowly dissolve in the tea, he again opened the envelope and withdrew the four enlarged snapshots.

They had been recovered from the body of a German soldier killed in the battle for Orel in November 1941 and despite having been re-photographed were of very clear definition. Arranged in sequence, they showed seven Russians, including a young woman, drawn up in line facing a German officer who appeared to be reading aloud from the millboard which he held before him. In the second and third exposures, the Russians were standing on a raised plank beneath the crude gallows, passively waiting their turn when the NCO in charge of the execution detail would tie their hands behind them before slipping a noose around their necks. Two other soldiers stood poised ready to whip the plank off the supporting trestles. The final shot was of the seven dead still hanging from the gallows, their feet pointing towards the ground like ballet dancers. The girl was in the centre and a placard had been pinned on to her blouse which read *Wir sind Partisan*. According to the information typed on the reverse, the executions had been carried out on the orders of a Lieutenant-Colonel Paul Heinrich Gerhardt, the then commanding officer of the 385th Panzer Battalion.

Superficially, there appeared to be a case against Gerhardt. There was no denying the fact that seven Russians had been hanged, and the Division at least had been identified by the formation signs displayed on the tunic worn by the officer in charge of the execution. There was, however, no positive evidence to show that the men concerned were drawn from the 385th Panzer Battalion or that the soldiers were acting on Gerhardt's orders. In any case, if the Russians were truly partisans, they were not protected by the Geneva Convention and the Articles of War did provide for the execution of captured guerillas. The Soviet Embassy had provided Pitts with some damaging material but their response to his request had been so swift, that even he felt it was suspect. He was anxious that his colleagues should not catch sight of the photographs while they were lying on the desk and he carefully put them away in the envelope before he touched his cup of tea.

Making use of the material posed a number of problems for Pitts. He could scarcely show them to the Minister without disclosing the source, which he was determined to avoid doing at all costs. In approaching his Soviet friends, he had already risked a breach of security, and there was a limit to how far he was prepared to go on Dryland's behalf. The last thing he wanted was a diplomatic row blowing up in his face.

Dryland was a young man with political ambitions, and if he wanted to make a name for himself with the Foreign Office, that was all right with Pitts as long as he himself was kept out of it. The war had embraced Dryland just as he was about to enter the Diplomatic Service, and now that the conflict was drawing to a close, it was natural that, with an eye to the future, he should want to ingratiate himself with the Carlton House lot. Giving the photographs to Tony was one way of getting rid of them, but the matter would have to be handled carefully and they would need to agree on how best they could be used. At the very least, they provided the bait which would lure Dryland round to his flat again, and once that pleasurable thought had occurred to him, Pitts made up his mind. He dialled Whitehall 9400 and asked for Dryland's office extension.

*

For a change, it wasn't raining but the sun looked watery and the small valley was in shadow. Nine Slim Jim figure targets had been arranged in groups of three against a dilapidated stone wall, and at fifty yards in the prevailing light, it was difficult to make out the detail on the playing cards which had been pasted on to the centre of each one. They were getting used to the feel of the Walther P38 9mm automatic but at that range most of the rounds were just clipping the edge of the target or falling short. No one in Force 272, apart from Ashby and Gerhardt, knew the precise nature of their intended enterprise but Stack could tell that, simply by handling the captured German weapons, the team as a whole had suddenly become imbued with a sense of purpose. You could see it in the way they eagerly inspected the targets after each detail had fired and compared their scores.

To everyone's surprise, Ashby was an outstanding marksman with the pistol. Style had a lot to do with it for, whereas they stood sideways on to the target like nineteenth-century duellists, he faced it squarely and kept the automatic in line with the centre of his body. They also dwelt too long in the aim and, as a result, the Walther began to waver in the outstretched arm.

Ashby, Ottaway and Cowper formed the last detail and as they came up to the firing point, Stack handed each man a magazine containing six rounds and then withdrew some distance to the rear to join the remainder of the party who were kneeling on groundsheets in a half-circle. He stood there watching them as they stripped and cleaned the Walthers and suddenly his eyes were drawn to Scholl's right hand, the knuckles of which were swollen and skinned.

'Been in a fight?' he said casually.

Scholl looked up and he was clearly worried. He opened his mouth but the crash of gunfire drowned his muttered reply. Stack wasn't calling for an explanation and really there was no need to because he could make a pretty good guess at what had happened. Most women and some men would find those long eyelashes and his open, almost feminine face attractive and he was prepared to bet that Remer had tried it on with the boy. Remer's mistake had cost him a fractured skull and, in Stack's view, it was no more than he deserved.

He winked at Scholl and said, 'You want to save your

strength until we get into a real fight, lad.'

Ashby fired two rounds into each target, cleared the automatic and then waited for the others to finish. He had seen the strike of each shot and he knew that they had hit dead centre, which was more than could be said for Cowper. His last bullet, missing the target altogether, clipped the stone wall and richocheted off at an oblique angle.

Ottaway said, 'If nothing else, Miles, I guess you would have scared the hell out of them.'

Cowper scowled, made the Walther safe and then turned to face the American. 'Only a fool would play around with a pistol at this range if it came to a real thing.'

Ottaway pointed to the row of Schmeissers laid out on the groundsheet behind the firing point. 'Do you fancy your luck with a sub-machine-gun then?'

'Maybe.'

'Bet you five you don't beat the Colonel.'

'Dollars or pounds?'

'Pounds, of course.'

'You know what we say about you Americans?'

Ottaway grinned. 'Yes,' he said, 'we're oversexed, overfed, overpaid and over here.'

'You said it, old boy, not me.' Cowper turned away and walked off the firing point.

'Now that,' Ottaway muttered, 'is what I call a real friendly ally.' He saw that Ashby had overheard and grinned sheepishly. 'I'm sorry about that, Colonel,' he said, 'but he has a knack of rubbing me up the wrong way.'

'He's the same with most people.' Ashby started to move down the range and then, calling back he said, 'Do you mind giving me a hand with these targets?'

For a moment, Ottaway was under the impression that the request was addressed to Cowper until he saw that Ashby was looking at him. 'It'll be a pleasure, Colonel,' he said.

Quilter saw that Cowper was moving in his direction and wished there was some way to avoid him. He disliked being patronised by the younger man in whose presence he felt totally inadequate. It was an irrational feeling which was partly engendered by the knowledge that Cowper had been decorated and was therefore a rather special person. There was nothing glamorous about being an electronic engineer,

73

but without Quilter's ingenious wireless sets, the SOE agents in the field would be helpless. He seemed a puny man but his appearance was deceptive, for within that wiry frame lay great reserves of strength, as those who had climbed with him on Snowdon, in the Cairngorms, the Alps and the Dolomites before the war would be the first to testify.

Cowper said, 'This is bloody silly.'

'What is?'

'Playing around with these toys. Someone should tell the gallant Colonel that, to survive in occupied territory, an agent depends on his wits and his cover story and no one in his right mind would carry a gun.'

'You never told me that you'd had practical experience at this sort of thing,' Quilter said mildly. 'Like me, I thought you'd only been on a course.'

'I played around behind their lines in the desert,' Cowper said defensively.

'Oh, quite.'

'If you're out to gather intelligence, you look, duck and vanish. You don't go around bumping off people if you can help it.'

'Who said we're to be employed on intelligence work?'

Cowper lit a cigarette. 'Good God,' he said quietly, 'it can't be anything else. Look around you, this lot couldn't fight its way out of a paper bag.'

The narrow stream entered the valley at a point some three hundred yards beyond the stone wall and then followed a meandering course. On either bank, spindly trees and clumps of bushes grew in sharp relief to the bare hills above and seemed out of context with the landscape. Anyone keeping close to the brook would have a restricted field of view and the targets which Ashby and Ottaway had concealed in the trees and undergrowth were meant to test each man's speed of reaction. The battle range would be a demanding test of skill especially as most of them had never handled a Schmeisser before.

Ottaway said, 'You believe in putting them through the hoop, don't you, Colonel?'

'There's no alternative; I don't have the time to waste on lame ducks.'

'You're planning on some wastage in training then?'

'Are you trying to pump me?'

Ottaway smiled. 'I guess I'm curious.'

'I can afford to lose one more before things get critical.'

'Of course, I don't know any of the details but I do have some idea of what you have in mind, which is more than can be said for the rest of your people.'

'Apart from Gerhardt.'

'Yes, well I guess he is the founder member.'

'Why don't you come to the point?' Ashby said quietly.

'I figure you're depending on the German Underground to set Bormann up for you, right?'

'Yes.'

'Can they do it?'

'I'll know ten days from now.'

'I just hope they don't let you down.' Ottaway picked up a stick and threw it into the stream. 'From what our agents over there tell us, I wouldn't bet on them.'

Ashby grinned. 'I'm not asking you to,' he said.

With only a slight variation in time alternating between nine o'clock and twelve noon, the 8th Air Force was beginning to establish a pattern of daylight attacks on the capital. Kastner, working at his desk in the Gestapo headquarters on Prinz Albrechtstrasse, ignored the alert and waited for his call to Dortmund to come through. The sudden urge to speak to Wollweber had been inspired by a photostat copy of a letter addressed to a Georg Thomas, care of the Bishop's Palace, Münster, Westphalia, which had been posted in Geneva on 24th September.

Following the July Bomb Plot, all letters addressed to local government officials and members of the church which bore a foreign postmark, had been subjected to a more rigid scrutiny than had previously been the case, and this note, signed by Baron Pierre Damon of the Credit and Merchant Bank, had been intercepted and opened at the main sorting office in Münster. It read:

I am pleased to report that your proposals have been most favourably received and I am very hopeful that in the near future I shall be asked to act as an intermediary on their behalf. I understand that they were much impressed by your representative, but I should warn you that they will require confirmation from the highest possible source that the articles of agreement can be implemented and if necessary enforced. In this connection they have stated that they are not prepared to deal with any of the present hierarchy with the possible exception of 'Rudi'.

I appreciate that in the circumstances it may be difficult for you to arrange a meeting at short notice but it is essential that I see 'Rudi' immediately I am authorised to do so. As a guide, the third week in October would be appropriate.

I am, of curse, sending a copy of this letter to Count Folke Bernadotte in order that he is kept fully informed.

Although it was written in veiled terms, Kastner felt sure that by implication Damon had agreed to act as an envoy in any peace talks with the British. Remembering his conversation with Osler, he was quite ready to believe that 'Rudi' was none other than Martin Bormann, and he wondered if Gerhardt was the representative to whom Damon referred in his opening paragraph.

The phone on his desk trilled and, answering it, he heard the girl on the switchboard say, 'I have Sturmbannführer Wollweber on the line for you, sir.'

It was, he thought, typical of Wollweber that he should use his SS rank whenever possible.

Kastner said bluntly, 'Has anyone been in touch with the Gerhardt woman yet?'

'No—she's leading a very quiet life—I'd soon know if she had a visitor.'

'You sound very confident.'

'With reason, Herr Kastner. I arranged for one of my ablest officers to be billeted in the house—Frau Gerhardt thinks she's been bombed out of her home in Essen.'

'Do I know this officer?'

'Her name is Ursula Koch; I think you met her about eighteen months ago.'

Kastner remembered Ursula Koch all right, a muscular woman of about forty-five with a face like granite. 'I think she'll serve our purpose,' he said.

Wollweber cleared his throat noisily. 'What purpose have you in mind, Herr Kastner?'

'I want Koch to harass the Gerhardt woman and frighten her out of her wits.'

'I see. You do realise that if, as a result, the Gerhardt woman makes a complaint to the police, I may be forced to remove Koch and it may not be so easy to plant another agent in the house?'

'If Koch plays it intelligently, I think she will get in touch with her friends and not the police.'

'Well, of course you know best, but I must point out that I am reluctant to accept...'

'The trouble with you, Wollweber,' Kastner said harshly, 'is that we all know you're afraid of responsibility and that's why you'll never progress further than Sturmbannführer. Now, just do as I tell you and stop arguing about it.' He slammed the phone down just as the battery of 88mm guns on top of the Zoo flak tower began to open fire.

There were six hundred B17 Flying Fortresses escorted by over four hundred and fifty P51 Mustangs and they were heading straight for the centre of Berlin. The first wave began to drop their bombs on the Lehrter Station north of the River Spree shortly before Kastner reached the air-raid shelter in the basement.

After spending more than two hours in the same room with Pitts and his Siamese cats, it was natural that Dryland should want to be with Laura Cole. From Cadogan Gardens to the flat in Grenville Place where she lived was just over a mile and, although he could have taken the tube out to Gloucester Road, he preferred to walk even though it was drizzling with rain. He needed a drink to take away the sour taste in his mouth but the only pub on the way to Laura's flat had a sign outside which read: Sorry we are closed—no beer.

The photographs which Leonard had given him could be a way of getting at Ashby through Gerhardt, but if it was handled badly, it would appear that he had a grudge against the man. Proving that his evaluation of Gerhardt had been correct had become something of an obsession, for it was his intention to enter the Diplomatic Service eventually and it had been suggested to Dryland that it would be to his ad-

77

vantage if he gained some experience with the Allied Control Commission before he applied. For the past year, he had worked to build a reputation for himself in Whitehall as an expert on German affairs to the point where he thought he was almost bound to be offered a post on the High Commissioner's staff when Germany was finally defeated and occupied by the Allies. Now, thanks to Ashby, his credibility was fast being undermined and that coveted post was in jeopardy. He had hoped that Pitts would be able to torpedo the Bormann project but clearly Leonard was too bloody windy. He had crawled, wheedled, lied and allowed himself to be pawed in return for a miserable selection of photographs which might do him more harm than good.

He turned into Grenville Place and with a sense of relief and impending pleasure, he rang the bell of the flat and waited for Laura Cole to answer it.

Presently, a muffled voice said, 'Who is it?'

'It's me, Tony,' he said lamely, 'may I come in?'

'Must you? Everywhere's in a frightful mess.'

'It's important I see you,' he said plaintively, 'really it is.'

'At this hour?'

'It's only just gone nine.'

'I wasn't expecting you to call round tonight.'

'Please let me in, I won't stay long.'

'Promise?'

'I've just said so.'

'Well, all right, but I warn you, I look awful—this is my make do and mend night.'

The door was opened reluctantly and he stepped into the room. Laura Cole was not the most glamorous sight. She was wearing her husband's dressing-gown over an apricot pink slip and her damp hair was up in curlers. Laid out on the bed was a triangular piece of nylon and what seemed to be a dressmaking pattern.

Dryland said, 'What's that in aid of?'

'I'm making a slip for myself. One of the girls in the typing pool has a boyfriend in the RAF and he scrounged the material—it's part of a nylon parachute and I'm hoping there will be enough left over to make a pair of panties as well.'

'Have you run out of clothing coupons?'

'Of course, ages ago, and at three shillings a coupon I can't afford to buy them on Black Market.'

Dryland removed his raincoat and hat and hung them on the back of the door. 'I'll get you some,' he said.

'I bet.'

'And they won't cost you anything either.'

'Why this sudden generosity?'

'Because I'm very fond of you.'

'Or because you want me to do something for you?'

'To me would be more appropriate.'

A blush suffused her face. 'You really are disgusting at times,' she said. 'To think that before I met you, butter wouldn't melt in my mouth. Would you like a cup of tea?'

'To start with.'

'That's all you're getting tonight.' She removed the pile of darning which littered the armchair and stuffed it into a drawer. 'Make yourself comfortable while I put the kettle on,' she said.

Dryland lowered himself gingerly into the chair in case he inadvertently sat on a needle. The photograph of the gallant warrior on her dressing-table, seemed to be watching him anxiously, and for a moment or two he spared a thought for Frank Cole in far-off Algiers. There was one soldier who, expecting to find the same demure little wife he'd left behind, was in for a big surprise when he returned home from the war.

Laura Cole said, 'I had a telephone call from Colonel Ashby this afternoon.'

Dryland rose from the chair and walked into the kitchen. 'Oh,' he said casually, 'and what did he want?'

'He's coming up to London tomorrow.'

'Is he now? Did he say why?'

'It's something to do with an exercise he's planning.' She shrugged her shoulders. 'At least, that's what I gathered. He's asked to see Truscott at two and the Director of Military Training at three, and he stressed that it was important.'

'I find that interesting.'

'I thought you would,' she said drily.

He caught hold of the cord around her waist and drew her close. 'What's that supposed to mean?'

'Can't you guess?'

'My guess is that you are a very provocative little minx.'

'I'm not sure I approve of that description.'

'Suppose I said you were a very attractive one?'

'Even with my hair in curlers?'

He untied the cord and slipped his arms inside the dressing-gown. 'Even with your hair in curlers.'

She let him kiss her, and her lips gradually parted, and there was this tingling sensation as he slowly raised the slip above her hips. 'The kettle's boiling,' she whispered.

'So what?'

'You wanted a cup of tea.'

'I've changed my mind.'

'I thought that was supposed to be a woman's prerogative.'

'A man should be allowed to change his mind occasionally.'

'We'd better turn the gas off.'

'Yes,' he said, 'you do that.'

She reached out, groped blindly for the tap and turned it off. The gas jet plopped into silence.

'I thought elastic was supposed to be a girl's best friend?'

'It is, but it's almost unobtainable now.'

'I can't undo this wretched button,' he said impatiently.

She placed both hands against his chest and half heartedly tried to push him away. 'What do you think you're doing?' she said quietly.

'I'm trying to undress you.'

'Is this the reason why you had to see me?'

'Can you think of a better one?'

'You've got a one-track mind,' she said weakly.

He moved forward and gently pushed her into the other room.

'The bed's in a frightful mess.'

'Who needs a bed?'

She sniggered. 'You really are a terrible man, Tony.'

He left her standing in front of the gas fire and, as he walked across the room to put out the lights, Laura Cole hastily grabbed hold of the photograph and laid it face down on the dressing-table.

8

THE FILE WHICH Heydrich had started in 1934 now ran to three volumes and it provided a rare insight into the private and public life of Martin Bormann. Its contents embraced hard facts, conjecture, rumour and malicious gossip, and although its principal contributors were Himmler and Kaltenbrunner, various observations made by Hitler, Goebbels, Goering, Ribbentrop, Keitel and Jodl over the years had been included without their knowledge. Seen on another plane, this portfolio also reflected the mutual distrust, petty jealousies, backbiting and schisms within the leadership, and not surprisingly, its circulation was therefore strictly controlled on a need-to-know basis. Excluded from this category, Kastner, aware that Himmler still maintained a tenuous friendship with Bormann, was obliged to seek out Kaltenbrunner who signed the necessary docket giving him access to the file.

In starting the search for a connection between 'Rudi' and Martin Bormann, Kastner checked the list of contents inside the flyleaf of the master file, turned to Index One and extracted the personal data card. As a means of refreshing his memory, it made dull but informative reading.

Bormann, whose father was a middle-grade civil servant in the post office, was born in Halberstadt on 17th June, 1900. Academically he was not gifted, and his formal education was interrupted briefly when he served as a gunner in the 55th Artillery Regiment from June 1918 to February 1919. Following his release from the army, he resumed his agricultural studies until, in August 1920, he obtained the position of farm manager on the Treuenfels estate near Parchim in the northern province of Mecklenburg. Bitterly resentful of conditions in post-war Germany, he joined the Rossbach group of extremists late in 1922 and became its section leader and treasurer in Mecklenburg.

On 31st May, 1923, Bormann and other members of this group murdered Walter Kadow, a twenty-three-year-old schoolteacher who had failed to repay a loan of thirty thousand marks to the Party funds and who was also suspected of being a communist informer. Since Germany was then in the grip of raging inflation, the value of this sum of money in real terms was about ten marks. Arrested two months later for his part in the crime, Bormann was eventually brought to trial before the State Court for the Defence of the Republic in Leipzig and sentenced to one year in prison.

After his release, he drifted into the Frontbann, a league of ex-soldiers who had supported Hitler in the disastrous Munich putsch of 1923, until on 17th February, 1927, he joined the Nazi Party in which, as a comparative latecomer, his membership card number was 60508. Thereafter, his rise to power was spectacular.

After a short spell as Press chief and Party business manager for the Thuringia province, he was appointed to the staff of the Supreme Command of the SA in November 1928, staying there until 25th April, 1930, when he left the Stormtroopers to head the Aid Fund of the Nazi Party. His advance to this post was not altogether surprising because, in the September of the previous year, Hitler had served as a witness of his marriage to Gerda Buch, the daughter of Major Walter Buch, chairman of the Nazi Party Court. From July 1933 onwards when he became Chief of Staff to Rudolf Hess, the deputy leader, he strove to make himself the indispensable confidant of the Führer, and in so doing, ultimately gained control of the Party machine.

In appearance he was unprepossessing. Short and stocky with hunched shoulders and a bull neck, his rounded face with its strong cheekbones, broad nostrils and wary dark eyes reminded Kastner of a sly but ruthless fighter. The straight black hair, thinning in front, was parted backwards and added to this first impression.

Contained in the three volumes was a wealth of information which showed Bormann in an unfavourable light and illustrated precisely why he was feared and hated by everyone except the Führer. He scorned popularity and made no attempt to establish friendly relations with his colleagues who privately referred to him as 'The Bull'. They believed that he was capable of almost any act which would enhance his power and influence and, when Walter Schellenberg who was then deputy chief of Amt VI, first heard the news that Heydrich had been assassinated in Prague in May '42, he immediately concluded that Bormann had arranged it.

He was devoted to Hitler and certainly this feeling also extended to his wife by whom he had fathered ten children but, surprisingly enough, Gerda's view of marriage was somewhat unconventional. Aware that he was having an affair with a minor actress whose fiancé had been killed in action, she proposed that they set up a *ménage à trois*, a suggestion which Bormann had rejected out of hand. Coyly referred to as 'M' in their letters to one another, Kastner was unable to discover any further clue to the identity of this little-known actress.

Of greater interest to him was a certain Margerete Axmann of the Linz Foundation. Although she still owned a small art gallery on the Kurfurstendamm, Axmann now spent most of her time scouring Europe for works of art for the Führer Museum and was in constant touch with Bormann. In a footnote to this item, Goebbels had hinted that they were on rather intimate terms, and if this was so, Kastner wondered if she had an endearing nickname for her lover.

If nothing else, the portfolio had convinced him that Bormann was quite capable of making a deal with the British if he thought it was in the Führer's interests, and although he had failed to discover a link with the man known as 'Rudi', he was not discouraged. He thought it would be politic to know a great deal more about Margerete Axmann.

*

Under the heading of *Escape and Evasion*, Ottaway wrote:

If captured, try to make a break before you wind up in a PW camp since it will be a damn sight more difficult to get away once you're inside—always remember to lie up during the day and move only at night because darkness can be a friend and for obvious reasons it's a lot safer if they start shooting.

He chewed on the pencil and then added:

Take someone with you but don't forget that while two's company three's a crowd—avoid villages and isolated farms if you can, because dogs have a habit of barking at strangers, and beware of children for their eyes miss nothing—a bicycle is the most popular form of transport in Europe today so steal one when you get the chance and stick to the side roads—don't ride a freight train unless you know for certain where it is going and watch out for security checks at railroad stations.

The notes were a little on the bald side but he figured that, with padding, he had enough there for a forty-five-minute lecture, provided they were interested enough to ask questions afterwards. Cowper would try to make him look small if he drew too much on personal experience to illustrate the points he wished to make, but that was a risk Ottaway was prepared to take.

It was laughable to think that one abortive mission in France could turn him into an expert on escape and evasion, but that was the way the Service worked. German was his strong suit but since his French was reasonably good, OSS had picked him for the St Etienne team. Hole up in the Massif Central, they said, and when the Anvil landings begin in the south of France, bring the Maquis out to hit the Germans as they withdraw up the Rhône valley.

The idea was sound, but unfortunately the SS were waiting for them on the DZ and they'd started shooting the moment the Maquis reception party had moved out into the open to meet them. The fire fight had been brief, confused and very one-sided, and everyone with the exception of Ottaway, had been scooped up. Luck had played a part, but it was a dark night and in going to ground and staying there, the SS had failed to notice him as they'd closed in on the rest of the party. He'd spent six weeks on the run before an FFI unit put him in touch with the 29th US Division at St Lo, and apart from the last five days when the French Resistance had taken him under their wing, he'd had to go it alone.

Ottaway pushed the completed notes to one side and stood up. He didn't relish the idea of lecturing to this particular audience and he was glad that Ashby would not be there to hear him. He consoled himself with the thought that if it got at all sticky, he would cut the period short and send them back to the gym for another session on unarmed combat under Sergeant Stack. It suddenly occurred to him that with Ashby away in London and only Cowper, Gerhardt and Quilter for company, there was reason enough not to spend yet another night in camp and he wondered if he could talk the attractive Corporal Bradley into a date. He left the office and set off at a brisk rate in the direction of the post room.

Anne Bradley was twenty-two years old. Born in Salisbury, where her father was the senior partner in a firm of solicitors, she had led a happy but uneventful life until 30th May, 1942. On that night her brother, a pilot in Bomber Command, had been shot down in the first 1000 bomber raid on Cologne. Barely six months later, her fiancé was reported missing believed killed over Hamburg, and this news following so closely on the other, had had a shattering effect. Close to a nervous breakdown, she had absented herself without leave from the officer cadet training unit and had gone to London where, some two days later, she had been arrested on Waterloo Station by the military police as she tried to board a train for Salisbury.

Subsequently, an unsympathetic company commander had told her that, as she obviously lacked moral fibre, she would be returned to duty in her former rank of corporal. A succession of dreary postings followed, until in May 1944 she arrived at Trawsfyndd.

From the moment he had asked her to direct him to Force 272, Anne Bradley had been aware of Ottaway's interest in her. He was, she thought, quite unlike her idea of a typical American, for although he was self-assured, he did not seem to be brash or pushing. In her own mind she had been quite sure that he would find an excuse to seek her out again, and was therefore not at all surprised when he strode into her office.

Ottaway cleared his throat and said, 'Good morning, I wonder if you can help me?'

She smiled. 'I'll try to.'

'Can I mail a letter to the States from here? I have no idea where the nearest FPO is.'

'Have you got it with you?'

'What?'

'The letter. I'm going into town to collect another batch of stamps and postal orders—I'll post it for you when I call in at the post office.'

'I couldn't put you to all that trouble.'

'I won't be going out of my way.'

Ottaway smiled sheepishly. 'I guess I haven't written it yet,' he said.

'Oh, I see—well, just pop it in when it's ready.'

'I was wondering...'

'Yes?'

'What do you do for entertainment in these parts?'

'There's a good hotel in Portmadoc but usually we go to the Wheatsheaf down the road.'

'Would you care to have a drink with me tonight?'

'I'm afraid I can't, I'm on duty.'

'That's too bad.'

'But there's an all ranks dance in the gym.'

'Oh?'

She flushed and hastily brushed a strand of chestnut hair out of her eyes. 'I don't want you to get the wrong idea—all the girls for miles around turn up at the dances.'

'And do you?'

'Sometimes.'

'Like tonight?'

'I thought I might drop in later.'

'When?'

'I'm on duty until last defaulters' call.' She saw his puzzled expression and said, 'Anyone who is confined to barracks has to report to the guardroom on the hour every hour until 2100 hours. I have to be here to check them off.'

'And after 2100 hours?'

'I'll go to the dance.'

Ottaway smiled broadly. 'You know, Miss Bradley, I think we're making progress.'

'Of a kind,' she said.

*

86

From her room upstairs in the attic, Koch saw Christabel Gerhardt leave the house and set off in the direction of the Schillerplatz to meet her children from school. It was a regular event on each afternoon at this hour and predictably she always looked back at the house as if to reassure herself that it would still be there when she returned. Knowing just when she would turn her head, Koch quickly withdrew from the window, for in her own mind she was quite certain that the Gerhardt woman was in fact trying to catch her out, and she took great pleasure in outwitting her. It was, of course, part of the cat and mouse game and there were a lot of cats after this particular mouse because Wollweber had seen to it that every policeman on beat duty would keep an eye on Christabel Gerhardt and report her movements.

A blind unswerving faith in the leadership of the New Order helped to make Ursula Koch the perfect police spy. She remembered all too clearly the last days of the Weimar Republic when there were eight million unemployed and she had known what it was like to go hungry before the Führer had come to power. No one had opposed him when things were going well, but now that there had been a few setbacks, the defeatists and traitors were busy at work. Perhaps not surprisingly, she had no time for Generals like Gerhardt who had so conveniently forgotten their oath of allegiance, and in his absence, she thought it only right that reprisals should be taken against his family. Satisfied that for the next twenty minutes at least she could work without fear of interruption, Ursula Koch descended the attic stairs and entered the master bedroom on the floor below.

It was easy to see that the clothes hanging up in the fitted wardrobe were of a far better quality than she could ever hope to afford, but Koch wasn't interested in the makers' labels. Piling everything on to the bed, she then tore down the hems and ripped out the linings of coats, dresses and skirts. For good measure, Koch selected three pairs of court shoes, and using the bedroom door as a crude vice, wrenched off the heels.

With this bogus evidence of a police search, the harassment of Christabel Gerhardt had begun.

Truscott stared at the large scale map which Ashby had

placed before him on the desk. From Wem in Shropshire a line had been projected north-eastwards across the width of England to Withernsea in the East Riding of Yorkshire. Parallel to this was another line which, running south of Chester, Manchester, Leeds and York, finished at Scarborough on the coast.

Truscott said, 'Would I be right in assuming that your exercise will be confined to the area within the tram lines?'

Ashby shook his head. 'Within reason the escapers can roam anywhere, but they will only have a sketch of the area I've enclosed on the map.'

Truscott looked up with a perplexed expression on his face. 'It might be as well if you went over the details with me before we go cap in hand to the Director General of Military Training.'

It was not a very subtle approach and Ashby sensed that Truscott, intending to do most of the talking when they saw the General, wanted to be quite sure that he had all the facts at his fingertips.

Placing a finger on the map, he said, 'I've chosen to start the exercise off from this point because there is a German POW camp near Wem, and as you will see later, this will give it an authentic flavour. It will end when either our people rendezvous at the safe house outside Market Weighton or when they are all recaptured. I'd like to see the exercise beginning on Friday the 29th of September and it should be over by Tuesday the 3rd of October at the latest.'

'May I ask why Market Weighton and not the coast between Withernsea and Scarborough?'

'My father-in-law has a farm just outside Market Weighton, which in view of its isolation, would make an ideal RV and exercise control point—it's as simple as that.' He waited to see if Truscott had any further questions before continuing. 'Now, I propose to put our people into standard POW clothing when we turn them loose—you know the sort of thing I mean—battledress with coloured circular patches sewn all over it—and they won't have more than five bob in cash on their person, and no food apart from a bar of chocolate.'

'You intend to make life difficult for them.'

'I do. They will get a head start of two hours and then I

88

want the commandant of the POW camp to raise the alarm.'

'And then what?'

'I expect the police, Home Guard and every RAF and army unit to be alerted from north of the Thames to the Scottish border.'

'That's rather a tall order.'

'We can't make do with less.'

Truscott picked up a pencil and tapped the desk. 'How is the team shaping up?' he said tentatively.

'I'm not too sure about Cowper, Scholl and Haase.'

'You know I've had no success with SOE over the extra men you wanted?'

'Oh?'

'They've no more to spare.'

'I can see I'm going to be in trouble if I lose anyone else,' Ashby said drily.

'I understood you were planning to use a team of eight?'

'Yes, I don't have much leeway.'

'You've still got Ottaway up your sleeve.'

'I thought he was merely attached to me as an observer and to help out with our preliminary training?'

'If he is, it's news to me.'

Ashby shrugged his shoulders. 'He seems quite certain of his status.'

'Talking of status, what do you make of Gerhardt? Do you trust him completely?'

'The short answer is no. Oh, I think he will be loyal enough unless we run into serious trouble and then he'll be looking after number one.'

'I'm glad you're aware of the risks.'

'I'm sorry, I'm not sure I follow you.'

Truscott opened a drawer in his desk and produced the series of snapshots depicting the execution of a group of partisans in Russia. 'Dryland uncovered these,' he said. 'I'm afraid that there is conclusive evidence to show that Gerhardt's division was involved in the atrocity.'

Ashby examined the photographs carefully. 'When were they taken?' he said.

'Some time in 1941.'

'Gerhardt was only a battalion commander then.'

'Quite.'

'What's Dryland's motive?'

'I beg your pardon,' Truscott said coldly.

'Why is he so interested?'

'You forget that he helped to screen Gerhardt when he first arrived in this country. He wants to be quite certain that we are not making a mistake.'

'Perhaps he ought to make quite certain of his facts before he starts making allegations. He should have taken a closer look at the NCOs in charge of the execution detail and then maybe he would have noticed the crossed Z emblem.'

'That has some significance?'

'It shows they belong to the 4th SS Police Division.'

'Well, that's quite a relief.'

'May I keep the photographs?' Ashby smiled. 'You see, I wouldn't say that Gerhardt was entirely in the clear and I'd like to hear his explanation some time.'

'Take them by all means.' Truscott frowned. 'We seem to have strayed a long way from the original point of discussion, and we don't have much time left,' he said. 'What happens to your men if they're caught?'

'I'd like them kept in custody until either Ottaway or I can arrange to collect them. I'll have Ottaway keep in touch with the commandant of the POW camp, and of course we'll both need transport.'

Truscott glanced at his wristwatch. 'We ought to be going,' he said briskly. 'The General doesn't like to be kept waiting.'

They called themselves 'The Five Swinging Metronomes' and not one of them was a day under fifty. A conspicuous lack of musical ability was more than adequately compensated for by their sheer, unbounded enthusiasm as each intrumentalist in turn tried to draw out the rest of the band. Piano, drums, saxophone, clarinet and piano-accordion were an odd combination but at least they produced rhythmic music to dance to.

Red, white and blue bunting had been draped around the wall bars to complement the Tricolour, Stars and Stripes, Hammer and Sickle and the Union Jack which hung from the retracted parallel beams in the roof of the gym. French chalk gave the floor a passable surface and a beer bar, which was closely supervised by the Orderly Sergeant wearing a distinctive red sash, had been set up in the changing room while, ignored by everyone present, a couple of regimental policemen stood in the entrance to the gym as a visible reminder that rowdy behaviour would not be tolerated. A pall of blue-grey cigarette smoke drifted like cirrus cloud above the heads of the assembled crowd.

The girls came from miles around on their bicycles, on foot or by bus and, regardless of their age or true reputation, the soldiers referred to them collectively as tarts, judies and crumpet, a slander justified in part by only a very few of their number. For the vast majority, the dance was no more than a welcome break from the grinding, monotonous drudgery of the war, and they were out to enjoy themselves.

Their gaiety was as infectious as it was spontaneous, and although he was frequently jostled as they tried to move around the crowded floor, Ottaway didn't care. Whether she wanted to or not, Anne Bradley was forced to keep close to him and through the heavy khaki skirt he could feel the softness of her thighs. Their heads were touching but she was looking past him and he wondered if she was remembering another time and another place and another man. From the stage, a soldier crooned:

'Missed the Saturday dance,
Heard they crowded the floor,
Awfully lonely without you,
Don't get around much any more.'

'Does that apply to you?' he said quietly.

She moved her head and smiled at him. 'Perhaps it did a few months ago.'

'Thinking about him?'

'Who?'

'Your boyfriend.'

'I haven't got one.'

'How about me? Will I do?'

She laughed and said, 'I'll think about it.'

'I'm free, white and over twenty-one and you would just love Cape Cod.'

'Is that where you live?'

'No, but some day I will.'

'Send me a postcard when you do.'

'Well, that may never happen—schoolteachers are badly paid.'

'I can't imagine you in a classroom.'

'I taught French and German for a year or so after I'd graduated.'

'You don't look old enough.'

'I'm twenty-seven, I guess that makes me an old man, or at least I will be before this war's over. Have you ever thought what you will do when peace finally breaks out?'

'Yes,' she whispered, 'I shall try to forget the war.'

'I could do with some fresh air. I don't suppose I could persuade you to take a walk with me?'

'As long as it is only a walk.'

A lopsided smile appeared on his face. 'What do you take me for?'

'A red-blooded American,' she said lightly. 'My mother warned me about men like you.'

After the humidity inside the gym, the night air seemed damp and chilly, and shivering, she drew close to Ottaway and was comforted by his arm around her waist. They walked briskly along the narrow path which led towards the Range Warden's hut on the perimeter of the camp, and half expecting him to produce the key, she was surprised when he made no effort to lead her inside.

'Now I know you were telling the truth.'

He stopped and turned to face her. 'About what?'

'Going for a walk. I thought it was just an excuse to get me outside.'

'You've got a very suspicious mind, Anne Bradley.'

'Perhaps I have.' She shivered. 'It's cold out here,' she said, 'let's go back.'

'Tell me about him,' Ottaway said firmly.

'Who?'

'The man you're trying so hard to forget.'

'There's nothing to remember,' she said coldly. 'He was a friend of David's.'

'Who's this David?'

'My brother, they were in the same squadron.'

'And?'

'He was shot down over Hamburg two years ago. We were

very close especially after David was killed.'

'I'm sorry.'

'Are you?'

'Of course I am. I like you very much.'

'Now perhaps, but you won't be here for much longer, will you? What is it they say?—out of sight, out of mind?'

He placed his arms around her shoulders and drawing her close, kissed her. 'I won't forget you in a hurry,' he said.

9

THE WIND WHICH had got up towards four o'clock in the afternoon lifted the tarpaulin covering the hole in the roof, and the loud, slapping noise of the billowing canvas eventually disturbed Quilter who woke up feeling stiff and cold. A draught whistled through the gap in the wall where the timbers of the barn had rotted away and aggravated the rheumatic ache in his right shoulder, putting him in a bad humour. Hunger pains gripped his stomach and not unnaturally his thoughts immediately turned to the question of food. Rummaging through his pockets, he brought out the last square of chocolate and, convinced that Stack was still fast asleep, he quickly popped it into his mouth like a guilty schoolboy. Although he tried to make it last, the morsel failed to take the edge off his appetite. Still feeling ravenous, he crawled across the loft, raised the trapdoor and looked down into the barn. A couple of hens pecking for corn in the loose straw attracted his attention and made his mouth water.

Stack said, 'What's up, sir?'

Quilter jumped and lost hold of the trapdoor which fell back with a clatter. 'Christ,' he said, 'must you do that? I thought you were asleep.'

Stack ignored the show of temper. 'Is someone poking around?'

'If there was,' Quilter said irritably, 'the noise we're making would soon bring them up here. As a matter of fact, I was thinking of grabbing a chicken.'

'I had the same idea, but I didn't fancy eating a raw bird.'

He reached out sideways and produced a couple of eggs. 'But I did find these while you were asleep. I hard-boiled them in a scoop which I found outside in the yard.' He saw the look of alarm on Quilter's face and smiled. 'It's all right, sir, nobody saw me.'

Quilter felt the stubble on his chin. 'I need a shave,' he said meditatively.

'There's a rainwater butt behind the barn.'

'Good, I'll just have a quick scrape and then we'll move on.'

'How far do you think we covered last night?'

'Not more than twenty miles.'

'We shall have to do better than that if we're going to be at the RV on time. Seems to me we've got to lay our hands on some form of transport.'

'Pinching a bicycle isn't as easy as Major Ottaway led us to believe—most people have got into the habit of chaining them up.'

'We can always bust the padlock.'

Quilter took out the rough sketch map that Ashby had made and studied it carefully. 'We could try Eccleshall, you never know, we might find something in a cinema car park.'

Stack nodded his head in agreement. He calculated that once they had the bicycles they would be able to average ten miles in the hour. Of course, they would need to allow an hour or more to find a suitable hiding place before first light, but even so, they would cover at least sixty miles during the night. They might do even better on a full stomach.

On the spur of the moment, he said, 'Do you want to eat the boiled egg now or later?'

Quilter looked up from the map. 'I didn't realise you meant me to have one,' he said awkwardly.

'I believe in share and share alike, sir.'

'Well, that really is very generous of you. Perhaps it would be better if we ate them now.' He took the proffered egg and peeled it carefully. To conceal his embarrassment, he suddenly said, 'I wonder how Captain Cowper is getting on?'

'You don't want to worry about him, sir,' Stack said firmly, 'if I'm any judge, he had his feet under somebody's table soon after he parted company with us.'

*

95

The Eastmans had made him very comfortable but it was no more than Cowper had expected, although his only claim to their hospitality was a casual friendship with their son George which had flowered during their last year together at Sherborne. Fortunately, he'd run across George again in Cairo early in '43 and this chance encounter had given him a valid excuse to call on the Eastmans. That they lived on the outskirts of Shrewsbury, which was less than ten miles from Wem, was not as fortuitous as it seemed because Cowper kept a list of potential hosts who were liberally scattered across the country.

The exercise had started at 2130, and ten minutes later Cowper had persuaded Quilter and Stack that it would be in everyone's interest if they split up. Knowing that the alarm would be raised within a couple of hours, he'd set off at a fast pace and had arrived at the Eastmans' before news of the escaped prisoners had trickled down to the police constables on beat duty. He'd openly admitted that he was taking part in an exercise but had implied that, in accepting their offer of a bed for the night, he was not breaking any rules. The problem now facing him early on Saturday evening was how to extend his stay. After some thought, he decided on the direct approach because he was convinced that his hosts would be too embarrassed to refuse him.

Cowper said, 'About the exercise...' Eastman lowered his newspaper and waited expectantly. 'It's really rather stupid.'

'In what way?' Eastman said mildly.

Cowper pointed to his suit of battledress. 'I'm supposed to be an escaped German POW.'

'So you said when you arrived last night.'

'Quite. The point is that I am being tested, not the police or the Home Guard or anyone else for that matter.'

'I'm not sure I understand.'

'If everything was reversed and the Krauts were after me, I would naturally seek help from sympathisers, wouldn't I?'

'Yes.'

'Which of course is exactly what I've done, and you were kind enough to put me up.'

Eastman removed his glasses and polished them with a handkerchief. 'It was nothing,' he said modestly, 'Molly and I were only too delighted. I know your parents would have done the same for George.'

'Of course they would, they're very fond of George.' The statement was untrue; Cowper's parents had met George only the once and they'd disliked him on sight, but he saw no reason to disillusion Eastman. 'And that's why I wondered if I could be bold enough to ask you for another favour?'

'My dear Miles,' Eastman said expansively, 'please don't hesitate to ask, we're always ready to help a friend of George's, especially in these days.'

Cowper did his best to look suitably embarrassed. 'Well then, since you put it like that,' he said, 'I wonder if I could stay with you both until Monday morning? I'll make sure my unit sends you a ration card when I return because I should feel awful if I ate my way through your larder.'

'My dear chap, I'm sure we could manage anyway.'

'And then I wondered if I could borrow some of George's old clothes which I could parcel up and send back when the exercise is over?'

'I think we can find something which might fit you.'

'You're very kind.' Cowper looked down at the carpet and shuffled his feet.

'Is there anything else we can do to help?'

'I don't really like to ask.'

'Oh, come on, there's no need to be so reluctant.'

'Can you lend me three quid?' Eastman looked astonished. 'You see,' Cowper said hastily, 'My Colonel made sure we only had five shillings in our pockets before the exercise began and I need the money for the train fare and so on. I could send you a cheque with George's things.'

'If I do as you ask, wouldn't that be cheating?'

'Oh, no. You see, it's a test of our initiative. I mean, if I was making my way through Holland at this very moment, I'd take money from a Dutch family if they offered it.'

'I see. Well, that puts everything in a very different light. I'm a bit short of cash just now, could it wait until I go to the bank on Monday morning? I mean, there's no desperate hurry is there, Miles?'

'Good Lord, no.'

'Well, that's all right then. How about a drink?'

'I'd love one.'

'I think we've got a drop of whisky left in the house.' Eastman regretted making the offer as soon as the words were out of his mouth.

It amused him to think that they had more in common than Gerhardt would ever care to admit. Physically, there was little between them although, at five foot seven, Frick was the taller of the two by almost half an inch and he was also about ten pounds the heavier. Four years the junior, Frick, despite his thin, receding brown hair, looked much younger than thirty-seven and, rather surprisingly, the years of being down and out in Paris and the experience of the Spanish Civil War had neither aged nor embittered him. Gerhardt might try to give the impression that he belonged to the traditional officer-producing class but Frick sensed that their backgrounds and childhood were not dissimilar. Both were essentially men of action who, given a common aim, could sink their political differences and, in pairing them off, Ashby had shown considerable insight into their characters.

Unlike Quilter and Stack, whose every move so far had been improvised, Gerhardt and Frick were working to a carefully thought out plan. They had conserved their chocolate ration by living off the land on a diet consisting of raw carrots and apples, and they were no longer short of money. Late on Friday night they had broken into a telephone kiosk which had yielded the sum of two pounds eleven shillings and five-pence in silver and copper. Now as they approached the outskirts of Market Drayton, they were on the look-out for a change of clothing.

It was Frick who noticed and immediately realised the possible significance of the signboard fixed on the door of a wooden hut which faced the caretaker's house in the entrance of the Wordsworth Central School.

'Do you see that?' he said quietly.

Gerhardt stared into the darkness, '2097 Squadron, Air Training Corps.' He paused and then said, 'I don't understand, should it mean something to me?'

'It's a cadet organisation—they have RAF uniforms.'

'In there?'

'They are bound to hold a small stock of clothing and we're both about average size.'

'But surely, they're only boys?'

'Sixteen-year-olds and above are encouraged to join by the Ministry of Labour when they register for service.'

Gerhardt looked up and down the street and satisfied that no one was in sight, he removed his boots and vaulting the low stone wall, landed quietly in the asphalt playground. Frick joined him a moment later, took one look at the Yale lock and realising that he couldn't force the door, checked the windows. He found one at the back which hadn't been fully closed because the wooden frame was warped, and using his jack-knife he prised it open. Once inside the hut he waited until his eyes became accustomed to the dark before he crossed the room and opened the door for Gerhardt.

The hut had been sub-divided by hardboard partitions to form a makeshift office in each corner facing the entrance. One was labelled 'Stores', the other 'Squadron Leader Mullins—Knock before entering'. As a gesture towards security, both office doors had been fitted with a frail-looking hasp, staple and padlock which they had no difficulty in forcing, but although there were a dozen suits of varying sizes in the stores, chest and waist measurements ruled them all out and their only acquisition was a forage cap which just fitted Gerhardt.

Frick said, 'I thought it was too good to be true.'

'You forget there is still the other room.'

'I doubt if we will find anything there, but maybe we'd better take a look before we call it a day.'

The moon broke through the scudding clouds long enough for them to see that, superficially at least, Mullins had created an air of efficiency about his office. A desk, filing trays, a folding chair and a wooden locker had been scrounged from an RAF stores depot and the walls had been covered with air-craft recognition posters. The locker was secured by a solid-looking combination lock but no one had thought to burr the screws holding the staple to the frame and, as Frick pointed out, a jack-knife made an adequate substitute for a screw-driver.

Neatly arranged inside the locker were two suits of RAF battledress, an officer's raincoat, a beret, and a service dress hat which had been deliberately bent out of shape to give the wearer a rakish air.

Gerhardt measured one of the suits against his chest. 'It

is a bit large,' he said, 'but I don't think anyone will take much notice of that. We are fortunate, are we not, that this Mullins is obviously a vain man—he has more clothes than a film star. If we unpick the shoulder flashes, people will think that we are in the RAF.'

'It might be safer if we claimed to be Poles, otherwise our accents might arouse suspicion.'

'I should have thought of that,' Gerhardt said tersely, 'it was stupid of me not to.'

The note of self-criticism amused Frick and he was not averse to reminding Gerhardt that he had overlooked yet another problem. 'Of course,' he said chidingly, 'we could dye our khaki shirts with ink but we'd still be short of a tie.'

Gerhardt frowned. 'I do not see the difficulty,' he said seriously. 'If this man Mullins has a pair of scissors in the drawer of his desk, we can cut a tie each out of the black-out curtains.'

Frick stared at the window and then a broad smile appeared on his face. 'You know,' he said, 'you've just provided the perfect answer. We'll remove the curtains, cut a hole in each one and then slip them over our heads. If I remember correctly there is a roll of white tracing tape in the stores which we can use to make a pair of collars.'

'I don't understand,' said Gerhardt, 'why should we want to wear a curtain?'

'We're about to become chaplains in the Polish Air Force. Don't you see—it's absolutely perfect. When they see a clergyman, the English seem to become embarrassed and they tend to look the other way. I tell you, Paul, with such a disguise we can travel anywhere without fear of being questioned and our appearance won't matter—no one expects a padre to conform with dress regulations.'

Every pigeon-hole in the desk was crammed with pamphlets, forms and leaflets issued by the Ministry of Agriculture. Neglected in peace time by successive governments, the war had brought expansion, subsidies and comparative prosperity to the farmer as well as a flood of paper work. Although in her letters Katherine had often said how hard she had to work on the farm, it wasn't until he'd seen some of the evidence for himself that Ashby realised that she had not been exaggerating. Arriving late at the farm, he had been hurt and angry to find that the children were already in bed and that Katherine had left for Beverley, where two evenings a week she helped to run a canteen for servicemen. But now that he'd had time to reflect, he was slowly beginning to realise that it was not the long bouts of separation which had caused the rift between them but indifference and a failure on his part to appreciate the many problems which she faced in bringing up their children alone. It was his fault that they had become accustomed to living separate lives and he knew that he would have to do something about it before their marriage finally broke up.

He was a regular soldier and for too long his energies had been directed towards one goal and in his desire to make a name for himself, he'd often failed to take leave when the opportunity had arisen. Now for the first time, he knew that this sacrifice had been absurd for he had only to listen to the noise around him to get things into perspective. From Marston Moor, Pocklington, Driffield and Riccall the Halifaxes of 4 Group joined the Lancasters of 6 Group RCAF from Linton on Ouse, Dishforth and Leeming to thunder across the night sky in a never-ending stream towards Holland and Germany. Night after night Katherine must have lain awake listening to them as they droned overhead and wondered how many would return in the morning. The men who flew in those Lancasters and Halifaxes were not strangers but faces she knew and when they failed to return, the loss was personal. Compared with the reality of their war, his must have seemed irrelevant and she would find his dedication to a futile desk job quite incomprehensible.

The phone rang and lifting the receiver off the hook, he heard the operator say, 'I'm sorry about the delay, caller, but I now have your Wem number on the line.'

Against a rushing noise in the background, Ashby said, 'Is that you, Jack?'

'I'm sorry, I can't hear you. Who is that?'

'My name's Ashby,' he shouted, 'am I speaking to Major Ottaway?'

'Okay, you're a bit clearer now, but this sure is one hell of a bad line, Colonel.'

'Any news?'

'What?'

Ashby counted up to ten and then started again. 'Has—anyone—been—captured—yet?' he said slowly and distinctly.

'No.'

'Not—even—Scholl or Haase?'

'No one's been caught yet. Where are you calling from?'

'Market—Weighton.'

'I thought it was the goddam moon, Colonel.'

'That's—funny—you—sound—as—if—you—were—in—the—next—door—room.'

'Yeah? It sounds to me like you're standing under a waterfall.'

'You—have—my—number?'

'Yes.'

'All—right—call—me—if—there's—any—news.' Ashby hung up with a sense of relief.

Of course, luck had favoured Scholl and Haase, but even so, their performance so far had exceeded his expectation. They were the youngest and the least experienced, but in pairing them together, he'd known that he would be able to assess their ability with greater accuracy. If they had been split up and teamed with older and more experienced men, their limitations might have passed unnoticed.

Ashby knew that they had run into trouble late on Friday night when they'd stolen a couple of boiler suits which had been left out overnight to dry off on a clothes line. A neighbour emptying rubbish into his dustbin had spotted them in the adjacent garden and had raised the alarm. They'd had a head start but within minutes every policeman in Whitchurch had been alerted. Since no one at that stage connected them with the escaped POWs, it did not occur to the station sergeant to warn the local Home Guard detachment, and that was their first stroke of luck. They were spotted later by an elderly Special War Reserve constable whom they managed to outrun with ease, and they were doubly fortunate in that there wasn't a call box in the area and that the police constable was out of breath by the time he remembered to use his whistle. Following that brush with the law, they had managed to stay out of trouble but Ashby doubted if they would continue to do so.

Ashby had had very little sleep in the last twenty-four hours and now it was catching up on him. He yawned repeatedly, fought briefly against the overwhelming desire to doze off and then finally gave in to it. He woke up about an hour later to hear the low murmur of voices in the hall and he quietly opened the door of the study to see who it was. Afterwards, he wished he hadn't. The way the airman held Katherine in his arms lent substance to a suspicion that they knew each other rather well.

After their experience in Whitchurch, Scholl and Haase had followed Ottaway's advice to the letter. Lying up during the day and moving only when it was dark, they had avoided all towns and villages until they reached Crewe. They had hoped to time their arrival to coincide with the clocking on of the night shift at Rolls-Royce but they had been forced to make a wide detour to avoid the road blocks on the outskirts of town and this had upset their schedule. To move through the streets when they were practically deserted would be asking for trouble and reluctantly they had come to the conclusion that it would be necessary to approach the railway marshalling yards by a more roundabout route.

Tired, hungry and dispirited, they began a wide circling movement in a north-westerly direction which brought them into the gusting wind and then, as if deliberately to add to their misery, it started to rain. In a matter of minutes they were soaked to the skin and shivering with cold but somehow, while on the verge of collapse, they managed to keep going. The uneven ground jarred their weary legs so that each pace forward represented a triumph of sheer will-power. A warm bed was waiting for them if they chose to walk into town and give themselves up, but although the idea was always present, neither man suggested it.

And then, when they believed themselves to be completely lost, the wind dropped a little and they heard from afar the discordant sound of grinding wheels and the clank of wagons being shunted in the yards. An hour later, they were lying in the long wet grass on top of a bank which overlooked the sidings.

'What can you see?' Haase whispered.

'There are some wagons about fifty yards away and I

can hear an engine shunting.'

'Voices, listen for voices,' Haase muttered impatiently, 'we don't want to be picked up by the railway police.'

'Nor the Home Guard.'

'Oh, don't you worry about them, on a night like this they'll be indoors brewing themselves a cup of tea.'

'You think so?'

'Sure, they're old men and boys—not proper soldiers,'

'Do you think this is wise?'

'What?'

'Riding a goods train; Major Ottaway said it was risky.'

'You have to take risks in a war, and besides we know what to look for. There will be chalk marks on the wagons to tell us—all we have to do is find one which is destined for York, Doncaster or Hull.' He grinned at Scholl. 'Are you ready?' he said.

'I think so.'

'All right; from now on you stay close to me, and remember, no more whispering. If you do see anything, grip my arm and make a hand signal.'

Together they rose from the damp grass and moved down towards the sidings.

The Home Guardsman saw them as they came over the top and then lost them almost immediately. There was no ambient light from the stars but his ears told him that they were moving in his direction. He was fifty-two years old and his eyesight wasn't as good as it used to be, but on a dark night there are other senses which tell you where to look and what to look for, and he was, after all, an old and very experienced soldier who'd been through the last lot at Mons, Ypres and on the Somme, and so, convinced that he was facing a couple of escaping Germans, he stood there in the shadow of the guards van and waited until they were less than twenty paces apart. The Candian Ross Rifle came up into his shoulder and he opened and closed the bolt with a precision which came from years of practice. His command to halt cracked like a whiplash.

The metallic sound of a round entering the breech was unmistakable yet Haase seemed unaware of its fatal significance. Pushing Scholl to one side, he turned about and started running. The shot, following instantly on the second challenge, hit him squarely between the shoulders and exited through his chest. He stumbled, fell on to his face, tried to raise himself up on his hands and knees, and then, finding the effort too much for him, sank back and died.

As the rifle swung in his direction, Scholl raised his hands. 'Don't shoot,' he screamed, 'for the love of God, please don't shoot!'

10

ASHBY WANTED TO hold her close but every time he tentatively slipped an arm around her waist, Katherine pushed it aside and drew farther away.

'This is ridiculous,' he said quietly, 'if you move again, you'll fall out of the damn bed.'

'You stay in your half then,' she said coldly, 'and stop pestering me; I'm trying to get to sleep.'

'And I'm trying to apologise.'

'You have an odd way of doing it, I must say.'

'I didn't mean to lose my temper with that man.'

'He does have a name, you know.'

'Indeed?'

'It's Norman Young.'

'Does it matter who he is? After all, I'm not likely to meet him again.'

'You might.'

Ashby rolled over on to his back. 'What's that supposed to mean?' he muttered.

'I'm fond of him, very fond of him. As a matter of fact, he wants to marry me.'

'There's such a thing as bigamy.'

'And divorce.'

It was out in the open now and suddenly he felt cold and numb with disbelief. 'It's come to that, has it?' he said thickly.

'Why not? There's nothing to hold us together.'

'You forget we have Jeffrey and Elizabeth to consider.'

'I wondered when you were going to bring them into the argument,' she said vehemently. 'How much of a father have you been to them in the last five years? They've seen more of Norman in these past three months than they ever have of you. Do you know what Elizabeth said to me the last time you came home on leave? She said, "When is that man going away, mummy?"'

'Things will be different after the war.'

'I can't see why you should suddenly change, we've always been a very poor second to your career. I could have lived through these long periods of separation if I could have seen some reason for it, but your work really isn't all that important, is it?'

'It could be now.'

Katherine raised herself up and plumped her pillow viciously. 'Oh, for God's sake,' she said impatiently, 'stop living in a dream world and face reality for once in you life.'

'What do you mean by that?'

'You know very well.'

'Now you're being cryptic.'

'Only because I don't want to hurt you unnecessarily.'

'Why hold back now? Perhaps it would help to clear the air between us if you said what you were really thinking.'

Katherine turned on to her back and stared up at the ceiling. 'All right, if that's what you really want,' she said dully. 'Why not admit to yourself that you've been left behind by your contemporaries? I don't make a habit of reading the Army List but even I know that two of your closest friends are already Major-Generals and they were only a year senior to you before the war. God knows no one could have been more devoted to the army, but where has it got you? You've spent the duration behind a desk in St Albans doing a job which some chit of a girl in the ATS could do just as well; and as far as we are concerned, you could have been serving at the far end of the world for all we've seen of you.'

'You just don't understand.'

'No, I don't,' she said acidly, 'I don't understand how someone like Norman can get leave every three months when apparently you can't be spared.'

'Perhaps he's got a cushy number.'

'That's a pretty cheap remark coming from you. Norman

has just completed his second tour on Ops and, thank God, he's earned a rest at least.'

'You really do care for him, don't you?'

The reply was a long time in coming, and he lay there in the dark listening to the rain spattering against the window.

'I think I'm flattered by his attention,' she said.

'What kind of an answer is that?'

'I'm thirty-two and he's not yet twenty-six—perhaps he's just infatuated with an older woman.'

'Infatuation passes, Katherine, and then what's left?'

'What we have now,' she said bitterly.

He turned on to his side to face her. 'We could try again; there must be something left because at least we're here together.'

'The only reason you're in my bed is that my parents would be shocked if it were otherwise.'

'We're just keeping up appearances, are we?'

'Yes, that's it precisely.'

'Well, I think we ought to dress it up a bit,' he said grimly. 'I mean we don't want your parents to get the wrong idea about us, do we?'

He pinioned both arms, leaned over and kissed her. Her legs threshed beneath him and a knee caught him a sharp blow in the stomach, and when he tried to force her mouth open, her teeth found his lip and bit it.

'You bastard,' she whispered fiercely, 'you're no better than an animal. Why can't you leave me alone?'

'Because I love you and you damn well know it.'

'Love,' she started to say, 'what the hell do you know about ...'

His mouth closed over hers, and although she tried to turn her head away and to claw his face, he remembered and exploited those secret places where she was vulnerable, and gradually her resistance faded and was replaced by an eagerness which began to match his own.

'I love you.'

'Then show me,' she said, and instantly despised herself for being so weak and vulnerable.

He began to raise the satin nightdress an inch at a time and was surprised by her sudden and impulsive response. Pushing him to one side, Katherine sat up in bed and removing the nightdress, tossed it to one side and then lay back. Crooking an arm around his neck, she drew him forward and rediscovered the old sensual pleasures which had been absent for so long. Her body arched, received and having coupled with his, moved with growing harmony to provoke a wild emotional spasm.

He was in bed with a stranger who writhed and twisted beneath him in an ecstasy which surpassed anything he had ever known before, and for a few brief minutes this woman filled and dominated his mind to the exclusion of all else. Nothing and no one was more important than Katherine, and he was consumed with a desire to prolong and preserve this feeling for eternity. For years he had carried a mental picture of a demure and unemotional woman but now, between the endearments, she whispered obscenities which shocked yet stimulated and excited him to a climax which drained them both so that at the end he lay inert and exhausted beside her.

Sleep tried to seduce him and the brass rails at the foot of the bed became blurred. From a long way off a drowsy voice said, 'Did you wear anything?'

A tired brain failed to comprehend the question at first and then its significance became apparent.

'No,' he said, 'I didn't think about it.'

'Oh, God,' she said wearily, 'isn't that just typical of a man.'

She raised the bedclothes and he felt a blast of cold air. Faintly, above the noise of the wind and the rain, the telephone began its insistent ringing.

'Now who on earth can that be?' she said.

Ashby rolled out of bed, slipped his feet into a pair of carpet slippers and reached for his dressing-gown.

'I expect it's for me,' he said. In a state of disenchantment he crept downstairs and entered the study.

Ottaway was a man with confidence in the efficiency of the post office. Without waiting to check that he was speaking to Ashby he said, 'We've run into trouble, Colonel.'

'What's happened?'

'Haase has been shot by a member of the Home Guard.'

'Is he badly hurt?'

'He was pronounced dead on arrival at the hospital. As near as I can figure it, they tried to board a freight train at

Crewe and Haase made a run for it when they were challenged.'

'And Scholl?'

'He was still pretty shaken up when the police took him into custody.'

Ashby took a cigarette from the packet of Goldflake on the desk and lit it. 'Did he say anything about it being an exercise?'

'I guess he must have kept his mouth shut because the police think they've got a Kraut on their hands.'

'Where are they holding him?'

'Crewe.'

'You'd better collect him before he starts talking. Call me as soon as you return to Wem with Scholl.'

'All right; but there is just one thing, Colonel. The commandant of the POW camp here wants to know if you're thinking of calling off the exercise?'

'That's quite out of the question.'

'It's easily done,' said Ottaway, 'you could speak to the duty officer at the War Office, couldn't you?'

'I could, but I'm not going to.'

'We have five other guys still on the loose, Colonel, and I don't think we can afford to have another death on our hands.'

'I'm deeply sorry about Haase,' Ashby said patiently, 'but cancelling this exercise won't bring him back to life. On the other hand, if I did call it off, I might unknowingly retain a weak man with disastrous consequences for all of us.'

'It's your decision.'

'I'm afraid it is, Jack. If it's any consolation to you, there will almost certainly be a court of inquiry, and I will put it on record that you advised me to stop the exercise before more casualties were incurred.'

'You don't have to save my neck, Colonel,' Ottaway said coldly. 'I'll call you again when I have Scholl.'

From the tone of his voice, Ashby knew that he'd been tactless but before he had a chance to put it right, Ottaway had rung off. He stared at the dead telephone wondering if he should call back and then he decided that there were more important matters to attend to. He dialled the operator, asked for Trunks and booked two calls to Sunningdale 88965 and Whitehall 9400 in that order.

He was unaware of Katherine's presence until she said, 'Who are you ringing at this hour?'

'The War Office.'

'Do you know what time it is?'

Ashby glanced at his wristwatch. 'It's ten to four,' he said.

'Then, for God's sake, come back to bed; whatever it is can wait until morning.'

'This can't; someone in the Home Guard has just killed one of my soldiers and I have to inform the War Office.'

'And the Sunningdale number?'

'I've got to alert Henry Irvine.' He stubbed out the cigarette in a brass ashtray on the desk. 'I don't want a court of inquiry.'

'Henry Irvine,' she said slowly, 'I remember him very well from before the war when he was a junior Major in the regiment—now he's a Major-General, isn't he?'

'He's also Director of Plans.'

'Should that mean something to me?'

'He's backing me, that's all. He used his influence with certain people in the War Office to push my ideas through the system.'

'What ideas?'

'I can't tell you that,' he muttered, 'I've said too much already.'

'It's a military secret, is it?'

'In the circumstances, I could do without the sarcasm.'

Her mouth set in a hard straight line. 'And I can do without you,' she said furiously, 'so you can just make up a bed for yourself on the couch.'

'Now we're both acting childishly.'

'You speak for yourself.'

'Must we quarrel like this?' He rose from the chair and moved towards her and then the phone began to ring.

'You'd better answer it,' Katherine said coldly, 'it's probably good old Henry Irvine and you mustn't keep him waiting.' She stalked out of the room and slammed the door on him.

It had stopped raining now and the first light of day was beginning to show in the east. Although wet through, both men had found that the physical effort of cycling mile after mile throughout the night without a break had kept the blood flowing warmly. Equally, they were aware that, once they stopped, their sweat would dry off and then the damp clothes would chill them to the bone.

No one in his right mind would have taken the bicycles as a gift, let alone go to the trouble of stealing them as they had done in Eccleshall. Of the two machines, Quilter's was in the poorer condition and barely roadworthy. It had worn brake blocks, a slightly buckled rear wheel and a slack chain which, as he had discovered, would slip off the crank if he attempted to coast downhill. By dead reckoning, Quilter had calculated that they had cycled just over seventy miles which, in one sense, was cause for satisfaction but in another was less so. The Peak District of Derbyshire offered little cover for the hunted and they were running out of time; wherever he looked he saw only bare rolling hills and he felt a tinge of apprehension. Although he was half convinced that this exercise was nothing more than a childish game, he was still anxious to succeed. To be caught, to have failed where others less intelligent, like Cowper, might not, would undermine his confidence.

Lost in thought, he failed to notice until it was too late that the road curved sharply and then fell away to the small town in the valley. The bicycle gathered speed and, although he jammed on the brakes, they did little to check the wild downhill momentum. Fields, hedges and isolated trees flashed by in a blur and the wind lashing into his face forced Quilter's lips apart. Each corner became a desperate gamble, and praying that he would not meet anything head on, Quilter was forced to use the full width of the road to get round. In less than a couple of minutes he was leading Stack by a good half mile and the gap between them was increasing with every passing second.

He came into the main street and, faced with a slow right hand bend, went into it at a speed approaching forty. The rear wheel slewed away, the ground came up fast to meet him and then, as if the smooth wet tarmac were an ice rink, he found himself sliding along on his right side until his feet, slamming into the kerb, brought him to an abrupt halt. For what seemed an age, he lay bruised and shaken in the gutter.

A voice above him said, 'Who do you think you are, Malcolm Campbell?' The policeman bent forward to get a closer look. 'What are you doing in Matlock at this hour of the morning? There's no army unit for miles around.' A flashlight moved quickly over Quilter's body and then snapped out. 'I thought so. You'd better come quietly, Fritz,' the man said heavily, 'unless you're looking for trouble.'

The tone of voice was meant to be intimidating but it had the opposite effect on Quilter. He began to laugh, silently at first and then out loud. Stack would never have appreciated the funny side of it but then he was not there to witness the absurdity of it all. Sensing that Quilter's headlong dash could only end in trouble, he had begun to look for an alternative route which would avoid the town.

Frick and Gerhardt left the train at York, walked over the bridge and passed through the barrier on platform one. Two Corporals in the Royal Military Police who were loitering by the bookstall in the entrance hall, ignored them and looked the other way. Their failure to salute irritated Gerhardt but he was sensible enough not to make an issue of it.

They were down to their last few shillings and they were not sure in which direction Market Weighton lay. Realising that the city would be quiet on a Sunday morning and not wishing to draw attention to themselves, they planned, rather than walk, to take a bus if they could find one which ran out to Hull.

As they came out into the station approach, a Hillman pick-up drew into the kerb and an RAF officer got out. Frick watched him collect a suitcase from the back and then, timing it perfectly, moved round to the offside, tapped on the glass and smiled at the WRAF driver.

The girl obligingly lowered the side window. 'Can I help you, sir?' she said in a quiet voice.

Frick smiled again. 'My friend and I are going to Market Weighton. Can you take us there?'

The girl frowned. 'It's a little off my route.'

'Where are you stationed, please?' Coupled with the assumed accent it was an unfortunate question, and he sensed immediately that the girl was suspicious. 'I'm sorry,' Frick said hastily, 'we are Poles and strangers in your country.'

'You speak very good English.'

'I have had much practice since my country was invaded, but sometimes it is not so good and peoples do not understand what I am saying.'

'I suppose I could return via Market Weighton.'

'You are most kind.'

'But my work ticket is made out to Great Driffield.'

Frick tried to hide his disappointment. 'I would not like you to be in trouble,' he said.

'I could give you a lift as far as Barmby Moor, if that's any help? It's only seven miles from there to Market Weighton.'

'Thank you,' he said eagerly, 'thank you again. My friend and I will ride in the back.'

'There's room for one up front, sir,' she said helpfully.

He could ignore the suggestion, make some feeble excuse or accept the offer for what it was, a kindly gesture. Frick chose the latter. Signalling Gerhardt to climb into the back of the pick-up, he walked round to the passenger's side and got in beside the girl.

'This,' he said cheerfully, 'is better than walking, I think.'

The girl made no comment until she'd completed a U-turn and they were passing Micklegate Bar towards the Hull road. "I didn't know we had a Polish unit in the area,' she said casually.

The remark left Frick with an uneasy feeling and he wondered if the girl was more intelligent than he'd first supposed. It was the sort of loaded remark he would expect from a knowledgeable NCO, not a mere Aircraftswoman who was still obviously in her teens.

'We were here in 1941,' he mumbled, 'but then we moved south. We are visiting old friends.'

He looked to see if her face showed any reaction but she sat there placidly chewing a piece of gum while her eyes remained fixed on the road ahead.

'That's nice,' she said vaguely.

Frick stifled a sigh of relief. 'Yes,' he said, 'it will be good to see all our old friends again.'

The houses thinned out to become a single ribbon on either side of the road and then they were out in the open country. Occasionally, a military vehicle passed them going in the opposite direction towards York, but apart from this traffic and a few cyclists, the road was practically empty.

Shortly before one o'clock the WRAF driver dropped them off at the road junction in Barmby Moor, and two hours later, Frick and Gerhardt arrived at the farmhouse without further incident.

Stack, who had been watching the army despatch rider for some twenty minutes, wondered how much longer it would take the man to repair the puncture. The Norton 500cc was his for the taking provided his luck continued to hold and no one else appeared on the scene at the wrong moment. There was little to choose between them in height, weight and build and he reckoned that the crash helmet, leather jerkin, breeches and riding boots should fit him perfectly. Getting close to the man without being noticed wasn't going to be easy but it wasn't an insuperable problem. The belt of trees would cover him for most of the way before he was forced to crawl the last fifteen yards along the roadside ditch. He started moving as soon as the man finished levering the outer cover on to the wheel rim.

The DR slotted the wheel into the front forks, tightened the securing nuts and then stood up. The first blow slammed into his kidneys, the second chopped into his neck and, as he twisted round and went down, a foot thudded into his stomach.

Stack raised the unconscious figure into a sitting position and then, stooping, hoisted him into a fireman's lift and carried him into the wood. Ten minutes later he reappeared dressed in the DR's clothing, kicked the Norton into life and rode off. He had less than four hours of daylight in which to reach Market Weighton but from now on it was going to be a piece of cake. The DR wouldn't make any trouble for him; since his wrists had been lashed together with a pair of bootlaces behind the trunk of a tree, it would be too late to matter by the time his shouts for help attracted attention.

It was just possible, through a gap in the trees, to see the waters of the Havel sparkling in the autumn sunlight, but Kastner was not in a mood to appreciate the view. He wondered why, on a Sunday afternoon, Obergruppenführer Kal-

tenbrunner had thought it necessary that they should meet in
civilian clothes at this particular quiet spot in the Grunewald. It had meant leaving his wife, Gerda, whom he rarely
saw these days, to brood alone in their apartment house off the
Chausee Potsdamer in the Zehlendorf District of Berlin. for
the dubious pleasure of an informal conversation with his
chief.

He paced the dirt road, growing more impatient as the
minutes slipped by and it became obvious that the former SS
Police Leader of Vienna was going to be late for their appointment. Expecting to see an official car, he took little notice of the grey-coloured Wanderer until it drew up beside
him and stopped.

Kaltenbrunner leaned across and opened the door on the
near side. 'Get in,' he said tersely, 'we have a great deal to
discuss.'

Precisely why Himmler had chosen this excitable, self-
indulgent and deceitful Austrian to succeed Reinhardt Heydrich had always mystified Kastner. Perhaps the scars on the
left side of his face, the large ears and his murderous attitude
which was utterly cold-blooded helped to make him a suitable
candidate. His instinct for self-preservation was quite remarkable.

Kastner said, 'Which subject does the Herr Obergruppenführer wish to discuss?'

'Axmann—Fraulein Margerete Axmann.'

'Yes?'

'Why was it necessary for you to question her?'

'I wondered if she knew of anyone called "Rudi".'

'And does she?'

'I'm not sure—she was very guarded.'

'The lady is not to be bothered again. Is that understood?'

'Is that an order?'

'A request from SS Reichsführer Himmler.'

Kastner nodded. 'Of course, I understand,' he said thoughtfully.

'I don't think you do. The request was made on behalf of
that odious individual, Bormann.'

'Am I to ignore it then?'

'Not unless you have a very good reason for doing so.'

'As yet, I haven't.'

'But you have a feeling that something is wrong?'

Kastner shrugged his shoulders. 'You've seen my report on Osler and a copy of the letter sent by Baron Pierre Damon of the Credit and Merchant Bank in Geneva to a Georg Thomas care of the Bishop's Palace in Münster, and you know the circumstances surrounding Gerhardt's disappearance. I think something may happen in Münster over the weekend of the 14th and 15th of October which could well change the course of the war.'

'For better or worse?'

'Worse.'

'After Stalingrad, that would be an impossibility. I thought everyone knew that.'

'I am to ignore the situation then?'

'I didn't infer so,' Kaltenbrunner said sharply. 'Last night our intercept service in the Leipzig area picked up a transmission to the British Station Greenline Two which operates in Geneva. The text read: "The deed is everything, the repute nothing." It is, of course, another quotation from Goethe.'

Kastner said, 'Is there anything else I should know?'

'Himmler wants us to concentrate all our resources on uncovering the disaffection within the army. No one who was implicated in the 20th of July Plot is to be spared, and you are to complete your investigation of Major-General Paul Heinrich Gerhardt by the 7th of October at the very latest.'

'That gives me less than a week.'

'You'll find a large envelope on the back seat of the car which may be of assistance to you. It contains a photostat copy of Gerhardt's personal file and record of service.' The Austrian smiled thinly. 'Colonel-General Jodl obtained it for me as a favour.'

Kastner turned, leaned over the back of his seat and picked up the fat manilla envelope. 'I'm grateful,' he said drily.

'It makes interesting reading. In 1938 Gerhardt was Adjutant of the 91st Infantry Regiment in Münster and was on very friendly terms with a Doctor Julius Lammers. In case you are not aware of it, Lammers is the Party Gau for Westphalia and still lives in Münster.' Kaltenbrunner paused briefly to allow this significant piece of information to sink in, and then said, 'Should you consider it necessary to place him under close surveillance, you will act with the utmost discretion.'

'But of course.'

'It is a thousand pities that Himmler ever went to Bormann and asked him for a personal loan from Party funds. It could make things awkward for us.'

Kastner opened the door of the car and got out. Turning about, he said, 'I will bear that in mind.'

'Good. I think we understand one another. Just remember to keep me informed at all times Herr Oberführer.' Kastner's puzzled expression etched another tight smile on the Austrian's face. 'Oh, didn't I tell you?' he said. 'You've just been promoted—my congratulations.'

The door slammed in Kastner's face, the engine fired into life and the car moved away. He stood there gazing after the Wanderer until it was a speck in the distance, and then he began walking towards the S Bahn at Nikolassee. The train would take him as far as the Anhalter station and from there it was only a short distance to his office in Prinz Albrechtstrasse. He had already decided that all letters addressed to Doctor Julius Lammers should be intercepted and scrutinised before they were finally delivered and he wished to set the necessary machinery in motion. He was not to know that events had already overtaken him.

Forty-eight hours previously, Julius Lammers had received a letter posted from Rastenburg. It said:

Dear Lammers,

I agree that Germany is facing difficult times and it is up to all of us to do everything in our power to ensure final victory. I think your suggestion for a levee en masse to defend our country has merit, but I do not think much of your idea that this force should be called 'The People's Army'. Such a description smacks of Bolshevism, and I consider that 'The Volkssturm' would be a more appropriate title.

As you can imagine, it is not easy for me to leave the Führer's side these days when he needs me so much, but in view of the importance you attach to your proposed meeting with the other Party leaders, I can arrange to be in Münster on Saturday, 14th October.

Regretfully, much as I would wish to see Fraulein Axmann again, I must decline your invitation to spend the
weekend at your house. Instead, I will order the Luftwaffe
to place a JU 52 at my disposal and I will fly to Loddenheide, arriving there at fourteen hundred hours. You
should arrange for a car to meet me at the airfield and note
that I intend to leave at eighteen hundred. Four hours
should be sufficient for our purposes, and I will expect to
chair the meeting.

                                    Martin Bormann.
                   *
Cowper spent Sunday evening composing a long letter to
Pitts which, in masterly terms, explained precisely why he
had so little faith in Ashby's leadership. He also made a point
of describing in detail everything about the exercise and his
part in it, hinting that Ashby would not approve of his meth-
ods and inferring that he was hidebound.

Cowper was a man who, once he was able to see the hazards
confronting him, believed in laying off the odds. Of all the
personnel from Force 272 taking part in the exercise, he
alone was destined to experience the least difficulty in reaching Market Weighton.

I I

THERE WERE DAYS when Truscott detested Whitehall and thought of it as a vast warren continually expanding and which harboured stoats, weasels and ferrets as well as the usual rabbits. He was essentially an honest and straight-forward man and deviousness was foreign to his nature. The greater part of his life had been spent at regimental duty where justice was done and seen to be done when the rules were broken. In Whitehall it was not always so, for here there were people who tended to seek an expedient solution if it meant they could avoid washing some dirty linen in public.

In a briefing lasting well over an hour, he'd gathered that the Director of Plans was very anxious that any court of in-quiry convened to investigate the circumstances in which Private Haase was shot and killed, should act with the utmost caution and discretion. It had also been made abundantly clear to Truscott that he was responsible for ensuring that Major-General Irvine's wishes were respected in this matter. Whoever he detailed to handle it would need to be urbane, tactful and completely unscrupulous if there were to be no repercussions from the civil authorities. Logically therefore, Tony Dryland was the only contender for the job.

Truscott said, 'Do sit down, Tony.' He pushed a box across the desk. 'Would you like a cigarette?'

Dryland shook his head. 'Thank you, Colonel, but I'd rather not; I've got a sore throat.'

'Sorry to hear that.'

'It's nothing really, just a cold.'

Truscott lit a cigarette and then closed the lid on the box. 'We have a difficult problem,' he said, 'which I want you to handle. You're probably aware that a Private Haase was accidentally killed on Saturday night while taking part in an escape and evasion exercise organised by Force 272?'

'I had heard something about it,' Dryland said quietly, 'you know how rumours get around.'

Truscott raised an eyebrow. 'Quite, and our job is to see that they're scotched before the affair is blown up out of all proportion. Fortunately, the Home Office has agreed that a coroner's court will not be necessary provided they receive a copy of the findings of our court of inquiry.'

'Is that normal practice?'

Truscott ignored the question. 'The Director of Plans is extremely anxious that the court proceedings should be conducted in a low key, and that's where you come in.' He opened a drawer in his desk, took out a sheet of paper and handed it to Dryland. 'Army Form A2,' he said, 'the convening order for the court of inquiry signed by the Adjutant General on behalf of the C in C Home Forces. You will see that a Lieutenant-Colonel Robinson of the Army Legal Services has been named as President to make the proceedings more acceptable to the Home Office, and you're down as one of the members. The court will assemble at Abercorn House tomorrow, Wednesday 4th October at eleven hundred and will take evidence from Lieutenant-Colonel Ashby, Major Ottaway, Private Scholl and a Mr Woodhouse.'

'Woodhouse?' said Dryland.

'The Home Guardsman who shot and killed Haase. He's been subpoenaed to attend.' Truscott raised his eyes and fixed them on a wall chart above and behind Dryland's head. 'The findings of the court should roughly take the line that, for some unaccountable reason and contrary to the briefing he'd received before the exercise began, Haase attempted to escape after he'd been arrested by a member of the crown forces.'

'From what little I've heard, they hadn't been arrested, had they?'

'In this instance,' Truscott said firmly, 'you could say that when they were challenged by the sentry they were technically under arrest. Certainly, all the evidence you will hear will point to that conclusion.'

'Supposing it doesn't?' Dryland said. 'What if Scholl's evidence differs?'

'That, my dear Tony, is your cue to suggest to the President that perhaps the witness is still suffering from shock.' Truscott smiled encouragingly. 'I'm sure you will be able to pull it off—everyone I've met thinks very highly of you.'

Dryland knew that he was being flattered but he still experienced a warm glow of pleasure. 'I'm still puzzled about one thing,' he said.

'What's that?'

'Why Abercorn House? I thought Force 272 was based on Trawsfyndd?'

'They've gone into quarantine; apparently, word came through from Germany that the operation is set to go, and the Director of Plans has given it his blessing. It seems that we are willing to try any hairbrained scheme if there is the slightest chance that it will help to finish the war this year.' Truscott suddenly busied himself with the papers on his desk. 'I'm afraid that's all I'm allowed to tell you,' he said. His tone of voice implied that they had nothing further to discuss.

Gerhardt was back where he had started almost six weeks ago, only this time he was not a prisoner. Abercorn House was one of those stately homes whose owner had been clever enough to sell it off to a government department before the repair bills got out of hand. Surrounded by spacious gardens and with a fine view of the rolling countryside, it was also cold, draughty and riddled with dry rot.

In its better days the ballroom had been impressive but now the chandeliers high up in the ceiling were coated with dust, and someone, thinking to preserve the wood, had dark-stained the oak panels around the walls. Elegant men and women had once graced this room, but now most of the floor space was taken up with a scaled model of the city of Münster and its surrounding area. Ashby checked the model against the mosaic of aerial photographs displayed under a sheet of perspex on the table.

'I can't see any errors of detail,' he said, 'can you?'

'Not with the model.'

'But you have other reservations?'

Gerhardt flushed. 'It's not for me to say.'

'Oh, but it is,' Ashby said coldly. 'After all, it is your friends who have made this operation possible.'

'Very well, since you put it like that, I think we should leave Scholl behind. He is too immature and unstable.'

'And what about the others?'

Gerhardt shrugged his shoulders. 'They will suit our purpose.'

'Even Cowper?'

'Of course, why not? I personally do not care for him but he has cunning and he can be ruthless, like the good Sergeant Stack.'

'And you?'

Gerhardt looked puzzled. 'I'm sorry,' he said woodenly, 'I do not understand you.'

Ashby slipped his left hand into the map pocket of his battledress and brought out an envelope. Tipping the contents on to the perspex, he arranged the four enlarged snapshots in their correct order.

'They're getting a little curled around the edges,' he said, 'but you should have no difficulty in recognising them.'

Gerhardt barely gave them a passing glance. 'If I so wished, I could deny that I was responsible.'

'You could.'

'I could draw your attention to the fact that the executioners were drawn from the 4th SS Police Division.'

'And I might believe you.'

'But it would not be the whole truth. I ordered the executions and I have no regrets. Does that shock you?'

'No, but I wish you'd seen fit to tell me when we met.'

'Should I then have made a confessional? Are you perhaps a priest who can give me absolution?'

'Don't get arrogant with me. If I am to be tarred with the same brush, the least you owe me is some sort of an explanation.'

'Explanations,' Gerhardt said irritably, 'of what use are they? Do you think you can fight a war without getting your hands dirty? I could talk all night and still you would not understand.'

'Try me.'

'Unless you have been there and seen it with your own eyes, it is impossible to imagine what it is like to fight on the Russian Front. It is ...' He paused, groping for an apt description. 'It is like stepping back into the Dark Ages. On the third day of the war, we found the body of a Luftwaffe pilot; he had been lynched by the peasants, you understand, and every orifice in his body had been filled with earth and stones. If one of our assault engineers was unfortunate enough to be taken prisoner, he was invariably burnt to death with his own flamethrower. I do not know who first started this brutality—it is like the chicken and the egg—but certainly we were not slow to respond. The partisans were the worst and we had good reason to fear them. It was easy to lose your way in Russia; there were few roads and our maps were hopelessly out of date and inaccurate. One night, early in September '41, we lost a truck on its way up to us from the supply point. I do not know how it happened, perhaps the driver missed a directional sign, but four days later we found the burnt-out truck in a wood some twenty kilometres off the route. The driver had been beheaded.' Gerhardt pointed to the photographs, 'Those seven partisans did it.'

'You sound very sure of your facts.'

'A detachment of the 4th SS operating in our rear area flushed them out of a woodcutter's hut. They were armed with a couple of bolt-operated Moissim Nagant rifles and a PPSH sub-machine-gun but they surrendered without firing a shot. When the SS searched them, they found the driver's pay-book.'

'And on the strength of that, they were hanged?'

'You might have acted differently,' Gerhardt said quietly, 'but it was enough for me. The partisan is a peasant working in the fields who expects to be treated as a civilian one minute and as a soldier the next. His kind come out in the night and kill the wounded. I should feel guilty about executing them?'

Ashby picked up the photographs, shuffled them into a neat pile and then tore them across. 'The subject is closed,' he said calmly. 'Please give Major Ottaway my compliments and say that I should like to see him.'

Gerhardt clicked his heels, bowed stiffly and then stalked out of the room. His face was white with anger. In being honest, he had been defiant and typically, he had expected understanding and sympathy for his point of view. In common with so many of his fellow countrymen, he was quick to shift the blame, and he had tried to give the impression that the conduct of the Wehrmacht in Russia, if not beyond reproach, was at least excusable in the circumstances. As Ashby knew well, this was complete nonsense, for in March 1941, informed by Keitel that they would be required to implement the notorious Commissar Order in the forthcoming campaign, the army chiefs had at first demurred and then reached a happy compromise. The secret field police and the SS commandos would administer the rear areas and were therefore free to execute captured soviet political commissars, provided the army didn't know about it.

Ottaway said, 'You sent for me, Colonel?'

Ashby turned to face him. 'I owe you an apology,' he said.

'Oh? Why?'

'For being dragged before the court of inquiry tomorrow. I didn't think it would come to that.'

'It doesn't bother me any.'

'It should be over in a day.'

'It's no sweat then?'

'No; in fact you should be able to leave first thing on Thursday morning.'

Ottaway looked puzzled. 'Leave? Why should I leave now?' he said.

'Because your job is finished. Believe me, I'm very grateful for all the help I've received from you.'

Ottaway pointed a foot at the floor model. 'Is this where it all happens?'

'Yes.'

'Enschede is in Holland, isn't it?'

'It is,' Ashby said guardedly.

'And if I read the scale correctly, it's about fifty kilometres away from the objective.' He looked up and smiled. 'At a guess I'd say the objective was somewhere in Münster. Would I be right?' He saw the change of expression on Ashby's face. 'Oh, I get it,' he said quickly, 'forget that I asked.'

'I'm glad you understand.'

'You're welcome, Colonel.' Ottaway produced a packet of Lucky Strike, offered one to Ashby and lit it with a Zippo lighter. 'Can I tell my people that everything is set to go?'

'Bormann has taken the bait.'

'Well now, that really is something.' Ottaway snapped his fingers. 'Have you got all the volunteers you need?'

'I haven't asked them yet but it will be a mere formality.'

'What makes you so sure?'

'I have my reasons.'

'I'd be interested to hear them.'

Ashby hesitated briefly. 'All right,' he said, 'why not? As the sponsor of the project, Gerhardt can't back out; for ideological reasons, Frick wants to be in at the death of National Socialism; and Scholl is romantic enough to see it as a glorious crusade. Stack will go because he can't tell the difference between a request and an order and obeying orders is second nature to him; Quilter has an outsized inferiority complex and when he hears that everyone else has volunteered, he will fall in line because otherwise he couldn't face himself. And Cowper? Well, it seems Cowper hopes to make the army his career after the war, so he'd have to think twice before refusing.'

'And where do I come in, Colonel?'

'You, Jack, are an observer for the State Department who are alarmed in case we do something which might upset that special relationship that Roosevelt thinks he has with Stalin. You weren't thinking of joining us, were you?'

Ottaway shook his head. 'Not on your life,' he said, 'I wouldn't even come along for the ride.'

'Well, of course, that leaves you with rather a difficult problem.'

'How come?'

'If you're not there to watch every move, how do you know that we won't make a deal with the German High Command?'

'How could I stop you even if I was there?'

Ashby shrugged his shoulders. 'Oh, I daresay your OSS would figure out a way. After all, once you got the message out, it would be up to your State Department to do the rest and I don't imagine that would present any difficulty. At this stage of the war we are very much the junior partner, and whether HMG likes it or not, we will follow the Washington line in the end.'

Ottaway said, 'When do you plan to move out?'

'Monday the 9th of October.'

'All right, Colonel, maybe I will take off on Thursday morning. I think I ought to have a long talk with my Director!'

Ashby stubbed out his cigarette in an ashtray crudely fashioned from the lid off a tin of Players. 'Shall I be seeing you again?' he said quietly.

'You know you will because after I've made my report, I won't have any choice.' He dropped his cigarette on to the floor and trod on it. 'I'll be back on Sunday afternoon.'

He was almost at the door when Ashby said, 'Give my regards to Miss Bradley when you see her.'

Ottaway looked back and smiled wryly. 'Colonel, if ever you get stuck for a job after the war,' he said, 'you could always take up mind-reading.'

As soon as Dryland finished speaking to him on the telephone, Pitts opened the drawer of his desk, took out Cowper's letter and tore it up. In the right hands and at the right time, it could have been used against Ashby with telling effect at the court of inquiry, but Dryland simply hadn't the courage of his own convictions. Clearly, no one in the War Office wanted the court of inquiry to probe too deeply into the Haase affair, and once that had been made clear to Dryland, he had performed a complete volte-face. Pitts was forced to the conclusion that, if it became necessary to stop Ashby, then Tony was not the man to do it. As an ally, he was totally unreliable and he was well shot of him.

Pitts got up, crossed the room and opened the large security cabinet which stood in the corner of his office. From the top shelf he lifted out a bottle of Cockburn and carefully filled a wine glass. In times of stress, a glass of port always helped to restore his sense of well-being and enabled him to see things in their true perspective.

The sonic boom was loud enough to startle him, the explosion which followed buffeted the windows, and the rushing noise at the end sounded like an engine blowing off steam. The glass slipped from his nervous fingers to shatter on the floor and, as the wine formed a pool about his feet, he stood rooted in fear, unable to move until the moment passed and gradually his heart ceased to flutter. However much the scientific advisers decried the effectiveness of the V2 Rocket as a strategic weapon, the fact remained that, not only was it impossible to give forewarning of its arrival, but there was also no defence against it. Its advent was another reminder to Pitts that war was just an obscene lottery.

The first item of any real intelligence value produced from the phone tap on Lammers reached the Gestapo Headquarters on Prinz Albrechtstrasse on the G-Shreiber teleprinter during the early afternoon of Wednesday, 6th October. The transcript showed that the call, routed via Cologne, had been placed by Fraulein Margerete Axmann, and at first, Kastner was inclined to believe that it had been made for purely social reasons. However, one passage towards the end of their conversation caused him to change his mind. In passing, Lammers had said, 'it is a pity that Rudi can only pay us a brief visit,' and Axmann had replied, 'One must not complain—in times like these we should be grateful that he is able to leave Rastenburg even for a few hours.'

It was not conclusive but it was enough to convince Kastner that he'd been right to continue the investigation; still, until he could show that Rudi was undoubtedly Bormann he thought it advisable to tread warily. Kaltenbrunner would never support him if he put a foot wrong because Himmler was ultrasensitive where Bormann was concerned. For the first time, he began to speculate whether Himmler, even if confronted with the most damning evidence, would ever find the nerve to take action against the Deputy Führer. And then, remembering the gossip which this timid, muddleheaded and hesitant man inspired, Kastner was left with the uneasy feeling that the Reichsführer SS would look for an expedient solution.

He knew only too well the treatment handed out to those who were no longer in favour. To be given command of an Einsatzgruppen, to become a mere butcher, was to take the final step over the abyss. In July 1941 he'd seen Artur Nebe's men in action outside Minsk and vividly recalled the sergeant who sat on the lip of the anti-tank ditch stupefying himself with Schnapps while he waited for the next batch of naked prisoners to climb down into the pit and lie face down on the pile of corpses. In the course of one day, this NCO had exterminated one thousand six hundred and eighty-three men, women and children and, breaking all previous records, had established a personal best. Six months later the sergeant was a confirmed alcoholic, a year later he was committed to an asylum for the insane, and Nebe himself had become sufficiently unbalanced to join forces with the traitor Stauffenberg and was now under sentence of death. And for a man credited with being the father of the gas chamber, this was perhaps the final ironic twist.

In this autumn of uncertainty, a man had to be careful even if Kaltenbrunner did want quick results. If an open breach with Bormann was to be avoided, it would be wise leave Osler well alone, but, on the other hand, Christabel Gerhardt was a woman without apparent influence, and since the policy of harassment had so far proved a failure, sterner measures were called for. It occurred to Kastner that, if the hints were broad enough, Wollweber could be prodded into arresting her and then, if anything unfortunate should happen during interrogation, he could always disclaim responsibility. The more he thought about it the more Kastner liked the idea.

12

HIS NAME WAS Yates, he was a twenty-six-year-old Major in the Rifle Brigade who, following his successful escape from Oflag VIIc at Laufen near Salzburg in the spring of 1943, had subsequently been attached to MI9. One month after the D-Day landings, he'd returned to France to participate in an operation which involved the rescue of some one hundred and thirty-eight Allied pilots who were being sheltered by the Maquis in the Forest of Fretteval close by Châteaudun. In August he was back in London again organising an escape network in Holland, and he had been ordered to report to Abercorn House because it was considered that his connections with the Dutch Underground would prove invaluable. He sat beside Truscott in the darkened room staring at the floor model which was barely illuminated by a chandelier high up in the ceiling, and wondered what the hell it was all in aid of.

A tall figure carrying a pointer staff, which was about the size of a billiard cue, stepped forward into the pool of light and said, 'Good morning, my name's Ashby.' He smiled warmly. 'I apologise for the somewhat dramatic entrance, I assure you it wasn't intentional.' The pointer staff dipped towards the floor model. 'For obvious reasons, I'm afraid I shall only tell you as much as I think necessary.'

Yates cleared his throat. 'Of course,' he said, 'I fully understand.'

The pointer swung and hovered over a town. 'This is Münster, and this building with the remarkable gable end, which stands in the Prinzipalmarkt is the Rathaus or town hall. On

Saturday the 14th of October an important meeting will be held in the council chambers historically known as the Hall of Peace. Among those known to be attending will be the Party Gauleiters of Westphalia, the Saar, Hesse, the Rhineland-Palatinate and Lower Saxony, and ...' Ashby deliberately, paused for effect, 'and the Deputy Führer and Party Secretary, Martin Bormann. We shall be the uninvited guests at this rally. Our problem is not so much how to get there but rather how to get away should anything go wrong—and that's where I hope you will be able to help us.'

Yates leaned forward in the chair, rested both elbows on his knees and clasped his hands together as if in prayer. 'Wrong is such a euphemistic term, Colonel. Could you be a little more precise?'

'All right then, in plain English, if there's a balls-up we're going to be bad news and I doubt if our friends will want to know us. That won't bother us too much if we can get across the border.'

'And link up with the Dutch Underground?'

'Precisely.'

'What about your German connections? Are you sure they won't be able to help you?'

'I've already implied that I think they will suddenly develop cold feet.'

Yates abandoned the thoughtful pose and his manner changed too, becoming brisk, almost curt. 'I don't like it,' he said. 'You could provoke a violent response which could make things difficult for us.'

'Us?'

Yates coloured slightly. 'I mean the Dutch Underground. I don't want to see our escape network broken up to no purpose, especially just now.'

'What's so special about now?'

'Several hundred survivors from 1st Airborne Division are hiding up in the forests around Arnhem. We're trying to get them back across the river.'

'When?'

'Soon.' Yates hesitated and then added reluctantly. 'As a matter of fact, planning for this is pretty far advanced.'

'If it became necessary, couldn't we latch on to this arrangement?'

Ashby was pressing hard and Yates felt uncomfortable. It was not an unreasonable request but if he agreed, other complications would arise. For one thing, Arnhem lay some seventy miles due west of Münster and it was doubtful if Ashby's force could make that distance unaided.

'I suppose it might be possible,' he said cautiously.

'I'll need a contact.'

Give this man an inch, thought Yates, and he'll steal a yard. 'Where?'

'Somewhere near Enschede, ideally. In case you're worried about security, I won't divulge the name to anyone until the final briefing.'

'When's that likely to be?'

'Saturday the 14th of October. And if you're still anxious,' Ashby said grimly, 'we'll each be carrying a cyanide capsule because most of us can't afford to fall into the hands of the Gestapo alive.'

Yates came to a decision. 'All right,' he said briskly, 'go to the Zwinjnenberg Hotel on Molenstraat and ask for a room. Say that you've come on the recommendation of your uncle— Jan Vrooburgh.'

'And is that all there is to it?'

'Yes.'

'Good. Let's hope the emergency never arises.'

As if on cue, Truscott suddenly came to life. 'Well, I'm glad that's all settled,' he said, 'now perhaps we can get some lunch.'

Ashby frowned. 'There are still one or two small details I should like to clear with you, sir,' he said. 'They won't take more than five minutes.'

'Do they concern Major Yates?'

'Hardly, they're purely domestic problems.'

Truscott glanced towards Yates and smiled sympathetically. 'I'm sorry about this,' he drawled, 'but perhaps you wouldn't mind waiting for me downstairs in the ante-room?'

'Of course not, Colonel.' Yates stood up, saluted and walked out of the room, conscious that his shoes made a loud clacking noise on the parquet floor.

Truscott waited until the door closed behind him and then said, 'I thought Yates was quite helpful really.'

'So did I, but if we're going to make use of his organisation we shall need some Dutch guilders—say about a hundred pounds' worth in small denominations. I'd like the currency delivered to me before Sunday. Can that be arranged?'

'There shouldn't be any difficulty. Anything else?'

'Albach and Remer are still in hospital. I want them confined and isolated for another ten days or so.'

'All right.'

'And finally, I want a message included in the German Language news broadcast on Friday night.'

'You know,' said Truscott, 'with all the jamming that goes on over there, it's a wonder that anyone ever receives your words of encouragement.'

'You can bet that their Intelligence service does.'

'Do you mean to say that all these quotations are for their benefit?' Truscott tried to appear casual but he failed to suppress the note of surprise in his voice.

'It's all part of the deception plan, Colonel.'

'And it seems the Gestapo were not the only people to be taken in,' Truscott said pithily.

Ashby took a slip of paper out of his pocket and handed it to Truscott. 'This is the text for tomorrow night,' he said.

'Well, I suppose it will help to get "Leopard" off the ground.'

'Leopard?'

'The code-name for your operation, derived from the biblical quotation: Can the Ethiopian change his skin or the leopard his spots?'

'Very apt and subtle.'

'Yes, I thought you'd like it.' Truscott smiled thinly. You see, Michael,' he said, 'I didn't arrive empty-handed after all.'

Pushed violently in the back, Christabel Gerhardt stumbled forward into the cell and, tripping over the urinal bucket, fell on to her hands and knees. Blood ran from her nose, and her right eye, bruised and swollen, was rapidly closing to a narrow slit.

'Next time,' Koch said harshly, 'perhaps you'll be more co-operative.'

The door slammed, the bolts thudded home and then the brilliant light in the ceiling came on, bringing the bare room into sharp relief.

Crawling across the stone floor, Christabel grasped hold of the bed and dragging herself up, collapsed on to the horse-hair mattress. Denied sleep, questioned for hours on end, subjected to psychological pressures and now physical intimidation, she had reached breaking point.

She thought about the children who had been taken from her and placed in the care of foster parents whom Wollweber had said could be relied upon to see that they became good Germans, and remembering their faces, the tears came to her eyes. Over and over again they'd said that Paul had betrayed her, and perhaps they were right. It had, so Wollweber said, become a habit with him; after all, he'd sent Hasso Jurgens into Berlin at the head of a company on that hot July afternoon and then had backed out at the last minute. And if that wasn't enough, the oh so gallant General, fearing that his part in the conspiracy would inevitably be uncovered, had sought refuge in Sweden.

It was possible, they said, to sympathise with Frau Gerhardt, whose loyalty to her husband was obviously misplaced, but no one could be expected to believe her story. Her husband had not run off with another woman, he had not been killed in an air raid on Dortmund, and even as he'd made his escape, he must have known that his plan to hoodwink the Gestapo was bound to fail. He had involved his wife in a fantastic web of lies and then callously abandoned her to face the consequences alone. As an intelligent woman, she must surely realise by now that such a man did not deserve her protection.

And then the questions had flowed once more like a river in full spate, and since it was impossible to think clearly, they'd tripped her up again and again until finally she had thought it safer to remain silent, and then, suddenly wearied of the whole business, Wollweber had signalled Ursula Koch to take her back to the cells.

The assault had been premeditated in order to show once and for all that obstinacy would not be tolerated. In the silent empty cell block, Koch had also shattered any illusion that, as the wife of a Wehrmacht General, Christabel Gerhardt would be treated leniently. In a demoralised state of mind, she began to think of her husband with loathing and resolved that if they came for her again, things would be different.

Next time she would name anyone and everyone and say any-thing which might please Wollweber so long as it kept her alive.

As soon as he entered the flat, Laura Cole could see that Dryland was more than slightly drunk. There was a silly smile on his face and he swayed visibly.

'I come,' he said, 'bearing gifts for a beautiful woman.'

'You're drunk.'

'Now that,' he said, wagging a finger under her nose, 'is no way to treat Father Christmas.' He thrust his hands into the pockets of his greatcoat, brought out a number of cellophane packets and then, raising his arms above his head, allowed them to fall to the floor. 'Nylons,' he said thickly, 'traded them for a bottle of whisky with a Yank I met. Christmas will be a little early this year.' Struggling out of the greatcoat he dropped it into a chair and then collapsed on to the bed.

'You need sobering up,' Laura said firmly. 'I'll make you a cup of coffee.'

'Not with that bloody awful chicory essence you won't.'

'Tea then?'

'Yes. Make it hot and strong like you.'

'Now, now,' she said indulgently.

'Don't forget your nylons,' he muttered.

'You pick them up for me while I'm making the tea.'

Dryland, raising himself up on one elbow, caught a final glimpse of her back as she disappeared into the kitchen. The straight grey skirt, hugging firm buttocks, gave the lie to the impression of a demure little wife created by the pink twinset and string of cultured pearls.

'Who else did you see besides your American friend?' Her voice coming from the kitchen sounded a long way off.

'Leonard Pitts.' Dryland got down on his hands and knees and scooped up the stockings.

'What did he want?'

'Nothing.'

'Something to do with your friend Ashby I expect.'

'He's not my friend,' Dryland said loudly.

'I bet you discussed him though.'

She was uncomfortably close to the truth but he wasn't go-ing to admit that Pitts had been slyly pumping him for information. 'What's eating you?' he said angrily. 'To hear the way you talk, anyone would think you had a crush on him.'

'Don't be ridiculous, I only met him once.'

'And you're not likely to meet him again either.'

'Oh, why's that?'

'Because he doesn't need your help any more.' Dryland picked himself up off the floor and sank down on the bed again. There was a definite sinking sensation in his stomach and he felt vaguely sick. 'The court of inquiry was a push-over.'

'I thought so too. Here,' she said, 'drink this, it will make you feel better.'

The cup and saucer rattled in his shaky hand. 'How did you know?' he said owlishly.

'I typed out the proceedings from the original, remember?' Laura picked up a packet of nylons. 'Are you sure these are my size?' she said.

'I don't know—why not try them on?'

She shook out the stockings and then sat down on a stool in front of the dressing-table. 'Your little ploy wasn't very suc-cessful, was it?'

'I'm not with you?' he said muzzily.

'Getting me to spy on Colonel Ashby.'

Dryland turned his head in Laura's direction. The skirt was bunched up in her lap and the sight of her thighs as she fastened the suspenders excited him. She caught his glance and pulled the skirt down, primly adjusting it to cover her knees.

'You've got a vivid imagination, Laura.'

'Have I? Well, I suppose we must be thankful that Frank hasn't.'

'What's that supposed to mean?'

'There was a letter waiting for me when I got home this evening. Frank's been posted to Worthy Down and hopes to be back in time for Christmas. I'm afraid that rather puts paid to our little affair, darling,' she said sweetly, 'unless you have a more permanent arrangement in mind.' She searched his face. 'No,' she murmured, 'I thought not. I can see that the idea of marriage doesn't enthrall you.'

'I didn't say that.'

'You didn't have to.'

Dryland averted his gaze. 'What will you do now?'

'Find another place. Fortunately, that shouldn't be too difficult; thanks to the V2, London has lost its attraction for quite a number of people.'

'Why must you move away?'

'Oh, for goodness sake,' she said irritably, 'use your head. How can I possibly stay here? The woman in the flat below thinks that you're my husband.'

'I can see that you've thought it all out,' Dryland said morosely.

'I have, and in the circumstances, I don't think we should see one another again, at least not outside the office.'

'If you're that damned sensitive about it, perhaps you'd like me to arrange a transfer to another department?'

'It might be a good idea,' she said coolly.

'Too bloody right it is.' Dryland struggled to his feet and lurched towards the door. 'I can't think what the hell I saw in you, Laura.'

'Now you're acting like a petulant schoolboy.'

'And you're behaving like a bitch.'

'I think you'd better leave before you say something which we both will regret later.'

'Don't worry,' he said, 'I've no intention of staying where I'm not wanted.'

'Don't forget to take your greatcoat with you.'

'Oh, yes,' he said nastily, 'we mustn't leave any evidence behind, must we?' He eyed the nylons in their cellophane packets scattered on the bed and retrieved them. 'You won't be needing these now, will you? Can't have you feeling like a kept woman.'

It was a childish gesture but the look of surprise on her face gave him some satisfaction and led him to think that he had handled the situation rather well. He told himself that there were plenty of other fish in the sea, but somehow, as the tube bore him towards Charing Cross, the thought of spending the rest of the evening in the Mess at Woolwich had a sobering and deflating effect on his spirit.

13

THE RAIN FELL steadily from a dull sky and the wind blowing from the east was a chilling reminder of the hard winter to come. A few dead leaves still floated on the surface of the flooded bomb craters in the Tiergarten but the trees which lined the Charlottenburger Chaussee were already bare. On such a wretched day as this, it was easy to believe that Berlin was slowly dying, but in the centrally heated offices of the Gestapo Headquarters on Prinz Albrechtstrasse the warm atmosphere cushioned the occupants against the reality of life outside in the sombre streets.

The file, which he had chosen to call *Münster—Case Black*, represented hours of hard work, yet Kaltenbrunner skimmed through it in less than ten minutes and then consigned it to the Out tray as if it were a matter of little consequence.

'Not very enlightening, is it?' he snapped.

The provocation was deliberate but Kastner remained cool. 'I believe there are certain points which are worthy of further consideration. For instance, as a result of the conversation between Axmann and Lammers, we know that "Rudi" is the code-name for someone at Rastenburg.'

'Well, I suppose we must be thankful that at least you've narrowed the choice down to one man out of possible thousands.'

'Most of whom we can safely ignore since we're looking for someone who is on a social par with Lammers and is important enough to impress Baron Pierre Damon.'

Kaltenbrunner inspected his fingernails. 'Oh, yes,' he said, 'what do we know about the good Swiss banker?'

'Our Embassy staff in Berne were a little vague.'

'I'm not surprised, but what else can you expect if we allow a champagne salesman like Ribbentrop to become our Foreign Minister?'

Kastner ignored the interruption. 'But they seemed to think that Damon was on good terms with the British Consul-General in Geneva.'

'And a certain Georg Thomas whose address is care of the Bishop's Palace in Münster?'

'Yes.'

'Do we know his identity yet, Oberführer?'

'No, but I suspect that Thomas and Lammers are one and the same man.'

'It is a pity that Frau Gerhardt was unable to help you over that, but despite supplying us with an impressive list of names, she failed to mention Thomas. Do you suppose that is significant? Or like me, do you believe that she simply named anyone she could think of as a means of placating that idiot Wollweber?'

'I think it's possible; she's certainly very frightened.'

'And imaginative—like you.' Kaltenbrunner pointed to the file lying in the Out tray. 'I mean, look at the title you've given to the file—*Münster—Case Black*. *Case White* was the attack on Poland, *Case Yellow* the attack on France and the Low Countries and I suppose you'll be telling me next that *Case Black* refers to a projected attack on Germany from within?'

'Yes, that's it precisely.'

Kaltenbrunner picked up a heavy steel ruler and slammed it against the desk. 'Where is your proof?' he shouted. 'All I hear from you in conjecture, rumour and gossip. I tell you frankly, I've had enough of this damned nonsense.' He turned his back on Kastner and faced the window. The rain tracing meandering streams on the panes of glass seemed to fascinate him. 'It has to stop here and now,' he said in a quieter tone of voice. 'Is that understood?'

'Perfectly. But there is just one thing—what if this "Rudi" is also the Soviet spy we've been looking for all these years?'

The suggestion was not lost on Kaltenbrunner and it left him shaken. Since 1942 it had long been apparent that someone in the Führer Headquarters at Rastenburg was supplying the Soviet High Command with high-grade intelligence. This information, which was thought to be relayed to a communist cell in Basle by a high-speed transmitter operating somewhere in the Leipzig area, usually concerned changes made in the order of battle and chain of command on the Eastern Front. It thus enabled the Russians to predict the Wehrmacht's operational plans with remarkable accuracy, so much so, that in July 1943 the great armoured battle at Kursk was lost before it had ever begun.

Kaltenbrunner said, 'It's an interesting theory but a dangerous one.' He sounded worried and uneasy and his thoughts were far from being coherent. 'There are occasions when it is unwise to disclose the true facts and then we have to look for an expedient solution to the problem.'

For a reason that completely eluded him, Kastner sensed that he was expected to agree. There were days when he was almost convinced that you had to be half crazy yourself to understand the way this man was thinking.

'I'll give you an example of what I mean,' Kaltenbrunner said dreamily. 'Take the case of the late Field-Marshal Erwin Rommel.'

'I didn't know he was dead. I thought he was still on convalescent leave?'

'He is at the moment, but I have it on good authority that he will suffer a fatal relapse one week from today. The state funeral is to be arranged for Wednesday the 18th of October in the Cathedral at Ulm. Field-Marshal Rundstedt will deliver the oration.' He swung round to face Kastner again and his voice became harsh. 'Of course we knew that Rommel was implicated in the July Bomb Plot but it was decided not to bring him to trial. Bad for the army's morale, you see. It would also look bad for the Führer—after all, he raised him from comparative obscurity and everyone knew that he was the Leader's favourite General.'

'I see.'

'Good. In that case, you can give your attention to more important matters.'

'Am I to abandon my investigation of the Gerhardt ring then?'

'No, it is merely to be given a lower priority. You should

arrange to transfer Frau Gerhardt to the Lehrterstrasse Prison here in Berlin. Similar action should be taken with regard to that suspect from the Technische–Nothilfe Battalion.'

'Johannes Lehr?'

'Yes, that's the man.' A chilly smile curled his top lip. 'You see, Kastner, it will make it that much easier for you to question them when you're not engaged on more pressing inquiries.'

'And what about Osler?'

'Oh, by all means have him arrested and brought to Berlin too if that pleases you.'

Kastner stood up. 'Will that be all, Herr Obergruppenführer?' he said.

'No, it will not be all. I have a special assignment for you. Next Saturday, an important Party conference is to be held in Münster and you will be in charge of the security arrangements.'

'Isn't that a job for the local office?'

'Perhaps you would like to take that up with Himmler?—after all, it was his idea that you should be in charge.'

Kastner swallowed nervously. 'May I ask who will be attending this conference?'

'A number of important Gauleiters.' The facial muscles twitched and the scars on Kaltenbrunner's left cheek were momentarily distorted and became more pronounced. He rearranged the blotter on his desk and then, almost as an afterthought, said, 'The meeting will be addressed by Martin Bormann and his speech will be recorded and then dubbed with applause where appropriate and later broadcast to the German people over Radio Deutchlandsender.' Like a rabbit mesmerised by a snake, Kastner watched him open a drawer in the desk and take out a sheet of paper. 'I believe you will find all the necessary details in this signal.'

The tone of voice was distant yet murderously hostile. A number of questions boiled in his mind, but in Kaltenbrunner's present mood, he was afraid to ask. His hand trembled as he picked up the signal, for he sensed that, in some obscure way, it could well be his own death warrant. Pulling himself together, he clicked his heels, raised one arm and in a loud voice said, 'Heil Hitler!' He walked out of the room on legs which, like the aged and infirm, moved stiffly beneath him and only when he reached the safety of his own office did Kastner begin to unwind.

He poured himself a large brandy and then seated himself in a comfortable armchair to read through the signal, carefully making a note of the points which he thought might require special attention. He missed lunch and worked on until late in the afternoon completely engrossed in the task of identifying the security problems arising out of the projected conference because this, at least, was a situation which he fully understood and one that did not raise confusing doubts in his mind.

Possibly Kaltenbrunner was right, perhaps the Gerhardt ring did not exist except as a figment of his imagination and the General was just one more of those treacherous swine bent on saving his own skin after the débâcle of the July Bomb Plot. God knows there had been enough of them; what with Beck, Witzleben, Stieff, Kluge, Stuelpnagel and now Rommel, it seemed that half the army had forgotten their oath of loyalty. The Leader was absolutely right to be suspicious of the cabal who represented the so-called traditional officer class, for events had proved that only the Party would remain unswervingly loyal in these times of adversity.

If the circumstances had been different, he might have accepted and been comforted by this simple, blind declaration of faith, but inwardly he knew that it was stupid to ignore the facts entirely. On the present evidence it would obviously be dangerous to take action against Bormann, but to sit back and do nothing about the situation was, in Kastner's opinion, equally hazardous since it might later be inferred that he had tried to shield the Party Secretary. Still, he could shelter behind the report he'd already submitted, and then it would be up to Kaltenbrunner to explain why he had seen fit to shelve the investigation.

His work almost finished, Kastner pressed the bell on the desk to summon one of the secretaries from the typing pool. Frau Bungert owed much of her popularity with the other secretaries to the fact that she could always be relied upon to volunteer to work late whenever the necessity arose. She did so, not because she was a devoted National Socialist who enjoyed her work in the Prinz Albrechtstrasse Headquarters. but rather because she was lonely and anything which helped to make the time pass quickly was to be welcomed. She was just twenty-four but, although quite attractive, had taken little pride in her appearance since her husband, an armament fitter in the Luftwaffe, had been reported missing following the encirclement of the 6th Army in Stalingrad. For twenty-one months she had nursed a faint hope that one day word would come through from the International Red Cross that he was a prisoner of the Russians.

Entering the office timidly, she said in a low voice, 'You sent for me, Herr Kastner?'

It was one of her failings that she never remembered to address the Gestapo officers by their SS rank, and although this habitual oversight did not bother Kastner, it certainly irritated everyone else.

'I rang for you, did I not?' he said sharply.

She nodded dumbly, afraid to provoke any show of temper.

'Very well then, I want you to check with Obergruppenführer Kaltenbrunner's office to see if they have registered the *Münster—Case Black* file.'

'I don't remember sending it to them,' she said hesitantly.

'Naturally you wouldn't since I delivered it personally. Just let me know if they have failed to book it in.'

She opened her pad, scribbled a note and then said, 'Oh yes, I nearly forgot. Your wife called a few minutes ago and left a message.'

'What about?'

'She said that she had agreed to work a double shift at the hospital and was also going to attend a civil defence lecture.'

'Did she say when she expected to be back?'

'Well before midnight, unless there was an air raid, in which case she would stay on at the hospital.'

The message annoyed him and he was irritated with Gerda. As a senior government servant, it was naturally desirable that his wife should be seen to be playing her part in the war effort, but it was futile to pretend that her work as a nursing auxiliary made a positive and significant contribution. They saw little enough of each other as it was without Gerda taking on extra responsibilities.

Kastner sighed. 'I missed lunch, Frau Bungert,' he said plaintively, 'and now it seems that I shall also forgo dinner.

Could you please therefore get me a bowl of soup from the canteen?'

The pilot was witty, good-looking and very personable. If you ignored the lines around his eyes, it was still possible to see that Lieutenant Manfred von Tresckow was only a young man of twenty-one who had had to grow up very fast in order to stay alive. In fifteen months of aerial combat on the Eastern Front he had shot down eighty-three Soviet planes, most of which were Stormavik Fighter Ground Attack aircraft. He was a long way from being a leading ace but his name was being mentioned with ever-increasing frequency in the Goebbels Press and Gerda Kastner had been flattered by his obvious interest in her.

Ostensibly, he had come to visit a friend who was slowly recovering from a nasty bout of jaundice, but as soon as he noticed Gerda, Tresckow's motive had been transformed by a swift and somewhat crude reappraisal. In Gerda he saw a dark-haired woman of thirty whose pouting lips and full but not too over-ripe figure suggested interesting possibilities to a man who had a weekend pass in his pocket. He had monopolised her to the detriment of the patients and the displeasure of the ward sister, and to avoid a scene with matron, Gerda had agreed to meet him later when she came off duty.

She had thought to avoid him, but he was there waiting for her on the pavement outside the hospital, and as he'd said, what harm was there in having a drink with a lonely pilot, and he'd taken her to a bar on the Kurfurstendamm, but it hadn't stopped at one drink, and when she was starting to get high on the cognac, Tresckow had suggested that perhaps Gerda and her husband would like to have dinner with him, but both of them had known all along that the invitation really only applied to her and that a restaurant was the last place he had in mind.

The flat in the Siemensstadt District belonged to a friend who, because he was unfit for military service, had been directed to work in a munitions factory in Spandau. It was no small coincidence that he was currently on the night shift. Compared with her own apartment, it was a poky little place but that hadn't seemed to matter. Dinner had consisted of Leberwurst and black bread and that hadn't mattered either because Manfred had bought a magnum of champagne on the black market and who wanted to eat when there was champagne to be drunk? And all along Gerda had known how it would end but that too hadn't mattered a damn because she and Erich had slept together rarely of late and when they had, his increasingly bizarre tastes had upset and unnerved her.

Making love with Manfred had seemed to be the most natural and pleasant experience, but now that the effect of the champagne had worn off, she felt ashamed and worried lest Erich had checked up on her. The light from a single table-lamp revealed an empty bottle and two glasses lying among a pile of discarded clothing on the floor, a lover in shirt-tails kneeling on the threadbare carpet, and a woman sprawled in an armchair naked from the waist up.

Gerda stirred and prodded Tresckow in the ribs with a stockinged foot. 'Get up,' she said thickly, 'you look silly crouching there on all fours.'

Tresckow grinned up at her. 'From where I am,' he said, 'you look positively marvellous.'

'Do I? I don't feel it, I feel more like a cheap prostitute.'

'Now you're reproaching yourself because you have a guilty conscience and really you have no cause.'

'How would you know, Manfred? Are you a mind-reader?'

'No, but I know the sort of man you're married to.'

Gerda stooped down and picked up her things. 'I must get dressed,' she said.

'What's the hurry? Why can't you stay longer?'

'I can't, you know I can't; Erich will be getting worried.'

'But he's not expecting you home much before midnight.'

The thinness of the excuse she'd made for her absence suddenly became blindingly apparent and for the first time she saw clearly the risks involved. 'I must have taken leave of my senses to give that message to Frau Bungert. He's bound to phone the hospital and then he'll know that I've lied to him.' She began to dress hurriedly as if every minute lessened the risk of discovery, and every hook which failed to mate with its eye, every press stud which did not fasten at the first attempt, brought her closer to the edge of panic.

Tresckow said, 'I've read about situations like this but this is the first time I've seen it happen with my own eyes.'

'Oh, for God's sake, Manfred, just don't sit there leering at me, do something useful.'

'Like what?'

'Like getting dressed,' she snapped. 'Is there a bathroom in this place?'

'I thought you were in a hurry?'

'Don't be facetious, I want to brush my hair.'

A distant siren started to wail and was instantly taken up by others in the immediate area as the outer Berlin defences came into action.

Treskow said, 'I'm afraid that does it, you're stuck with me whether you like it or not. But don't worry, there's an adequate shelter in the basement.'

'I'm going home.'

'Don't be stupid, you won't be allowed to move on the street.' Tresckow tucked the shirt into his trousers and shrugged on his jacket. 'Oh, come on,' he said, 'don't look so worried. The worst that can happen to you tonight is that a lot of people in the shelter are going to make nasty remarks about the Luftwaffe.'

The Mosquitoes of Pathfinder Force, preceding the main bomber stream, put down the marker flares over Spandau and then veered away from the target area. In the space of the next twenty-five minutes, six hundred and forty Lancasters and Halifaxes from Groups 4 and 6 unloaded a shade over three thousand tons of high explosive and incendiary bombs into the area defined by the clusters of green, white and red magnesium flares. Years of hard, bitter experience had gone into perfecting the technique of saturation bombing but, inevitably, a number of aircraft bombed short or overshot.

'Golden Miller' was already notorious for two reasons. Despite bearing the name of a famous Grand National winner, it enjoyed the reputation of being the slowest Halifax of any based on Riccall and it also carried the least experienced crew. On this night, as it pitched and yawed over Berlin, 'Golden Miller' maintained its reputation for being cussed by refusing to part company with its cargo despite the frantic efforts to the bomb-aimer until they were clear of the target and over the Siemensstadt District.

No one at the time, and certainly not the crew of 'Golden

Miller' whose eight-thousand-pound blockbuster quite by chance levelled the apartment house in Gartenstrasse where Gerda Kastner was sheltering, could have foreseen the ripples which would spread outwards as a result of her death.

Monday, 9th October to
Saturday, 14th October, 1944

'The chapter of accidents is the longest chapter in the
book.'

ATTRIBUTED TO JOHN WILKES BY SOUTHEY IN *The
Doctor*, 1837

14

IN THE LONG hot summer of 1940, Northolt had been a fighter station but now that the war had moved on, it had become a quiet backwater on the outskirts of London and the bomb shelters around the dispersal aprons were empty. The time for heroics was past and the Spitfire had given way to the strictly functional Douglas C47 Dakota of Transport Command.

They arrived from Abercorn House in a fifteen-seater bus and no one came down from London to see them off. Ashby much preferred it that way; this was his moment of personal triumph and he was loath to share it with anyone. He had schemed, cajoled, lied and used every connection he had to force this project through. Against all expectation, he had gathered a team from diverse and often hostile sources and welded them together, but watching them now as they filed into the waiting aircraft, even he was forced to admit that they weren't impressive dressed in civilian clothes. He tagged on to the end of the crocodile and sat down in a canvas seat on the starboard side facing Ottaway.

A crew member closed and locked the door as each engine in turn whined and coughed into life. The Dakota rolled forward, taxied out on to the runway, turned and braked to a halt. The throttles were opened on the twelve-hundred-horsepower Pratt and Whitney radials until, like a dog straining to get off the leash, the plane vibrated from nose to tail. The revs fell away, rose, died and then built up once again, and suddenly they began to move, slowly at first until with increasing momentum they reached the point where the eye no longer saw the passing landscape except as a totally blurred image. It was not a good day for flying and the Dakota seemed to stagger into the air as if reluctant to leave the safety of the ground behind. They climbed steadily through the overcast, reached the optimum ceiling, levelled out and then throttled back to a cruising speed of 164 mph. Allowing for head winds, Lyon was just over five hours flying time away.

Ottaway closed his eyes and thought of Anne Bradley. Descending on her parents with little warning late on Friday night had not been a very good idea, but Anne had wanted it that way and he had allowed himself to be talked into it because it was difficult to find rooms in a London hotel. He wondered if she had planned to show him off for the approval of her parents, but if that was her intention, it hadn't worked out too well. Old friends of the family who were staying the weekend had been an embarrassment; they had teased her as if she were still a twelve-year-old schoolgirl with braces on her teeth, and after a while,, he could see from the expression on her face, that the jokes had worn thin. He'd been an outsider scarcely understanding a word of their conversation, but every now and then they'd thrown a question his way out of condescending politeness. It soon became obvious that they weren't really interested and gradually he'd lapsed into silence, disappointed that Anne hadn't come to his rescue.

And how much time had they had together? A sightseeing tour of the cathedral and a couple of hours in the cinema watching Bogart and a dewy-eyed Ingrid Bergman acting out their hopeless love affair in *Casablanca*. And, on reflection, hopeless just about described that last weekend. It seemed that her parents had been determined never to leave them alone. Even when everyone else had gone to bed and they'd had the lounge to themselves for once, he'd heard them moving about upstairs like sentries on the prowl and their unseen presence had soured everything. They were old and the war had already cost them a son whose room they preserved like a shrine, and perhaps, in their loneliness, their love for Anne had become totally possessive. He wondered if she could love him enough to want to break this umbilical cord which threatened to strangle them both, but he knew only too well that it was a pretty academic question now.

*

The man who sat on a bench seat in the Place des Alpes pretending to read a newspaper was fast becoming a familiar sight. At first, his presence had annoyed Pierre Damon but now he was beginning to see the funny side of it. Keeping the Credit and Merchant Bank under surveillance was probably the most time-consuming and useless job which could befall anyone employed by the Abwehr, and he sometimes wondered if the man himself had long since lost interest in the assignment and was merely going through the motions. It was, of course, pure speculation and in no way altered the fact that the tame watchdog would stay on his heels until, at the end of the day, he returned to his villa which overlooked the Parc de la Grange on the far side of the lake.

Baron Pierre Damon was forty but looked much younger. He was a slim and precise little man who, despite a quiet sense of humour, was inclined to be pompous. He had an attractive wife and three young children all of whom were devoted to him, but such was his interest in banking affairs that he tended to neglect them. Money was a subject which had always fascinated him and, although his title and family connections would have eventually ensured that he became a director, it was widely acknowledged that business had trebled following his appointment to the board in the spring of 1939.

A considerable amount of this capital inflow had come from Germany and stemmed from the numbered bank accounts which certain officials in the Nazi Party had opened as a hedge against the future. Perhaps not surprisingly, these monetary deposits had increased dramatically after the disaster at Stalingrad. As befitted one of a neutral country, the Credit and Merchant Bank also kept a watching brief on certain British investments in the form of factories which had been temporarily absorbed into the war economy of the Third Reich. In fulfilling the bank's obligations to the UK parent company, Damon found it necessary to visit Germany periodically in order to estimate the current value of these sequestered assets. In doing so he frequently came into contact with businessmen and Party officials, among whom was a certain Doctor Julius Lammers.

Using their business acquaintanceship as a springboard, Lammers, in the early summer of 1943, began to use Damon

as an unofficial diplomatic courier. There was nothing unusual in this, for a great many others had been similarly exploited as a means of gauging British and Allied reactions to
various peace proposals which had been made from time to
time. It was all rather futile because the Casablanca Conference had made it quite clear that the Allies were interested
only in unconditional surrender, but the myth persisted in
the minds of Himmler and others that a deal was still possible, given the right conditions. Kaltenbrunner was known
to harbour the illusion that the Western Allies would be prepared to negotiate with the SS whom he saw as the bulwark
against communism. Lammers, on the other hand, while con-
ceding that the SS might have a say in the final settlement,
recognised that negotiations were impossible while the present leaders of Germany remained in power.

This assessment was, in Damon's view, quite realistic and
throughout the winter months of 1943 he entered into a
series of informal talks with officials at the British Consulate
in Geneva in the naïve belief that he was dealing with diplomatic staff. He would have been shocked and affronted had
he known that he was, in fact, being debriefed and manipu-
lated by MI6. Until recently, he had been convinced that the
British were merely feigning an interest in the overtures
made by Lammers but then, quite suddenly, they became
very keen to meet face to face with the man known as 'Rudi'.
Nothing could have given Damon greater pride and pleasure
than the idea that he was helping to bring about a peaceful
settlement, and nothing could have been farther from the
truth. He was just the bait in the trap.

The phone trilled and, picking it up, Damon heard a
cheerful voice say, 'Good morning, my dear Baron. I've some
splendid news for you.'

Damon's heart began to beat a little faster. 'Oh yes?' he
said quickly.

'I've just been informed that the Embassy has heard from
London. It seems that our people are on the way and they
will be in Geneva this evening. Now what do you think of
that?'

'I think that's wonderful.'

'I knew you'd be pleased. We'll send a car for you at nine if
that's convenient? We're rather anxious to hold a prelimin-

ary discussion as soon as possible.'

Damon glanced towards the window which overlooked the square. 'Do you think that's wise?' he said. 'I'm being watched.'

'Chap in the Place des Alpes reading a newspaper?'

'Yes. How did you know?'

Laughter boomed in his ear. 'Oh, we get around. You don't want to worry about him, he's working for the Abwehr. As a matter of fact, you're meant to see him; it makes life much easier for the other two who are also watching your every move.'

'Why all this sudden interest in me?'

'Perhaps they think you're a spy, but after tonight they'll know different, won't they? I suppose nine o'clock is convenient?'

'Yes, that will be all right,' Damon said reluctantly. 'I'm quite free this evening.'

He hung up and walked over to the window again. The man was still reading his newspaper.

On the night of the raid Gartenstrasse had collected more than just one blockbuster. A two-thousand-pound HE bomb, one of a stick of four, had cratered the road at the junction with Dolandweg severing the mains and flooding the cellars of the houses near by. Now, some forty-eight hours later, the hard-pressed city fire brigade had managed to provide a single tender which was slowly pumping out the flooded crater. A gang of workmen, waiting to replace the shattered pipe, stood back from the lip of the crater smoking and talking among themselves.

By taking the Volkswagen up on to the pavement, Kastner managed to squeeze past the fire appliance and the crater, but farther up a barrier across the road eventually forced him to stop and get out. He walked forward, ignoring the notice chalked on a piece of wood, and stepped over a red and white striped pole which was supported at either end by a knife rest. A shrill voice shouted a warning but in his dazed condition he was quite unaware that anything was wrong until someone running after him, grabbed hold of an arm and tried to pull him back. Instinctively, he turned round and lashed out.

The boy caught a glancing blow on his shoulder, staggered backwards and, tripping over a lump of masonry, sat down heavily. Behind the thick pebble lenses, tears of anger welled in his eyes.

'I'll report you for that,' he said in a high shrill voice.

Kastner stooped and held out his hand. 'I'm sorry,' he said, 'I didn't mean to strike a member of the Hitler Youth.'

The boy pushed Kastner's hand to one side, scrambled to his feet and brushed the dirt off his trousers. 'You'll get into serious trouble for ignoring that warning notice.'

'What notice?'

'The one back there which says there are unexploded bombs in the area.'

'So?'

'So I'm in the messenger service and it's my job to see that no one goes past the barrier.'

Kastner stared at the boy with loathing. 'It's all right,' he said grimly, 'I'm in the SS. Take a look at my identity card if you don't believe me.'

The boy glanced at it quickly and then drew himself up like a soldier on parade. 'How can I help the Oberführer?' he said parrot fashion.

'I'm looking for my wife, she was visiting friends who lived at Number 64.'

A thin arm pointed up the street. 'I think that's the house you're looking for.'

Beyond the outstretched arm he could see a vast pyramid of rubble which had spewed out into the road, and in that instant he knew that the search had ended. Somewhere beneath the heap of masonry, Gerda lay dead in the arms of her lover.

'You bloody whore,' he said viciously.

The boy stepped back a pace and blinked up at him. 'We have a list of names at the post,' he said helpfully.

'Did anyone get out of there?'

The boy shook his head. 'They're still in the cellar. The Tenos said there was no point in digging them out.'

'Then your list is no damn good to me, is it?' He pushed the boy out of the way and walked back to the car.

No one would dare to say it openly but a lot of people would take pleasure in knowing that Gerda had been unfaithful to him. He'd refused all offers to help in the search for her when he found out that Gerda had left the hospital at her usual time and had been seen to meet Tresckow outside. Obviously, word had got around.

And Kaltenbrunner had known all right and enjoyed watching him squirm. 'Take all the time you need,' he'd said, 'Wollweber can do the spade work in Münster until you've got everything sorted out.'

He supposed he had Frau Bungert to thank for that.

He tried taking his anger out on the car but punishing an inanimate object gave him little satisfaction, the tolerances were too high; the engine might scream but it would survive his rough treatment and driving the Volkswagen at speed over the wet cobbled roads only invited an accident. He decided that what he really needed was a drink, several drinks in fact.

Werner's bar near the Innsbrucker Platz, looked seedy and rundown, but as soon as he entered the dimly lit cellar beneath the S Bahn, Kastner knew that he had found exactly the right place in which to get quietly drunk. Nobody from Headquarters would have been seen dead in it and that suited his purpose. The last thing he wanted was sympathy from that two-faced crowd. He sat down at a table in a dark corner of the room and ordered a Schnapps with a beer to chase it.

A woman seated on a stool at the bar smiled in his direction and then brushed an, imaginary speck of fluff from her tight, short skirt. A tramp on the make, he thought, a tramp with dyed red hair, plucked eyebrows and too much make-up on her face. Even on a dark night any man would think twice before picking her up. He watched her open the cracked patent leather handbag and take out a packet of cigarettes and then lean forward to catch a light from the candle on the bar. In the space of the next hour she showed everyone present what she had to offer but no one, not even the sailor who looked as though he was just out of High School, was interested.

The Schnapps and beer chasers following one on top of the other warmed his belly and, for the first time in two days, he began to see things in a new perspective. Gerda was a stinking little bitch and he was well shot of her, for it was pretty obvious to him now that this fellow Tresckow wasn't the only man she'd slept with. He'd been away from home so often, that probably half the male population of Berlin had shared her bed at one time or another and then boasted about it afterwards.

'Cheer up, *Liebling*, the world hasn't come to an end yet.' He looked up and saw her there, smiling at him across the table and smelling of cheap scent.

'Who invited you over?' he said thickly.

A hand with long red nails reached out and covered his wrist. 'You're lonely,' she said, 'and so am I.'

'I don't need you.'

'You need someone, you've been drinking steadily all afternoon—I've been watching you.'

She was wearing a black satin blouse which was stained under the armpits and he could tell from the way it clung to her that she hadn't got a damn thing on underneath it.

'Let's have one more drink,' he said aggressively, 'and then we can decide whether to go to your place or mine.'

She leaned back and patted her hair modestly as if shocked at the suggestion. The charms on the bracelet which hung loosely about her wrist jangled with the movement of her hand. 'You've got a nerve,' she said. 'What do you take me for?'

'A whore—correct me if I'm wrong.'

'I'm not sure I like you.'

'Well, I'll tell you something,' he said drunkenly, 'I'm not sure I like you either.'

The woman started to rise and then changed her mind. It might be a long time before she found another prospective client and she was too old a hand at the game to let this one off the hook.

'All the same,' she said, 'I don't see why I should sit here and be insulted by you.'

'I was married to a woman like you. Would you believe that?'

'Keep your voice down,' she hissed, 'everyone's staring at us.'

'Well, let them.' He looked across the room and tried to catch the barman's eye. 'What's the matter with the bloody service in this place?' he roared.

The woman stood up and dragged Kastner on to his feet. Her lips were set in a falsely bright smile. 'Come on,' she said coaxingly, 'let's get out of here before they call the police.'

Kastner began to laugh because the whole thing was so ridiculous. 'Oh my God,' he spluttered, 'that's rich, that's bloody rich.'

Her arm was about his waist and he was leaning on her shoulder and without him really being aware of it, she began to steer him towards the staircase which led up to the street above.

'We'll go to my place,' she said, 'it's nice and cosy.'

Kastner wagged a finger under her nose. 'I've got a better idea, we'll go to mine.' He belched loudly. 'You'll like it there. You know what I think?'

'No, but you're going to tell me just the same. Careful, *Liebling*, mind the last step.'

'The world,' Kastner said loudly, 'the world is full of whores and lonely men who can't afford them.'

'Ten marks isn't asking too much, is it?'

For no reason except that he was feeling maudlin, the tears began to stream down his face. 'I really loved that woman,' he said thickly, 'but you wouldn't understand that.'

The woman sucked on her teeth. It was, she thought, just her luck to end up with a crying drunk.

They arrived in Geneva late in the afternoon after transferring to a Swissair JU 52 in Lyon. While Gerhardt and the others faced a long journey by road to the villa outside the village of Schaffhausen close to the German border, Ashby and Ottaway were met by Richard Holmes of the consular staff and conducted to the Hotel Beau-Rivage on the Quai du Mont Blanc. It was hoped that their meeting with Damon would help to allay the suspicions of the Swiss authorities and would provide the Abwehr with further evidence indicating that peace talks were secretly being initiated. So far, everything had gone pretty much their way, but Ashby knew that the real test would come the following night when they crossed the Swiss frontier and entered Germany. The time was fast approaching when Gerhardt's friends in high places would have to deliver.

15

THE VILLA WAS more than a mile from the railway but in the stillness of the early morning, the sound of a locomotive blowing off steam as it waited in the station at Schaffhausen seemed close at hand and roused Ottaway from a fitful sleep. Other sounds began to reach him now, the cistern flushing in the lavatory across the landing, while in the adjoining room, Quilter's radio oscillated as he searched across the waveband. He tried pulling the blankets over his head to shut out the row, but it was no use. The house was alive with the noise of banging doors, heavy footsteps on the stairs and Stack whistling off key.

Bowing to the inevitable, Ottaway sat up in bed, drew back the curtains and looked out of the window. A thin veil of ground mist swirling above the meadow created the optical illusion that the cattle grazing near the stream had been hamstrung. Through the haze he could just see the pine forest on the distant hills.

Ashby knocked and pushed open the door. 'I thought you'd like a cup of coffee,' he said. 'At least, Stack assures me it is supposed to be coffee, although I have my doubts.'

Ottaway looked at the pale brown liquid in the chipped enamel mug and resisted a shudder. 'The colour's vaguely familiar,' he said dubiously.

Ashby closed the door and sat down on a chair. 'I'd like to have a chat with you before I brief the others.'

Ottaway grinned. 'I wondered when you were going to get around to it, Colonel.'

'Oh?'

'Last night on the way here from Geneva, I had a feeling that you were on the point of telling me something.'

'I almost did, but then I had second thoughts.'

'And now you're sure?'

'Yes, I've had time to think it over and I'd like you to take command if anything happens to me. I propose to tell the others if you've no objection.'

'Why me? Why not Gerhardt? He set the whole thing up.'

'I think you're the best man for the job, it's as simple as that. Besides, if this operation goes sour, Gerhardt will try to save his own skin and then it will be every man for himself.'

'And you think I can save the others?'

'I think you'd have a damn good try.'

Ottaway shook his head doubtfully. 'You flatter me,' he said.

'You'll have an even chance of bringing it off. I've made certain arrangements with the Dutch Underground should things go wrong, and that's another reason for not taking Gerhardt into my confidence. I don't want them betrayed to the Gestapo.'

'I thought you trusted him?'

'Only to a point, Jack. When you have to work with men such as Gerhardt and Kaltenbrunner it's as well to keep both eyes open.'

Ottaway's jaw dropped. 'Kaltenbrunner?' he said faintly.

'You're surprised? How else do you think our conspirators could remain at large in Germany today if they didn't enjoy the protection of the head of the RSHA? Someone has to steer the Gestapo agents of Amt IV away from them.'

'I can't believe it, Colonel.' His voice rose sharply. 'Why should he help them?'

'Because, like a great many others close to Hitler, he wants to see Bormann dead. The trouble is that if things get rough, Kaltenbrunner won't hesitate to change sides again.'

'Jesus, what are we letting ourselves in for?'

'The chance perhaps to save thousands of lives.'

'Or throw our own away.'

'I wouldn't do it if I thought it was a suicide mission.'

'No, I don't suppose you would, but who wants to take a major risk when the end is in sight?'

'As things stand, I think the war will drag on into the spring of next year, but if we succeed in killing Bormann, it might not. That's why I say we could save thousands of lives.'

'Maybe we don't share your vision, Colonel,' Ottaway said quietly, 'but at least we're here with you and I suggest we leave it at that.'

'You're right, of course, our various personal motives are immaterial.' Ashby leaned back in the chair and crossed his ankles. 'Tonight we shall cross the frontier in two groups—Cowper, Quilter, you and I will form one party, Gerhardt will be in charge of the other. I'm not anticipating any trouble.'

Ottaway smiled wryly. 'I wish I shared your confidence,' he said.

'We're moving on a proven route through Singen, Stockach and Ulm.'

'Who proved it?'

'A number of our escapees,' Ashby said coolly, 'and unlike us, they were trying to get out of Germany, which is much more difficult.'

'We could still run into trouble when we cross the frontier.'

'We might,' Ashby conceded patiently, 'and then we must take evasive action.'

'And if we can't?'

'Then we shall just have to kill anyone who gets in our way, won't we?'

Kastner opened his eyes slowly and found himself staring at an unfamiliar ceiling but, because his skull felt as though it had been split in two and there was a thick coating on his tongue, it was some minutes before he realised that he was lying in a strange bed in a strange room. He was also alone and that too was odd because he vaguely remembered a woman with red hair who'd tried to pick him up in a bar somewhere. He kicked the blankets to one side, swung his feet on to the bare floorboards and sat on the edge of the bed nursing his head in both hands. His eyes peering through the spread fingers focused on a black satin blouse and suddenly his heart began to thump wildly, because it was at that same moment that he noticed the scratch marks on his chest.

He squinted blearily at the room but there were no outward signs of a violent struggle and he sighed with relief. The woman must have risen early and walked out on him in disgust, and it was typical of a slut like her to leave her blouse lying on the floor where she had dropped it the night before. As he stared at his own clothing piled in an untidy heap in the overstuffed armchair, the thought occurred to him that she might have gone through his wallet before she left. He lunged across the room to his jacket and took the wallet out of the inside pocket, checked the contents and found that he had misjudged her. Whatever her faults, the woman was not a thief.

And now, despite the hangover, he felt much better in himself. Some of the bitterness which Gerda had provoked had drained away, and for some reason that defied logical explanation, he believed that this chance encounter with a common prostitute had a lot to do with it. Of course, he'd taken a risk in allowing her to pick him up, but apart from the few scratches on his chest, it had been worth it. Kastner changed his mind as soon as he entered the tiny washroom.

Partially dressed in her underclothes, she was lying in the bath with her neck resting between the taps, and seeing her again, he immediately had total recall. She had laughed at him because the alcohol had made him impotent, and in a fit of blind rage he had grabbed her neck with both hands and choked the life out of her. And afterwards, he had dumped her in the bath and tried to flush her skirt and slip down the lavatory and the water had overflowed and spilled out across the floor. It was still damp underfoot but most of it had drained away, and somewhere in the flat below he knew that there must be a tell-tale patch on the ceiling and it was only a question of time before someone noticed it.

Although his one desire was to get out of the flat before anyone called, Kastner steeled himself to act calmly and methodically. He dressed quickly, checked his appearance in the mirror on the dressing-table and satisfied that, apart from the stubble on his chin, he looked presentable, he went to the door and opened it stealthily. Hardly daring to breathe, he moved out on to the landing, crept down two flights of stairs, cautiously opened the front door and stepped out into the street. Werner's bar was just around the corner and now he understood why she had thought it unnecessary to wear a coat over her skirt and blouse.

And even worse was the sudden realisation that he had left the car all night in the side street facing the S Bahn. From past experience he knew that the detectives of the Criminal Police Division would soon put two and two together if some officious Berliner had thought to make a note of the registration number. So what if they do trace the number, he thought uneasily, they'll simply find that it's one of the pool cars belonging to the Prinz Albrechtstrasse Headquarters, and why should they bother to pursue that line of inquiry in a city where there were thousand upon thousand foreign workers any one of whom might have committed the crime? He took comfort in the knowledge that the population of Berlin still numbered close on four million and that he was therefore worrying himself unnecessarily, but obviously the longer her body remained undiscovered the better it would be for him.

It was essential that he left the city at the first opportunity and fortunately he had a cast-iron reason for doing so. Having already convinced himself that he would be safe once he left Berlin, Kastner had closed his mind to the fact that he had no alibi to account for his movements on the night of the murder.

The farm which was situated two kilometres north of Gremmendorf and about a kilometre east of Route 51, was too big for one man to handle, especially for a man like Gunther Jost who had lost an arm in Russia with the 16th Oldenburg Airborne Infantry Regiment. He was for ever badgering the State Labour Office in Münster for additional help and they, in their turn, were growing more than a little tired of his complaints. In the past three months he had rejected no less than fourteen of the men they'd sent him and, as one harassed official remarked, the trouble with Jost was that he seemed to think that the pool of foreign labour was a bottomless well which existed solely for his benefit. Fortunately for their peace of mind, Gauleiter Lammers had taken a personal interest in the problem of labour supply and demand, and thanks to his influence, Albert Speer, the Minister of Armaments and War Production, had agreed to increase their quota of foreign workers. Such was Lammers's concern that he had even gone to the trouble of personally sorting out Jost's problem. With four foreigners reporting to the farm on Thursday and with the promise of help from soldiers who were awaiting posting from their depot, the officials at the State Labour Office were agreed that Jost would have no difficulty in lifting the potato crop.

The potato crop was the least of Jost's worries. Since ten that morning he had been waiting for a load of chemical fertiliser which, for the fifth day running, the Department of War Agriculture had promised to deliver without fail. He was, by nature, a sceptical man and had learned never to accept their word on anything but today they'd sworn that the truck had actually left the depot yard and he'd been inclined to believe them this time. No doubt, if he phoned them again, they'd say that the lorry must have broken down on the way.

From behind the railway embankment in the far distance, a Fiesler Storch rose lazily into the air from the airfield at Loddenheide and banking sharply, headed towards the village of Telgte. As it passed low overhead, the loud puttering noise of its tiny engine disturbed the grazing cattle and sent them galloping across the field. Jost spat expressively into the dirt and walked into the barn. The trouble with the Luftwaffe, he thought, was that whenever you really needed them, they were never around. Leastways, that had been his experience in '41 when the Oldenburg Regiment had emerged from the wooded and hilly country of Moldavia-Bessarabia and entered the endless Steppe of the Ukraine.

God, but that had been a bloody awful country. It was just one vast plain covered with corn and sunflowers and damn all else apart from a few peasant huts. And we could have been alone out there for all we knew because for days on end, the regiment never saw a sign of a flanking unit, and half the time it was out of contact with Divisional Headquarters. And we were short of just about everything—transport, mortars and field guns—you name it, he thought, we hadn't got it. And Christ help you if you were unlucky enough to get hit because there weren't any ambulance cars to whisk you back to a nice base hospital where there were clean sheets on the bed and pretty nurses to look after you. The only thing we had in the way of ambulances were horse-drawn carts and it took them bloody near three days to get me back to an advanced dressing station. He looked at the empty sleeve on his jacket and smiled bitterly. The grenade which had wounded him had smashed his hand—the delay in medical treatment had cost him the arm.

A heavily laden truck, its worn propshaft whining in the differential and slapping against the universal joints, ground its way into the yard and slowly backed up to the barn. The engine died in a fit of coughing and the door slammed as the driver jumped out of the cab.

He shouted, 'Is anyone at home?'

Jost walked out into the sunlight. 'I am,' he said. 'What do you want?'

'Your name Jost?'

'It is.'

The driver removed his flat cap and scratched his head. 'I've got thirty sacks of fertiliser for you.' He eyed Jost's missing arm. 'I don't suppose you can give me a hand to unload them, can you?

'You'd be surprised what I can do with one arm.'

'Well, that's a relief. I've got a bad back and I didn't fancy shifting that lot on my own.'

'We're not going to shift anything if we stand here gabbing all day.'

The man replaced his cap and dropped the tailboard. 'You've got a point there,' he said. 'Tell you what though, I don't fancy the look of the stuff inside the sacks.'

Jost's heart skipped a beat. 'What's wrong with it?'

'Well, I mean, it's just a heap of grey ash.' Blackened teeth showed in a ghastly smile. 'Manufactured in Poland they do say. No knowing what it started out as.'

Jost stared at him with loathing. 'I'd watch my tongue if I were you, friend,' he said coldly. 'You've got a warped and dangerous sense of humour.'

'What are you getting so het up about?'

Jost grabbed hold of a sack and swung it over his shoulder. 'Jokes like that make me sick.'

'Supposing there's a grain of truth in it?'

'The suggestion made him sick with anger. 'If such things

166

are being done in our name,' he said savagely, 'then God help Germany.'

'You can say that again.'

'All right, let's get on with it, I can't stand here gossiping all day—I've got work to do even if you haven't.'

It took them under forty minutes to unload the truck but after the carrier had departed, Jost spent considerably longer than that searching for and identifying the specially marked sacks containing the arms, ammunition and uniforms which Force 272 would need.

Once the lights of Schaffhausen were behind them, they struck out in a northerly direction through the woods, and keeping roughly parallel to the railway, they crossed the frontier road without incident just before midnight. Moving on a compass bearing of thirty degrees to avoid the village of Singen, Ashby then led his group through the hills towards Stockach which he planned to reach in time to catch the first train to Ulm. MI9 had been correct in forecasting that he would experience little difficulty in crossing the frontier in the Schaffhausen area because it was ill-defined and infrequently patrolled, but, until they were clear of Stockach, he'd known all along that, as strangers, they had more to fear from the suspicious nature of the local inhabitants than from the police or the army.

Gerhardt had already discovered this truth. His party, crossing the frontier an hour ahead of the others, had veered too far to the east and, emerging from the woods, had found themselves on the wrong side of Singen. In trying to work their way round the village, they had bumped into a far too friendly drunk who, despite every effort to shake him off, had followed them at a discreet distance like a stray dog looking for someone to adopt him. His nerves stretched to breaking point, Gerhardt had finally sent the others ahead, and lying in wait, had killed the man with a knife.

The victim was not a friendly drunk. He was, in fact, feeble-minded and was treated like a child by the villagers of Singen; he was amiable, anxious to please and he talked a lot but nobody really paid much attention to him. In killing him, Gerhardt had made his first error of judgment.

16

COWPER JOINED THE queue which had formed outside the booking office in time to see Ashby and Quilter show their tickets at the barrier and pass through to the platform. He tried convincing himself that, if they'd got away with it, there was no conceivable reason why he and Ottaway shouldn't, but this piece of logic failed to stop the churning sensation in his stomach. He fixed his eyes on a propaganda poster in the entrance hall which showed a group of three small children gazing up in admiration at the bareheaded figure of a godlike infantryman whose face, turned towards the east, defied the Bolshevik hordes. The legend underneath stated that he was the saviour of Europe, but there was little resemblance between this figment of Goebbels' imagination and the pale, short-sighted Wehrmacht soldier queuing beside him.

The queue moved slowly forward and as they drew close to the window, the soldier elbowed Cowper to one side and pushing in front of him, asked for a return to Pfullendorf. All it needed to turn one insignificant little man into an arrogant lout was a badly fitting uniform. There was a time, earlier in the war, when any civilian would have given way to a serviceman, but not any more. Now only the foreign workers were expected to show respect.

The woman behind the counter said, 'Next.'

Cowper placed the suitcase on the ground. 'Two to Stockach,' he said hastily.

'Don't waste my time—this is Stockach.'

It was a stupid error, the sort of childish mistake that drew unwanted attention to himself. 'I'm sorry,' he stammered, 'I meant Ulm.'

'Single or return?' the woman said grumpily.

'Single.'

'Thirty-eight marks.'

Cowper pushed four tens through the grill, waited for the change and the tickets, and picking up the suitcase, walked towards the barrier where Ottaway joined him. The ticket collector barely gave them a second glance but a man in a dark overcoat did. He stood in their way and as they came closer, he snapped his fingers officiously.

'Your papers,' he said abruptly.

Cowper took out his leather wallet and exposed the identity card behind the piece of celluloid.

'You're a foreigner?'

'Belgians,' said Ottaway. 'We volunteered to work for Germany.'

'Did I ask you?'

Ottaway smiled apologetically. 'No,' he said, 'but we are together.'

The man ignored him and turned his attention to Cowper once more. 'Where are you both going?'

'Ulm. We've been ordered to report to State Labour Office; our work here is finished.'

'There are no foreign labourers in Stockach,' he said icily.

'We were working near Singen.'

'Yes? Doing what?'

Cowper moistened his lips. 'Felling trees.' He remembered Ashby's briefing and had a flash of inspiration. 'We didn't get on with the Poles—they were uncivilised.'

'*Untermenschen.*'

'Yes, that's it precisely.'

'I can understand how you felt. It is quite wrong that such good friends of the Reich as you should be forced to share their company.' A gold tooth flashed as he smiled at Cowper for the first time. 'Your wallet,' he said cheerfully, 'I hope you have a pleasant journey.'

He waved Ottaway through, scarcely bothering to give his papers a second glance. Cowper, his legs shaking beneath him as he walked to the far end of the platform, thought it was bloody unfair.

His sense of grievance was increased when Ottaway said, 'Well, I guess that wasn't too bad.'

'How would you know? You weren't taking the brunt of it.'

'What were you worried about? Our papers were in order.'

Ottaway took out a cheap cigar and lit it. 'You want to learn to relax,' he said.

'Go to hell,' Cowper whispered furiously, 'I don't need your advice.'

It was not the sort of reaction he'd come to expect from a man like Cowper whose record suggested that he would remain calm under stress. If any one of them had a reason to be nervous it was Quilter, who was carrying an HF transmitter concealed inside the false bottom of his suitcase, yet watching him as he chatted happily with Ashby outside the waiting room, Ottaway was amazed by his air of confidence. He began to think that he had underestimated him.

The train appeared as a black dot in the distance and for some time it seemed to the impatient eye to draw no nearer, and then, as if the whole process of motion had been speeded up, it rumbled into the station. As it squealed to a halt, the waiting passengers surged forward and Ottaway was separated from Cowper. He managed to find himself a seat next to a stout woman on the outside edge of the hard wooden bench but Cowper was forced to stand in the gangway. A porter walked the length of the platform slamming the doors, a whistle shrilled and the train lumbered slowly out of the station.

Thirty years experience with the criminal police had taught Detective Emil Maurice that the investigation of any murder was nine tenths routine to one tenth inspiration, and that was true of this particular case which seemed straightforward enough. According to the doctor who'd made the preliminary medical examination, the woman had been dead for almost thirty-six hours before her body was discovered by the old man who lived in the flat below. The deceased was Hildegarde Dollmann, a known prostitute with an impressive list of convictions for soliciting, causing a disturbance and drunkenness, but apart from making a formal identification, the old man had not been very helpful; discharged after a week in hospital with broncho-pneumonia, he had returned home to find a damp patch on the ceiling of his living room and had immediately called on Dollman to complain. Getting no reply, he had tried the door to her flat and finding it unlocked, had walked in and discovered her dead in the bath.

Tracing men who had consorted with a prostitute was never an easy business and sometimes it called for a great deal of tact. Maurice usually made a point of starting with the protector but, in this instance, it was known that she did not have a man pimping for her. She was a ten-mark, short-time whore who on a good night had been reputed to make as much as two hundred. Unless the killer had gone through her purse, and there was no evidence to suggest that he had, Monday had been a bad day for business. As far as he could tell, she'd taken thirty marks in fives and tens, which suggested that Dollmann had picked up a total of three men or one big spender. The list of convictions for soliciting indicated that she worked the Innsbrucker Platz, but since he'd been informed by the uniformed branch that she frequently picked up men in Werner's bar, Maurice decided that it was as good a place as any to start asking questions.

Even at eleven o'clock in the morning, the air inside the cellar smelled strongly of yesterday's tobacco smoke blended with stale beer, and the short tubby barman was badly in need of a wash and shave. The wary expression in his brown eyes also suggested that in or out of uniform, he knew a policeman when he saw one.

Maurice perched himself on a stool. 'Are you open?' he said.

The man rinsed a glass under the tap and dried it on a grubby towel. 'We are,' he grunted. 'What'll you have?'

'Do you serve coffee?'

'Only substitute.'

Maurice pulled a face. 'I'll have a beer then.'

'Draught or bottled?'

'Anything—they all taste much alike these days.' Maurice took a photograph out of his pocket and placed it on the bar. 'Do you know this woman?'

The barman knocked the cap off the bottle and deftly poured the beer into a glass. 'No, I don't think so.'

'Oh, come on, don't be coy, we already know that she frequents this bar.'

'Are you a policeman?'

'No,' he said sarcastically, 'I work for the Winter Relief Fund.'

'Tough.'

'It'll be tough on you all right if you continue like this.'

'You're all alike, you love to push people around.' The barman studied the photograph. 'Hildegarde Dollmann, right?'

'Yes. Have you seen her lately?'

'Is she in trouble?'

'You could say that—someone strangled her.'

The barman whistled softly. 'Poor kid,' he said.

'She was forty if she was a day and she'd been on the game long enough to know the risks she was taking. She picked a bad one and her luck was right out, and that's all there is to it, so spare me the tears.'

'It's a damn shame and I only wish I could help you.'

Maurice drained his glass and banged it down on the counter. 'I'll ask you just once more,' he said nastily, 'and then if you're still unco-operative we'll take a walk round to the police station and I'll let them soften you up a bit. Now, when was the last time you saw Hildegarde Dollmann?'

'She was in here the night before last.'

'And?'

'She picked up a man.'

'Good, we're getting somewhere at last. Would it be asking too much for you to describe him?'

'He was a big man in his late thirties, a real blond strength-through-joy type with a mean and arrogant streak. He wasn't a Berliner.'

'A foreigner?'

'How many arrogant men have you met among the foreign workers in this city? No, he was German all right; seemed quite well off too. You might say that he was slumming it.'

'Did you see Hildegarde again that night?'

'No, leastways she didn't come back here, but she could have been walking the streets.'

'And the man?'

'Haven't laid eyes on him since.'

172

'Do you live on the premises, Herr——?'

'Fischer. No, I rent a room on the Wielandweg facing the S Bahn.'

Maurice rubbed his chin thoughtfully. 'Have you seen anything unusual on your way to and from work over the past couple of days?'

'Like what?'

'Anything that didn't seem to fit in with the neighbourhood.'

'I don't think so.'

'You're absolutely sure?'

Fischer said, 'Well—there was a Volkswagen parked outside the bakery on Wielandweg late on Monday night that was still there yesterday morning when I came to work.'

'I don't suppose you thought to take its number?'

'I didn't reckon it was any of my business.'

Time could have been saved and unnecessary work avoided if Fischer had been a little more inquisitive, but at least he had something tangible which the local police could follow up. Maurice slid off the bar stool. 'I must be on my way,' he said, 'what do I owe for the beer?'

'It's on the house.'

Maurice nodded curtly and strolled towards the exit. 'You can expect to see me again,' he said.

Fischer waited until the detective was out of earshot before he made any comment. 'Not if I see you first you won't,' he said.

Doctor Julius Lammers was quite unlike any other Gauleiter whom Kastner had met. His background had been entirely intellectual until 1934 when he had suddenly left the University of Münster to become an active member of the Party because, in National Socialism, he had seen the means of curing Germany's economic ills. He was a large shambling man of untidy appearance whose shock of unruly brown hair belied his fifty-three years. His office in the Party Administrative Building overlooked the Dom Platz and was within easy walking distance of the Prince Bishop's Palace which the mysterious Georg Thomas had been using as a forwarding address.

Kastner said, 'It's very good of you to see me at such short notice but, as you'll appreciate, my arrival in Münster was unavoidably delayed and naturally I want to catch up on lost time.'

Lammers removed his horn-rimmed glasses and polished the lenses with his handkerchief. He had been warned that the Oberführer was a very difficult man and he was anxious to create a good impression.

'Please,' he said, 'there's no need for you to apologise—my time is yours. As a matter of fact, I hope you'll find that Sturmbannführer Wollweber and I have made all the necessary arrangements.'

Wollweber nodded vigorously. 'We've been all over the council chambers,' he said smugly, 'and I can assure you that security there will be as tight as a drum.'

'Then you won't mind if I check it out, will you?' Kastner said coldly.

'Of course not, Herr Oberführer.'

That each man disliked the other was very apparent, but of even greater interest to Lammers was the knowledge that Kastner had scant regard for Wollweber's abilities. Later, these weaknesses would prove useful, but this was not the moment to exploit them and, for the time being at least, he wished to appear neutral.

'We'd certainly feel much easier in our own minds if you did examine our tentative arrangements,' he said smoothly, 'just in case there is some vital point which we may have overlooked. Is this your first visit to Münster, Herr Oberführer?'

'Yes.'

'I think you will find that it is a beautiful and yet fascinating city. That oil painting on the wall to you left shows the interior of the council chamber as it used to be in 1939. The Treaty of Westphalia which ended the Thirty Years War was signed in that very room in 1648, since when it has been known as the Hall of Peace.'

'And that is where Party Secretary Bormann will address the Gauleiters on Saturday?'

'Yes. Of course, it looks much barer now that we've removed all the paintings and precious wood carvings. We couldn't risk having them destroyed in an air raid.'

'Quite. Perhaps we could take a look at the building and

also the route out to the airfield at Loddenheide?'

'Certainly. When would be convenient?'

'Now,' said Kastner. 'We can use Wollweber's car.'

Lammers sensed a note of hostility which made him feel uneasy. He wondered how much this man suspected and whether his appearance on the scene indicated a change of heart by Kaltenbrunner, for if this was so, they were in serious trouble. He saw that Kastner was watching him closely and with an effort he forced a reassuring smile on to his face.

'I'll just put my coat on,' he said, 'and then we can go.'

There was a great deal more to the city than the Hall of Peace and by the time Lammers had finished his conducted tour, Kastner knew all about the Anabaptist riots and had even seen the cages on the tower of St Lamberti Church where the bodies of the ringleaders were exhibited after they had been executed on the scaffold. He had also been told that nearly a quarter of Münster had been destroyed in the Seven Years War and that the city had suffered further damage in the French occupation of 1806. This cultural monologue, which had seemed to go on interminably, was not the only distraction. No matter how hard Kastner tried to close his mind on the subject, the nagging fear persisted that somehow, someone in Berlin would find a way to link him with the dead prostitute.

The sheer complexity of the council chambers, with the armoury, cellar restaurant, banqueting room and the Hall of Peace, posed any number of security problems which required his undivided attention. The connecting passages with the adjoining Stadtweinhaus needed to be sealed off, the public right of access to the cellar restaurant would have to be restricted and he made a note to ensure that both buildings were searched from attic to basement an hour or so before the conference assembled and that the civil servants and the technicians who would record Bormann's speech should be vetted and issued with special passes.

In normal circumstances, Kastner would have experienced little difficulty in dealing with these and a score of other points, but now, with other pressures building up on him, he was strangely hesitant and indecisive. If he had been capable of rational thought, Kastner would certainly not have overlooked the fact that, when the special guard company from the Waffen SS Training School at Brunswick detrained in Münster on Friday, they would be required to implement a plan of operation which, apart from a few minor changes, owed much of its concept to the combined efforts of Wollweber and Lammers.

Nearly twenty-four hours had passed since they had crossed the frontier at Schaffhausen and of the four men, Scholl was now the least apprehensive. He had developed an almost childlike faith in the efficiency of the German Resistance from the moment they had made contact with the cell in Tuttlingen, and without a second thought, he had accepted that they were able to transform him into a Gefreiter of the 421st Jager Infantry Regiment. It simply did not occur to him to question how many people had been involved in supplying the necessary uniforms and papers, otherwise, like Frick, he might have been worried.

With his experience as a communist agitator in the Hamburg shipyards to draw upon, Frick knew that, to escape detection, an underground organisation had to have a foolproof cut-out system, but all the indications showed that the Tuttlingen group was in direct contact with other cells. He did not believe that a unit whose security was that bad could possibly remain intact for long, and despite what Gerhardt had said, he was sure that it must have been penetrated by the Gestapo and that it continued to survive because someone in authority was tolerant of its aims. He took little comfort from the fact that he was carrying orders to report to the Reserve Army Replacement Centre at Handorf because, although the papers would pass inspection, he feared that at any time the Gestapo might grow weary of the charade and decide to end it. Even in the darkness of this cinema in the suburbs of Stuttgart where Gerhardt had taken them to pass the time while they waited for the next train to Münster, he did not feel safe.

Sandwiched between a plain, shabbily dressed young woman and Gerhardt, Stack also felt uncomfortable, but for very different reasons. He had nothing against officers, even German officers, but he liked to keep them at a distance. The film was no distraction either and he was growing tired of watching the simpering blonde heroine evade a host of admirers all of whom were intent on seducing her; for the life of him, he couldn't see why they were so eager because she was nothing to look at. The plot was heavily laced with lavatory humour which, although it lacked subtlety, appealed to the audience, and for the sake of appearances he was obliged to laugh in the right places. It was, he supposed, an antidote to the newsreel which had surprised him. He had always believed that the Germans were presented with a totally false picture of the war, but in this instance the camera had shown the truth, and no one seeing the devastated cities of the Ruhr could have any illusions about the outcome. Yet strangely enough, when the lights came on in the interval most of the audience seemed a long way from being depressed and without any prompting, they sang the *Horst Wessel* with defiant enthusiasm.

It was the first time he'd been to the cinema since leaving Kirkkudbright to join Force 272 and he suddenly found himself thinking about Janet and wondering if she'd ever really cared about him. Whoever said that absence made the heart grow fonder was barking up the wrong tree; absence just made it easier for someone like Janet to forget. For no reason which came to mind, her letters had gradually tailed off and then ceased altogether just before they moved to Abercorn House. Looking back now, he supposed that he should have listened to the other sergeants in the Mess at Kirkudbright. Perhaps they had been right all along, perhaps the only thing she had ever wanted from him was a good time. He tried telling himself that he was better off without her but still he remained unconvinced.

At the end of the day, Detective Emil Maurice had sufficient evidence to justify an arrest if he felt so inclined. He had witnesses who not only recalled seeing the Volkswagen parked in Wielandweg on the Monday night but who could also testify that it was still there the following morning until it was collected by a man answering to the description that Fischer had given him. Indeed, one of the witnesses had been so incensed by this apparent misuse of transport that he had made a note of the registration number.

By now, Maurice also knew that the car belonged to the Prinz Albrechtstrasse Headquarters and so, instead of taking further action himself, he simply prepared a report and submitted it to the Berlin Police President for consideration. In his considered opinion, there were times when it was politic to be discreet, and this was definitely one of them.

17

KALTENBRUNNER REPLACED THE phone and leaning back in his chair, clasped his hands behind his head. As a result of his conversation with the Police President he now had a perfect excuse to so worry and harass Kastner that his mind would be anywhere but on the job he had to do in Münster. A more direct man would have seized the chance, but Kaltenbrunner was devious and he wished to sit on the fence for as long as possible in case the assassination ended in failure. He had no intention of being implicated in the plot, and if he allowed the police to interrogate Kastner at this delicate moment, someone might infer later that he had tried to sabotage the security arrangements for the conference.

Lammers and his fellow conspirators were hopeless amateurs. The idea of killing Bormann as a necessary prelude to negotiating a separate armistice with the Western Allies behind the Führer's back was sound enough in principle but, from the very outset, these people had shown a remarkable talent for bungling even the simplest of plans. The arrangements for smuggling Gerhardt out of Germany had been particularly inept, with the result that Osler had immediately become a prime suspect. It was almost as if they had deliberately set out to draw attention to themselves and perhaps, in a curious way, this lack of secrecy had worked to their advantage.

Obviously Kastner had gained the impression that Bormann was behind the move to seek a peaceful settlement of the war and this explained why, despite obtaining authority to do so, he had still not arrested Osler. In common with so many others Kastner was trying to keep a foot in each camp, and the memorandum he had prepared under the title of *Münster—Case Black* was merely an elaborate form of life insurance.

Kaltenbrunner leaned forward and rifled through the contents of his pending tray until he found the docket which Frau Bungert had produced for his signature. Since Monday it had been lying there awaiting his attention and he wondered how much longer he could ignore its presence. To sign it would be an admission that the file existed, yet to pretend that he had never seen it would be equally dangerous because the Bungert woman had retained the carbon copies and once she produced them, the officious superintending clerk in charge of the central registry would insist on a complete check of all documents.

Faced with a difficult situation, Kaltenbrunner looked for and found the perfect compromise. He signed the docket and then telephoned Kastner to ask him to account for his movements on the night of Monday, 9th October. He was, in fact, still playing both ends against the middle.

The long wait from eight to eleven thirty was over, and Ashby was relieved when at last Jost arrived to pick them up with a horse and dray. The waiting room in the labour office in Münster had reminded him of a shelter for down-and-outs where, under the watchful eye of a uniformed official, twenty-five apathetic, shabbily dressed men drawn from practically every occupied state in Europe, passed the time until they were collected by their German employers. A few, like Quilter and Cowper, had dozed fitfully on the hard wooden benches, while the rest, with the exception of one man who was deep in a newspaper, had stared blankly at the array of propaganda posters displayed on notice boards around the room.

At his bidding, they followed Jost into the cobbled, tree-lined square of the Dom Platz, threw their belongings on to the cart and then, without a word being spoke, climbed aboard. The German gathered the reins in his right hand, whistled to the horse and then slowly they began to move forward. It was a grey, chilly day and no one in that windswept square, least of all the two priests scurrying between the

Cathedral and the Bishop's Palace, took any notice of them.

Jost said, 'Where do you come from?'

He spoke with a thick Westphalian accent which was difficult to understand and, playing for time, Ashby asked him to repeat the question. He wondered how much this man knew and whether he could be trusted.

'I was born in Strasbourg.' The lie came easily and Jost appeared to accept it readily.

'Your first job in Germany?'

'No, we've just come from the labour camp at Singen.'

Jost nodded thoughtfully. 'Must be nice and quiet down there with no air raids to worry you. Mind you, we haven't had much to grumble about either—you could say we've been lucky up to now.'

He reined the horse in at the junction and waited for a tram before turning up the Prinzipalmarkt towards St Lamberti Church. Another tram passed them going in the direction of the Rathaus but otherwise, apart from a number of cyclists, there was very little traffic about.

Ashby said, 'The town seems more dead than alive.'

'We've had a few raids, nothing like the Ruhr, but enough to drive the rabbits out into the country. It's bad around the station.'

'So we noticed.'

'Our turn is yet to come,' Jost said grimly, 'and then, God help us, because Münster will go up like a torch, especially the old part of the city. That'll shake some of those fat slobs in the Aegidii Barracks, I can tell you. Most of those cooks and bottle-washers have never been anywhere near the front.'

Ashby tried to place the location of the barracks in his mind and then remembered from his study of the aerial photographs that it faced the junction of Johannisstrasse and Rothenburg, less than four hundred metres from the council chambers where Bormann was due to address the meeting of Party Gauleiters. Gerhardt had said that if any reinforcements were brought in to strengthen the security arrangements, they would probably be accommodated there rather than in either of the supply depots on the other side of the Aa river.

They came up to the church and then turned right into Salzstrasse passing a large conical-shaped funnel on the street corner which reminded Ashby of the public urinals he'd seen in Paris before the war.

'What's that?' he said.

'An inspection shaft leading to the sewers,' said Jost.

If Gerhardt's friends had managed to obtain the maps of the city drainage system from Bürgermeister's office, thought Ashby, he might be able to put this newly acquired information to good use. Although it was their intention to pose as SS security guards, there was an alternative approach to the Rathaus through the sewers.

'Something worrying you?' Jost's voice broke through his concentration.

'No, I was just thinking of home, that's all.'

'Are you married?'

'Yes.'

'Cheer up, the war will soon be over if you do your stuff on Saturday.' Jost favoured him with a bleak smile. 'Either that or we'll all be dead and buried.'

Two kilometres beyond the station they crossed the bridge over the Dortmund Canal and left the city behind them.

Dryland walked into the pub on Northumberland Avenue and looked for Laura Cole among the lunchtime crowd. Given any choice, he would have preferred a quieter venue where they were unlikely to be seen by any of his colleagues but the terse note which she'd slipped into his tray had ruled that out. He didn't see her at first but as his eyes scanned the room a second time, he suddenly spotted her sitting in a booth near the bar and he noticed that she had kept a place for him. He gave her a cheery wave, pushed his way to the bar, ordered a small beer and a medium sherry and then carried the drinks across to their table.

'I'm afraid they're out of gin again,' he said, 'so I got you a sherry, okay?'

Laura Cole pointed to the glass in front of her. 'You needn't have bothered, I already have one, thank you.'

'Never mind,' he said lightly, 'I'm sure it will go down well.'

'Thanks. Have you got a cigarette?'

Dryland took out a packet and offered her a Craven A. As she leaned forward to take a light from his match, he noticed that the cigarette was shaking between her fingers.

'What's the matter, Laura?' he said quietly.

'I had another letter from Frank this morning. His posting has been cancelled.'

'I see.'

'Do you?' she said quickly.

'Well, of course I do recall you saying that you didn't want to see me again, but this puts things in rather a different light, doesn't it?'

'You mean we can take up where we left off?'

'Something like that.'

She puffed nervously on her cigarette. 'Is that all you have to say?'

'What else do you want me to say? You must know how I feel about you.'

'Do I?'

'This last week has been absolute hell for me,' he said smoothly, 'I've missed you terribly.'

She looked down at the table and toyed with the glass of sherry. Presently, in a low voice, she said, 'I think I'm going to have a baby.'

Dryland felt as if he had been winded by a blow to the stomach and he was slow to react. 'Are you sure?' he said hesitantly.

'I'm five days overdue.'

He almost sighed with relief because clearly she was panicking unnecessarily. 'I expect it's a bit late, that's all,' he said confidently. 'Have you tried to bring it on?'

'With a hot bath and plenty of gin?' Laura said coldly.

'I believe that is the usual remedy.'

'Oh, for God's sake, Tony, do try and be your age for once. Don't you think I've already tried that dodge? I've never been late before, so it's no use you telling me not to worry. I'm almost sure I'm pregnant and the question is—what are you going to do about it?'

Laura had been an entertaining diversion but she had never figured in his plans for the future. For the first time in months he was out of the red, but twenty-three pounds was hardly enough for what he had in mind and he wondered how much he could raise from the bank.

'I think I can get an overdraft,' Dryland said cautiously.

'Are you trying to buy me off?'

'Of course not,' he said hastily, 'I was just thinking...' He felt the colour rising in his face and he tried to skate round the point. 'Well, there are people who know about these things and I thought that when you're quite sure, we could perhaps arrange something?'

'If you think I'm going to let some old hag perform an abortion on me, you're very much mistaken.'

Her voice had risen sharply and, to his embarrassment, heads were beginning to turn in their direction and he knew from that moment on, everyone within earshot would be listening to their conversation. Somehow they had to find a more private place.

'We can't talk here,' he said.

'Where do you suggest then?'

'We could go for a walk.'

Laura Cole picked up her handbag. 'All right,' she said abruptly.

They walked down Northumberland Avenue, along the Victoria Embankment and thence back to Whitehall through Horse Guards Avenue. For Dryland it was an interminably long half mile because in that short space of time, she made it very clear that there would be no abortion and that if it came to a divorce, she expected him to stand by her.

That final cliché of hers could nevertheless spell ruin for his career. The war might have changed attitudes and shaken up the social order but the Foreign Office still clung to its old code of moral behaviour and they would never accept him if he was cited in a divorce case. Marrying Laura would entail living in a semi-detached house in the outer suburbs and commuting to an office job in the City for the rest of his working life; marrying Laura would involve bridge nights, membership of the local golf club, shopping in the High Street on Saturday afternoons and a fortnight's holiday in Bournemouth every year; marrying Laura meant embracing everything he abhorred.

There was perhaps a way out of the mess. If he could wangle an immediate posting to South East Asia Command, then in his absence Laura could work out her own salvation and there was just a chance that if Frank was reasonable, there might not be a divorce. His mind made up, Dryland, later that afternoon, asked for an interview with Truscott.

Inserting the key in the lock proved unusually difficult but Pitts managed it at the fourth attempt and pushed open the door to his flat. He knew that he had drunk more of the Algerian wine than was good for him and that he'd regret it in the morning, but he had enjoyed himself immensely and these parties which Anna Peach held once a fortnight to promote a better understanding of the Soviet way of life were always something of an occasion. Invariably among her guests there was someone who was worth meeting, and although the food was rather unappetising, at least Anna made sure that your glass was never empty for long.

He turned on the lights, closed the door and immediately both Siamese cats bounded towards him, and, as was their habit, they followed him into the kitchen flicking at his ankles with a paw. He filled two saucers with water from the cold tap and placed them on the floor. Lifting the lid from the saucepan on the gas stove, he ladled two equal portions of offal into their eating bowls and then stood well back knowing that, despite his efforts to distract them with a judas saucer of water, the cats would leap up on to the draining board once their food was ready.

He watched them with tolerance and great affection as they gobbled at the offal, conscious that these Siamese gave him more pleasure and comfort than most humans. If they were moody he could rub their ears and they would soon snap out of it, which was more than could be said for Major-General Vassily Kurochkin whom he'd met that evening at Anna's. A fascinating yet suspicious man whose mistrust of the British was complete and irrevocable, he'd spent two years in the Volkhov sector of the Leningrad Front where, in the heavily wooded marshes, they had waged trench warfare on the bitter, bloody pattern of '14–'18.

While Kurochkin was justly proud of the Red Army and was loud in its praise, he was equally emotional about the Western Allies who, he alleged, had failed to open a second front in 1942 and 1943 because it was not in their long-term interests to do so since the capitalists wished to deal with a weakened Soviet Union in the post-war world. As Pitts knew well, it was a monstrous distortion of the truth, but as an admirer of the Soviet Union and a communist sympathiser, he could fully understand and share their fears and anxieties for the future. With the Soviet army bogged down in front of Warsaw, Kurochkin had stated point blank that the Eastern Front had been reinforced by additional formations which until recently had been opposing the British and American armies in the west, and in his view, this was clear evidence that a secret agreement had been made with the Fascists contrary to the principle of unconditional surrender. In warming to his theme, he had hinted that a team of negotiators under the leadership of a British army officer was already in contact with representatives of the German High Command to finalise arrangements for ending hostilities.

This absurd accusation had angered Pitts and the wine had made him indiscreet for, in rebutting Kurochkin's theory, he now realised that he had said far too much about Force 272 and its objective. Although he had been unable to give the date, time and place of the assassination, in the heat of the moment he had named the target. Now, as the effect of the alcohol began to wear off and his befuddled mind cleared, something of the enormity of his crass error of judgment came home to him and he was afraid. He wondered if it would be advisable to report their conversation because there was no getting round the fact that he had been guilty of a gross breach of security but then, on reflection, he took refuge in the conviction that Kurochkin would not betray a confidence.

It was a stupidly naïve and false assumption. Kurochkin, whatever Pitts had been led to believe, was not a Red Army hero but a Major-General of the NKVD whose presence at Anna's party that evening had not been coincidental. In fact, it was the logical result of the squalid manoeuvres which he and Dryland had pursued in their attempt to stop Ashby.

The Soviet Military Mission, having provided Pitts with a series of photographs taken of Gerhardt's men as they witnessed the execution of Russian partisans, had naturally been anxious to see some return for their co-operation.

Blissfully unaware of the train of events that he had set in motion, Pitts fetched out a hot water bottle, filled the kettle and then turned on the gas. As the match touched the jet, the wall behind the stove bulged outwards and the floor started to give way beneath him. Deep fissures appeared in the masonry and the slates were plucked off the roof and sent skimming through the air. The timber joists splintered like matchwood, the windows shattered, plaster rained down from the ceiling and water poured out of the fractured pipes, and suddenly, as the world around him became a dark and terrifying place, he was falling over and over into a bottomless pit. Each load-bearing wall caved in under the blast and the building collapsed like a pack of cards. A giant hand was slowly crushing his chest and he tried to call out for help, but the words wouldn't come, and there was this numb, dead feeling in his limbs and he knew that his back must have been broken in the fall. And the brick dust was in his nose and mouth and ears and eyes, but now, in the comparative silence, he could hear something creaking and he became aware that above him was a wooden beam which seemed to bend in the middle like a drawn bow as it slowly gave way under the weight of the rubble. Final oblivion was but a few seconds away.

The V2 which fell in Cadogan Gardens had been launched from a site just outside The Hague. In addition to Pitts, it claimed twenty-eight other victims.

Shortly before midnight, the duty radio operator in the Soviet Embassy sent a Flash message to the Kremlin for the attention of the State Defence Committee. The text was necessarily vague. Decoded it read: FROM RELIABLE SOURCE HAVE HEARD THAT WITHIN NEXT SEVENTY-TWO HOURS ATTEMPT WILL BE MADE ON LIFE OF MARTIN BORMANN BY BRITISH COMMANDOS. TIME AND PLACE NOT KNOWN BUT INFORMANT CONFIDENT IT WILL SUCCEED. MESSAGE ENDS.

18

KASTNER HAD SPENT a sleepless night in the stuffy hotel bedroom on the shores of the Aa See. Grey ash and cigarette stubs filled to overflowing the heavy glass ashtray on the writing desk, and two empty packets of Lucky Strike lay crumpled on the carpet. The screwed-up sheets of notepaper which were scattered untidily around the waste bin represented hours of fruitless work.

The statement accounting for his movements on the night of Monday 9th October, which he had been ordered to produce had been on his mind from the moment Kaltenbrunner had called him late on Thursday afternoon. For some reason he had been kept completely in the dark about the progress of the police investigation, and it was difficult to know what evidence they already had in their possession, but he could make a pretty shrewd guess. Obviously they had traced him through the registration number of the Volkswagen which had been parked overnight in Wielandweg, but in order to connect the vehicle with the murder, two other links in the chain had to be established. Someone who had seen him leave Werner's bar with the woman had given a description of his appearance which was accurate enough to jog the memory of yet another witness who recalled that he had collected the car on Tuesday morning.

Once Kastner accepted this hypothesis, it was extremely difficult to invent a story which, in establishing his innocence, did not conflict with the presumed facts. Throughout the night, he had drafted one statement after another and even now he was far from satisfied. The final version read:

Herr Obergruppenführer,

I can remember very little of what actually happened on the night of Monday the 9th of October, 1944. I do know that I was extremely upset and emotionally disturbed when some time that afternoon, I established beyond doubt that my wife aad been killed in the air raid during the night 7/8 October. I recall that, after driving around in an aimless fashion, I visited a bar in the Schoneberg District which I believe is known as Werner's. I must have stayed there for some hours drinking heavily, until eventually, in an intoxicated state, I was picked up by a woman. We left the bar together and went to her flat, which was only a short distance away, where she said I could stay until I sobered up. It soon became clear to me that she was a common prostitute and I immediately left. I think I gave her ten marks as a small present because I naturally wished to avoid any unpleasantness.

I felt sick and unwell and I completely forgot about the car which I'd left in Wielandweg. After walking around a bit, I discovered that I had missed the last train on both the S and U Bahns, and I remember being distinctly annoyed. From that point on, my mind was and still is a complete blank until I awoke the following morning to find that I had passed an uncomfortable night in the cellar of a derelict building on Becke Strasse. Despite the compassionate circumstances which I feel accounted for my unusual behaviour, I realised that my conduct was likely to bring discredit on the SS. I made no mention of the incident to you because I had hoped that it would have passed unnoticed, but obviously this is not the case.

I, of course, immediately collected the car and since there was no longer any reason for me to stay on in Berlin, I came to Münster to take charge of the security arrangements in accordance with your previous instructions.

I await your further orders,

Heil Hitler!

Reading it through again, it still seemed more like a confession than an explanation, and he wondered if Kaltenbrunner would accept it as such. To be indicted for the murder of a common prostitute would be a travesty of justice for a man with a record like his. No one, he thought savagely, had done more to protect the Reich. He had played a significant part in destroying the White Rose Movement among the university students in 1942, and he believed, with some justification, that he had been outstandingly successful in exposing the conspirators who had been involved in the July Bomb Plot. For the good of the Fatherland, it was essential that he should be allowed to continue his work in this field, and surely even Kaltenbrunner could see that.

He rose stiffly from the chair and, walking to the window, drew back the curtains. In turning about, he caught a glimpse of himself in the mirror above the washbasin and was shocked at his appearance. His eyes looked puffy and beneath the thick stubble, his skin seemed almost yellow.

There was a knock on the door and, obeying his answering grunt, Wollweber strode into the room. In uniform, despite the limitations imposed by a corpulent figure and poor eyesight, he tried to cultivate a proud military bearing. His jacket, and breeches were immaculate and the leather belt, pistol holster and jackboots reflected hours of hard work on the part of his HIWI orderly. The hat, crushed out of shape, was modelled on the style favoured by Himmler. His hand wavered and the Party greeting died in his mouth when he saw the change in Kastner. The man seemed to have aged ten years overnight.

Kastner said, 'Did you want something?'

Wollweber stared at him open-mouthed. 'The Special Guard Company...' he said lamely.

'What about them?'

'You said you wished to meet them at the station when they arrived; they're due in forty minutes.'

It was obvious to Wollweber that he'd forgotten all about them, but Kastner recovered quickly.

'Is everything arranged?' he said. 'Transport to meet them and take them to the barracks?'

'Yes, I've checked the details personally with the Transportation Officer at the Wehrkreiskommando. Everything is in order.'

Kastner nodded. 'I still have one or two matters to attend

to, so I won't be able to come with you. You'd better tell the Hauptsturmführer in command that I'll meet him in the Gauleiter's office after his company has settled in at Aegidii Barracks.' He glanced at his wristwatch. 'Let's say at eleven thirty, that should give him plenty of time.'

'Very well, Herr Oberführer.' Wollweber hesitated briefly and then said, 'There are two other points which I should mention.' He unbuttoned his tunic pocket and took out a small notebook. 'Herr Lammers had a telephone call from Fraulein Margerete Axmann of the Linz Foundation at eight o'clock last night. She's decided regretfully to decline his invitation to spend the weekend in Münster.'

'Any reason?'

'Her exact words were, "I've had a letter from Rudi and in view of what he said, I feel I would be imposing on your hospitality unnecessarily." She sounded very angry; do you suppose it is of any significance?'

He had more than enough evidence to satisfy even Kaltenbrunner that Bormann and Rudi were one and the same man, but it no longer seemed important. There could be any number of reasons why Axmann had changed her mind about coming to Münster, but perhaps the most simple explanation was that Bormann had grown tired of her. In any event, that too was no longer important.

In a tired voice, Kastner said, 'I wouldn't attach any significance to it, Wollweber. Is there anything else I should know?'

'The recording engineers will arrive this evening and will be staying at the Kaiserhof, and finally, Herr Lammers is giving a dinner party tonight at his house. I understand you are invited.'

'Who are the other guests?'

'The Bürgermeister, the President of the Reichsbank and their wives, Lieutenant-General Graf von Macher from the Wehrkreiskommando on the Hindenburg Platz and Colonel Vietinghoff who commands the Replacement Centre at Handorf, plus the Gauleiters who are attending the conference tomorrow. Will you be going, Herr Oberführer?'

'I'll think about it.'

He turned his back on Wollweber in a gesture of dismissal and gazed out of the window. The sun was beginning to break through the overcast and it looked as though they would have a fine, crisp autumn day. Unlike yesterday, the waters of the lake were calm and placid but Kastner derived little pleasure from the view from his room for the smell of death and total defeat were all around him now.

The chauffeur-driven Citroën entered the forecourt of the Gare de Cornavin and stopped outside the main entrance. The driver alighted, opened the nearside rear door for Baron Pierre Damon and then, having collected his suitcase from the boot, handed it to a waiting porter. Damon was starting out on a journey which could well be the most important undertaking of his life and one which could well have a profound effect on the course of history. He had been told that he was an officially accredited representative of His Britannic Majesty's Government empowered to enter into negotiations with the leaders of a German Peace Movement, and he saw nothing incongruous in the fact that a provincial Swiss banker, with no diplomatic skill or previous experience to draw upon, should have been entrusted with such a delicate mission. Instead, he saw himself as a latter-day Metternich redrawing the map of Europe.

Officially, as far as the German Embassy was concerned, Damon had received permission to visit Hamm, which was a mere thirty kilometres from Münster, for purely business reasons, and although he fully understood the need for secrecy, he felt a little deflated that no one was there to see him off. In this he was wrong, because the Abwehr had him under surveillance and British Intelligence would have been very disappointed had they failed to be so obliging. It had been Ashby's intention from the very outset to use Damon as a tantalising piece of window dressing.

The barn was an integral part of the farmhouse and although they ate with Jost in the kitchen, their living quarters were in the loft above the cattle stalls. They slept on straw-filled mattresses in double-tiered bunks which stood on either side of a small window. Apart from this rudimentary item of furniture, there was a wash-hand-basin and a metal jug which had to be filled from a tap outside in the yard, and to complete their discomfort, a strong smell of dung was always present even when Ottaway was smoking one of his cheap German cigars. Although the single electric light bulb, suspended from a beam high up in the roof, cast a dim pool of light around the loft steps, most of the room was in darkness.

They had spent a long, hard day in the fields lifting the potato crop but there was to be no let-up for them yet. They sat in a semi-circle just outside the sphere of light and stared at the map spread out on the floor.

Ashby glanced at the ring of expectant faces and said, 'Until the day before yesterday, this map was lodged in the government offices on the Dom Platz. The Gauleiter, whose name is Julius Lammers, sent it to Colonel Jochem Vietinghoff, the commanding officer of the Replacement Centre at Handorf, and it reached us through Gerhardt who passed it to me during the lunch break today. I mention this to show once more that we do have allies among the Germans who are prepared to help us, because I know some of you felt that this operation was almost certain to be a disaster and that we would be extremely lucky if we even reached Münster in one piece.'

'I don't want to seem a pessimist, Colonel,' Cowper said stiffly, 'but I'm afraid it will take more than a map to convince me that we have a reasonable chance of success.'

'Would it make you feel any happier if I told you that, in the morning, we shall know exactly what security arrangements have been made by the Gestapo?'

Quilter said, 'Have we got an informer, sir?'

'Yes indeed, it's our friend Lammers. He's arranged a special dinner party for tonight and among the invited guests will be Colonel Vietinghoff.'

Ottaway leaned forward to get a closer look at the map. 'It looks like a spider's web,' he said. 'Do those superimposed hairlines represent the water mains or the sewerage?'

'The sewage system.'

'I thought we were going in through the front door?'

'That is the general idea but we might need an alternative way out if it gets rough.' Ashby's finger stabbed at the Rathaus. 'You see that dot in the Gruetgasse behind the council chambers? That's an access point to a feeder channel which runs into the main sewer under Klemensstrasse. We don't

193

have to wade through the muck because there is a raised walk running all the way to the Dortmund Canal on the outskirts of town. If they try to intercept us, we'll dodge through the feeders running north into Salzstrasse or south-east towards Windthorststrasse.'

'We could get ourselves lost down there in the darkness.'

'It's possible.'

Quilter cleared his throat nervously. 'Colonel, wouldn't it be easier to ambush Bormann when he's driving from the airfield to the Rathaus?'

'It's too open and unless we mined the road, which would be difficult, we could miss him. Besides, he'll probably have a strong escort and we wouldn't get a crack at the Party Gauleiters, and finally, we want everyone to think that the Gestapo engineered this assassination.' Ashby rolled up the map. 'When are we scheduled to go on the air?'

Quilter peered at the luminous face of his wristwatch. 'We have about ten minutes in hand.'

'All right, you'd better get ready. Is there anything you want to send to your people, Jack?'

Ottaway shook his head. 'I guess not,' he said.

Their call went out at 2335 hours and was picked up by Station 53B at Aylesbury. Getting an acknowledgment from the Home Station, Quilter rapped out the message on the morse key. It was brief and to the point and, in a way, inspiring, or so the girl at Aylesbury thought. It said: WE ARE READY.

Other messages were abroad that night. One beamed from Moscow was intended for the 'Choro' Group of the Rote Kapelle or Red Orchestra network operating in Berlin. It was captured and decoded by Station III of the wireless intercept service, who in turn passed it to the Headquarters of Signal Security in the Matthaikirchplatz. It gave warning of an intended assassination but since it was couched in deliberately vague terms, it avoided mentioning Bormann by name, although it did warn all Soviet agents to remain dormant until further orders.

Abwehr Signals Security were more than a little puzzled for the simple reason that, between 22nd December, 1942, and 5th August, 1943, all thirteen members of the 'Choro'

Group had been tried and executed. As a matter of routine, the message was referred to the Gestapo Headquarters on nearby Prinz Albrechtstrasse. It was not, however, given a priority precedence.

19

THE TRUCK, AN Opel 'Blitz', swung into the yard and, on Ashby's signal, drove straight into the barn and stopped just short of the far wall. Before the engine died, Cowper and Ottaway had closed both doors so that the vehicle was completely hidden from view.

Gerhardt climbed down with a confident smile on his face. 'Well,' he said, 'what do you think?'

Ashby pointed to the formation signs on the mudwings. 'Apart from these, which will have to be changed, it's just what we want.'

'There's no need to change the signs.'

'Why not?'

'Because the special guard company from the Waffen SS Training School at Brunswick arrived here without any vehicles and the Wehrkreiskommando had to order local units to provide them with a pool of transport. In the circumstances, divisional signs are irrelevant.'

'Where did you learn all this?'

'From Vietinghoff. Lammers gave him some interesting news about the security arrangements for the conference.'

'Good or bad?'

'A little of both.'

Quilter, Stack, Frick and the rest gathered in a tight circle around them and he could see by the set expression on their faces that they were keyed up and anxious to hear what Gerhardt had to say. He was tempted to let them stay on if only to satisfy their curiosity, but apart from this, their presence would serve no useful purpose until he was ready to brief them in full.

Ashby turned to Ottaway. 'All right, Jack,' he said firmly, 'briefing will be at twelve. In the meantime, let's act as if we've nothing to hide—that means all of you outside.'

'You want us working in the fields, Colonel?'

A low, disgruntled voice said, 'Christ, potato-picking again.'

Ashby glanced in Cowper's direction. 'At a time like this we'll get on each other's nerves if we just hang about waiting for something to happen.'

There was a moment's hesitation before they turned away and slowly filed out of the barn.

Ashby waited until they were alone and then said, 'All right, now you can tell me the bad news.'

Gerhardt cleared his throat. 'I think Kaltenbrunner is trying to sit on the fence. He's sent one of his top men from Berlin to take charge of the security arrangements.'

'Who?'

'Oberführer Kastner. I personally don't know him but I've heard that he has quite a reputation.' His forehead creased in a frown. 'Although, oddly enough, I understand Lammers isn't very impressed with him; he said that Kastner is hesitant and indecisive.'

'Maybe that's just a pose?'

'I don't think so, he made very few changes to the outline plan, most of which came from Lammers.'

Ashby unfolded the street plan and laid it out on the bonnet of the truck. 'Suppose you tell me about it?'

Gerhardt lit a cigarette. 'Well, as you would expect, Bormann will have a strong escort to meet him at the airfield—one platoon—say forty men in two trucks—one in front, the other close behind his car, plus four outriders on motorcycles. A guard of honour of about the same strength will be drawn up outside the Rathaus, but all that is for outward show because, once he's inside the council chambers, they will return to Aegidii Barracks leaving only fifty men in the immediate area, and it's these people we have to worry about. Pedestrians won't be allowed on the east side of the Prinzipalmarkt, which will be closed to vehicular traffic from St Lamberti Church to the junction of Rothenburg, Ludgeristrasse and Klemensstrasse. There will be a standing patrol of six men stationed behind the council chambers and four sentries inside the building.'

'I presume they're using road blocks to close off the street?'

'Yes, and the west side of the road will also be lined with troops spaced at five-metre intervals to keep the crowd in check.'

'We're expecting crowds, are we?'

'Bormann's visit hasn't been publicised but people are bound to collect when they see the road blocks established.'

'I'm counting on you to get us through the check points.'

'Do you think they are going to argue with a Major-General of the SS and his aide?'

'Not if you play your cards right.'

'You don't have to worry on that score. They'll take one look at the Mercedes and its occupants and the battle will be half won.'

'The car is definitely fixed, is it?'

'It will call for me at Lammers's house; Vietinghoff is also providing me with a reliable driver.'

'His house is how far from here? Two kilometres?'

'Less than that across the fields.'

'And in broad daylight you propose to walk there in uniform?'

'Why not? Who's likely to see us?'

'Anyone could, the countryside is flat and open.'

'If we're stopped, we'll say that we are guests of Herr Lammers taking a stroll after lunch. We Germans are a regimented people; no civilian is going to question the right of a General and his aide to cross a piece of farmland.'

Ashby folded the map away and stuffed it inside his jacket. 'This is going to be a long shot,' he said quietly, 'but I believe we can pull it off as long as the weather holds good over East Prussia. It would be ironic if poor visibility forced Bormann to cancel his visit at the last minute, wouldn't it?'

He turned away from Gerhardt and without waiting for an answer, climbed the steps to the loft above.

The dull brooding sky over Berlin matched Kaltenbrunner's mood exactly. He arrived at his office in a state of nervous tension and began sifting through the correspondence lying on the desk, hoping to find among the pile of letters, signals and reports some item which would enable him to resolve his dilemma over Bormann one way or the other. Until now he had been content to let things drift, knowing that he had not committed himself to any definite course of action, but today, because of certain events which might happen in a small city with a population numbering less than a hundred and forty thousand, he had to arrive at a decision. If Bormann was liquidated, he could establish himself as the most powerful man in Germany, but if the plan miscarried then suicide might well be the only choice left open to him.

A report from Amt VI, the foreign intelligence section of the SD, caught his eye and noticing that it referred to Baron Pierre Damon, he picked it up and read it eagerly. The text merely set out the itinerary for Damon's visit to the Reich but underneath it, Schellenberg, the department head, had penned a note which was of interest. It said:

'You may recall that on a number of occasions in the past, Damon, at the request of our Foreign Ministry, has had informal talks with representatives of the British Government in Switzerland. I understand that he has, as a result, enabled us to determine the attitude of the British towards a peaceful settlement of the war which, until now, has always been unfavourable. During the last week however, reports from Abwehr agents in Geneva suggest that Damon has frequently been in touch with officials of the British Consulate and this unusual activity could indicate a change of mind on the part of the British.'

Kaltenbrunner looked at the itinerary again and suddenly the town of Hamm became very significant, for Damon was now within easy reach of Lammers. It was not quite the omen he'd been seeking but it did cast a more hopeful light on the situation and he began to unwind a little. He placed the report to one side and picked up a letter addressed 'Personal for Obergruppenführer Ernst Kaltenbrunner, RSHA, Berlin'. The handwriting was unmistakably Kastner's, and in pleasurable anticipation, he slit open the envelope with a paper-knife and extracted two sheets of foolscap.

The statement which had been prepared at his insistence was unconvincing and only confirmed his opinion that Kastner had murdered Dollmann. Coupled with the chain of circumstantial evidence that Detective Emil Maurice had uncovered, there was every reason for allowing the criminal police to have jurisdiction over Kastner, but although tempted to adopt this course of action, he eventually decided to refer the matter to the legal department. Kastner was obviously a worried man and, at this moment in time, it was possibly more advantageous to leave him in charge of the security arrangements in Münster than to have him arrested and charged. There was also the comforting throught that no one could subsequently accuse him of having an ulterior motive if he acted on the advice of an independent team of lawyers. The decision taken, Kaltenbrunner pressed the buzzer on his desk to summon a secretary from the outer office.

Five hundred and sixty kilometres to the east of Berlin the captain of the JU 52/3M completed his pre-flight check and taxied out on to the runway. Knowing that Martin Bormann had already left Rastenburg for the departure airfield, he was anxious to take off as soon as his passenger arrived. The latest forecast showed that visibility over Berlin was down to less than two thousand metres and decreasing, and he had been advised by air traffic control to use the alternative flight plan. Instead of overflying the capital, they would now be routed via Hamburg, and he calculated that despite the assistance of a strong tail wind, their estimated time of arrival at Loddenheide might have to be adjusted by as much as fifteen minutes. He checked the time and then scanning the perimeter road, was relieved to see a Mercedes moving towards them at speed. Bormann was arriving ahead of time and with any luck, and if he pushed the aircraft to its limit, it might not be necessary to amend their schedule after all.

Less than five minutes later the tri-motor Junkers roared down the runway and lifted off. The time was 1109 hours.

The message intended for the 'Choro' Group which Station III had captured and decoded had followed a tortuous path before it reached Fraulein Erica Abetz. Referred to Prinz Albrechtstrasse by the headquarters of Signal Security on nearby Mattaikirchplatz, it had been seen and initialled by every section head in Amt VI. Only two people however had seen fit to make any comment. An unfamiliar hand scrawled

'Surely those stupid idiots in Moscow must know that the Rote Kapelle no longer exists?' while underneath, in a flash of rare but laboured humour, Schellenberg had added, 'Apparently not—should we tell them?' and then, as if wishing not to appear too facetious, he'd written, 'A crude attempt at psychological warfare?'

Erica Abetz might be a plain, unattractive spinster of thirty-five but she was one of the few women on the staff of the Gestapo Headquarters able to deal with Kaltenbrunner when he was in a foul mood. This reputation was not entirely justified, because over the years she had developed a nose for impending trouble and was particularly adept at avoiding it. Although she did not appreciate the significance of the Moscow signal, Abetz realised that Kaltenbrunner would demand to know why it had been shuttled back and forth.

She looked up and smiled at her assistant. 'Irmgard,' she said sweetly, 'I have to deliver a highly confidential file to the legal department. While I'm away, you might take this signal into the Chief.'

Kaltenbrunner did not fly into a rage; fear, not anger, drained the colour from his face. Schellenberg might dismiss the message as a piece of crude, black propaganda but he knew better. How the Russians were aware that there was a plot to kill Bormann and why they should broadcast this fact to a spy ring that no longer existed was something of a mystery. Faced with the need to act quickly if he was to protect himself, Kaltenbrunner was not inclined to question their motives too deeply.

Looking up from the desk, he said, 'Tell Fraulein Abetz that I want a top priority call to Rastenburg.'

The girl hesitated and then reluctantly said, 'She's taken a file down to the legal department, Herr Obergruppenführer.'

Somehow, because it was important that this girl should not become flustered, he managed to control his temper and a ghastly smile appeared on his face. 'Then perhaps you would attend to it immediately?' he said.

As the first step towards self-preservation, he hoped to persuade Bormann to cancel his visit to Münster. But it was already too late for that. By the time he was connected with Rastenburg, the JU 52 had been airborne for twenty minutes and local air traffic control was unable to raise the aircraft. In a bid to have the plane diverted, Kaltenbrunner then spoke to the senior air operations officer on duty at the Air Ministry but, since Amt VI saw the warning as a piece of black propaganda, there was little he could say which did not sound incriminating. Of necessity, his reasons for wanting the aircraft recalled were vague, and although he tried to convey a sense of urgency, the duty officer appeared reluctant to take any action unless it was first cleared with Goering.

Only one man could give him the proof he needed, and from 1147 hours onwards he made strenuous efforts to contact Kastner. At long last Kaltenbrunner had climbed down from the fence and the tide was now on the turn and running against Force 272.

They were preparing for battle now and there was an air of suppressed nervous excitement within the group. No one was in the mood for jokes and Ashby was not inclined to make one, for they were keyed up and anxious to get the job over and done with. They looked to him seeking reassurance and he knew that this would be his last opportunity to instil them with confidence and most certainly it was not the moment for posturing or for rhetoric.

He turned to the map which, pinned to a piece of softboard, was propped against the truck.

In a clear, sharp voice, he said, 'At 1415 hours Martin Bormann will enter the Rathaus on the Prinzipalmarkt to address a meeting of Party Gauleiters in the Hall of Peace. We know that the enemy will seal off the immediate area with road blocks positioned here at the St Lamberti Church and at the Klemensstrasse, Ludgeristrasse and Rothenburg road junctions. Sentries will also be posted inside the building and there will be a standing patrol in the Syndikatplatz behind the council chambers. No doubt they are satisfied with these security arrangements and since no unauthorised civilian will be allowed near the building, they have reason to be confident—as were the Trojans until the Greeks produced their wooden horse.' He paused briefly and then said, 'General Gerhardt is our Trojan horse.'

He could see from the intent expression on all their faces that he had their undivided attention now and that they were his to shape and mould as he wished. Aware of this, he endeavoured to communicate a sublime confidence which would disperse every nagging doubt and fear.

'Our strength lies in having a simple plan which, if boldly executed, will not fail. At 1415 hours an open Mercedes staff car will collect General Gerhardt and Scholl from the Gauleiter's residence on the Wolbeck road. As the car passes the bottom of the lane leading to this farm, we shall move in and stay behind it all the way into the city. It's important that no other vehicle should be allowed to get between us and the Mercedes because I'm counting on General Gerhardt to get us through the road block at the St Lamberti Church. When we stop outside the Rathaus, the General, accompanied by Scholl, myself, Stack, Quilter and Ottaway, will go inside, Frick will join the driver in the Mercedes and Cowper will stay behind the wheel of the Opel 'Blitz'. Bormann will be escorted out of the building by the General and Scholl, who will be posing as his aide, and at that stage, because we have such a good cover story, he will not realise that he is under arrest. In fact, as far as outward appearances are concerned, Bormann will help to create the impression that we are acting under his orders.' He pointed to Route 51 on the map and then said grimly, 'I don't think we'll have any difficulty persuading the assembled Gauleiters to accompany us, and once they're in the Opel, we shall move out on Route 51 until we reach this point eight kilometres to the north-east of the town where there is a track leading towards a large wood. Representatives of the German Resistance will be there to meet us and to take our prisoners into custody. Bormann, of course, will be dead long before then.'

In a voice which scarcely rose above a whisper, Cowper said, 'Supposing they don't show up? What happens then?'

'I'm afraid we shall have no alternative but to execute them.'

'All of them?'

'There are no rules in this game that I know of,' Ashby said coldly. 'Do you suppose that when the war is over we shall forgive and forget what they've done? It matters little whether it happens today, in six months' time or in a year from now, because these men are dead already.'

He waited to see if there were any other moral objections

but the brief note of protest had withered away and he began then to brief each man in detail.

Kastner was a man drained of all confidence and will-power. He ate, he slept, he spoke, he moved, his body functioned, but his brain was dull and he was no longer capable of making a decision. Unable to shape events, he merely responded to them like an automaton. He had known all along that Kaltenbrunner would never believe his statement and that it was only a question of time before he was arrested and tried for murder. As he sat there in the car speeding towards the Wehrkreiskommando in the Hindenburg Platz, he wondered why Kaltenbrunner had thought it necessary to summon him to the local army headquarters when it was so obviously a matter for the criminal police. It did not occur to him that the Wehrkreiskommando was the only establishment in Münster which possessed a secure telephone link. He was therefore even more surprised when he was met on arrival and shown into the office of Lieutenant-General Graf von Macher.

The General's handshake was firm but the smile on his face was a little strained. 'We'll have your call through to Berlin in just a few minutes, Oberführer,' he said.

'Do you know what's happening?' Kastner said in a tired voice.

'I'm as much in the dark as you are but I believe it has something to do with the conference. Naturally you'll wish to be alone when you speak with Obergruppenführer Kaltenbrunner'—he indicated the armchair behind the oak desk—'please make yourself comfortable,' he said. 'I'll wait in the adjoining office until you've finished.'

The room was full of photographs and everywhere he looked there was von Macher staring at him with the same set expression on his face—Macher as a young officer cadet in 1914, as a lieutenant posing with his officers and men of his battery in the Flanders mud of 1917, with the General Staff at the end of the autumn manoeuvres in '36, and in the dress uniform of a Major-General on the steps of the Madeleine in June 1940. The photographs showed a lion in uniform but in the presence of a Gestapo officer, von Macher had been as timid as a fieldmouse. The irony lay in the fact that Kastner too was afraid and when the phone rang, he answered it with great reluctance.

Kaltenbrunner said, 'I wish to speak to Oberführer Kastner.'

Kastner cleared his throat nervously. 'I'm here,' he said in a strained voice.

'Good. We'll go to secure speech now. Are you ready?'

Kastner moved the button to scramble, waited for the green light to show on the box and then said, 'I'm on secure now,'

'I won't waste any words with you ...'

'But if you just give me the chance I can explain everything.'

'What the hell are you talking about?' Kaltenbrunner said angrily. 'This is a matter of supreme national importance. We've just received information that there is a plot to assassinate Bormann while he is addressing the meeting of Party Gauleiters. I'm trying to get his plane diverted, but if I'm too late, you are to ensure that he does not leave the airfield until you are personally satisfied that his safety can be guaranteed. I want Lammers arrested and interrogated forthwith and you have my authority to cancel the conference if you should think it necessary. Is that understood?'

'Yes, perfectly. May I ask one question?'

'Well?'

'About my statement?'

There was a longish pause and then Kaltenbrunner said, 'The Dollmann case is closed as far as you are concerned.'

'Thank you.'

'And Kastner...'

'Yes, Herr Obergruppenführer?'

'I want you to know that the Führer and I have complete confidence in you.'

Kastner slowly replaced the phone. The reprieve was totally unexpected and almost beyond belief. His mind found it difficult to accept the fact that the danger had passed and he had nothing to fear.

Von Macher said, 'I'm not disturbing you, am I? I was told that you'd finished talking to Berlin.' He drew closer, puzzled at the expression on Kastner's face. 'You look pale,' he said, 'is anything the matter?'

'What?'

'Do you feel unwell?'

Kastner shook his head. 'No,' he said vaguely, 'I'm all right —it's Bormann...'

'What about him?'

'Someone means to kill him this afternoon.'

'Nonsense.'

Kastner looked up sharply. 'If that is your considered opinion, General,' he said spitefully, 'perhaps you'd like me to pass it on to the Führer? I'm sure he'd be very interested.'

The colour drained from von Macher's face. 'I spoke in haste and without being in possession of all the facts.'

'Quite so. In view of the situation, I would like to think that I may call on you for assistance should it prove necessary?'

'Of course. I'll confine the garrison to barracks and warn all units to be at fifteen minutes notice to move.'

'I appreciate your co-operation,' Kastner said drily, 'and I'll make a point of mentioning in my report how helpful you have been.'

Ten minutes after Kastner had left the Wehrkreiskommando, von Macher telephoned Vietinghoff and in veiled speech warned him that the Gestapo was on the alert. Acting on this broad hint, Vietinghoff decided not to send the Mercedes staff car to the Gauleiter's residence that afternoon. He was a man of straw and in placing too much reliance on him, Gerhardt had made his second error of judgment.

The time was 1337 hours and Lammers had already left for the Rathaus.

From the small window in the loft above the barn, Ashby watched Gerhardt and Scholl as they strolled unconcernedly across the fields in the direction of Wolbeck. He could not help thinking that Scholl was just the sort of good-looking aide that a vicious degenerate would choose. Most of the team had wondered why he had persevered with Scholl when common-sense told them that the boy should never have been selected in the first place, but now perhaps they understood his motives; no one else looked the part or could have played it with any conviction. He waited until they were out of sight beyond the distant hedgerow and then left.

Jost had been drinking steadily since eleven that morning. Sprawled in a wooden armchair, a glass clutched in his hand, he stared at the half-empty bottle on the kitchen table with bloodshot eyes as if trying to remember where all the Schnapps had gone.

He looked round as Ashby entered the room and raised the tumbler in a mocking salute. 'Heil!' he said thickly, 'Welcome to the SS fraternity; the uniform suits you down to the ground.'

'You're drunk.'

'No, not yet, but I intend to be before this day is over.'

Ashby placed a small pill on the table. 'You might need this,' he said.

'What is it?' Jost said suspiciously.

'A cyanide capsule.'

Jost placed the tumbler carefully on the table, picked up the capsule and aimed it at the fire. It struck one of the narrow bars on the grate and fell back on to the hearth.

'You bastard,' he said angrily, 'that's what I think of your bloody death pill.' He reached for the bottle and filled his glass to the top. 'Why should I cheat the Gestapo if it all goes wrong?'

'It might save you a lot of unnecessary pain.'

'Maybe I want it that way. You think I like being a traitor, because that's what I am and nothing you can say will change that?'

'Why did you do it then?'

'Christ knows. Maybe because no matter how hard I try to close my eyes and ears to it, I know what's going on in our concentration camps and I believe those rumours about the gas chambers. And maybe it's because I know that we've already lost this damned war and yet hundreds upon thousands of decent Germans are going to die because the gang of criminal lunatics who govern this country won't face up to the fact.'

'Whatever your motives, I admire your courage.'

'And that's supposed to make me feel better, is it, Englishman?'

'I wouldn't know, I'm not your keeper.'

Ashby left the room and quietly closed the door behind him. The time was 1348 and he had just under half an hour in hand. With Gerhardt out of the way, he considered it was now safe to let each man know how to get in touch with the Dutch Underground should the need arise.

Hamburg was behind them now and they were out of the murk and the sun to starboard flashed on the perspex and, half blinded by the glare, the pilot of the Junkers was unable to see their escort, but every now and then he could hear their laconic voices in his headset, and he knew that somewhere above him at twelve o'clock high were twenty-seven FW 190s in three Staffels each of nine aircraft. This protective umbrella was changed on each occasion when the Junkers 52/3M left one sector control and entered the air space of another.

Since the beginning of October, the day fighter strength of the Luftwaffe had stood at three thousand one hundred machines but a scarcity of petrol had severely limited operations. Yet on this day, according to the pilot's calculations, no less than one hundred and fifty sorties would be mounted for the sole purpose of ensuring that one man reached Münster in order to address a meeting. It was, he thought, a damn silly way to run an air force and a guaranteed recipe for total defeat.

The navigator broke into his chain of thought. 'We're coming up to Osnabrück now,' he said, 'we're on course and only two minutes behind schedule.'

The pilot acknowledged tersely and then slowly began to lose height.

They were five in number—Kastner, Wollweber, two burly SS men and Lammers, who looked pale but dignified. They were in a room directly under the Hall of Peace and, in the short silence which had followed Kastner's announcement, Wollweber was almost sure that he could hear the faint murmur of voices from above.

Lammers said, 'Have you taken leave of your senses, Oberführer?'

'I don't make a practice of arresting people without good reason.'

'Then I should like to know why I am being detained.'

'Because I believe that you intend to kill Martin Bormann.'

Lammers smiled easily. Turning to Wollweber, he said, 'I owe you an apology; you were right about this man and I was wrong. It's now quite obvious to me that he is on the verge of a nervous breakdown.'

'I said nothing of the kind, you're putting words into my mouth.'

'My dear Wollweber,' Kastner said smoothly, 'there's no need to be alarmed; Herr Lammers is just trying to drive a wedge between us. Behind that false smile he is a very worried man.'

'If I'm about to kill Bormann, why don't you search me? Perhaps I have a gun in my armpit?' He unbuttoned his overcoat and jacket and held them open. 'There, does that satisfy you now you can see for yourself that I am unarmed?'

'The demonstration was hardly necessary, I don't think you are the killer, Doctor.'

'I think this foolishness has gone on for long enough . . .'

'I agree with you.'

Lammers passed a hand through his unruly brown hair. 'My God,' he said, 'you'll have some explaining to do when Bormann arrives.'

'I doubt it. You see, I've already spoken to the escort commander and, on my instructions, the Party Secretary will remain at Loddenheide airfield until I consider it is safe for him to leave.'

'You're quite mad.'

'You're the one who's mad, Doctor. How long do you think you can go on bluffing me? We've had you under surveillance and we know all about 'Rudi' and Georg Thomas and Pierre Damon.'

'You say I've been watched?'

'Certainly.'

'On whose orders?'

'Kaltenbrunner's.'

'And now on his instructions you have arrested me?'

'Yes.'

'You're a fool, Oberführer; you're being used and you can't see it. Why do you think Bormann is coming here today? To address a meeting of Party Gauleiters? That is just a smoke screen to hide the real purpose of his visit. With the full knowledge and consent of the Führer, he has come to Münster in order to meet Baron Pierre Damon.' Lammers stopped and pointing to the SS troopers said, 'I don't think I should say anything more than that in front of these two men.'

Wollweber licked his lips. 'Perhaps we should hear what Doctor Lammers has to say in private, Herr Oberführer?'

'Oh, he'd like that,' said Kastner, 'because the good Doctor is playing for time.'

'But perhaps he's telling the truth.'

'Then he won't mind repeating this ridiculous story in front of Frau Lammers, will he? In fact, I think it would be a very good idea if you borrowed the Doctor's Mercedes and fetched the dear lady. And perhaps you'd better take a couple of men with you in case she proves stubborn.'

'Is that an order, Herr Oberführer?'

'Yes, it is.'

'Very well, but I must say I think you're making a mistake.'

'Do you now?' Kastner said icily. 'Well, understand this, Wollweber, if you fail to carry out my orders to the letter, I'll see to it that they hang you from a butcher's hook in Plotzensee.'

He waited until Wollweber had left the room and then still smiling, he smashed his right fist into Lammers's face and broke his nose.

'You're a bastard,' he said quietly, 'and that's only a sample of what is in store for you.'

The Bürgermeister and the Haupsturmführer in command of the escort stood some distance apart from each other as they watched the aircraft coming in on its final approach. This was a proud moment for the Bürgermeister and he was very grateful that Lammers had accorded him the privilege of meeting Bormann at the airfield; a lesser man would not have allowed anyone to share the limelight, but then the Doctor was noted for his generous nature. He was conscious that this was a great occasion and something to tell his grandchildren about when they were old enough to understand.

The Haupsturmführer did not share this feeling of pleasurable anticipation for it was his unpleasant duty to inform

Bormann that he must stay within the confines of Loddenheide airfield until his safety could be guaranteed. He knew
full well that no matter how tactfully it was put to him, Bormann was bound to take offence and there would be an em-
barrassing scene. With a sour taste in his mouth, he watched
the Junkers 52/3M make a perfect landing and roll to a stop.

The time was 1403 and Bormann was just three minutes
behind schedule.

The inverted L-shaped house which stood well back from
the road, owed much of its privacy and seclusion to the fact
that it was screened by an orchard in the front and by a
vegetable garden enclosed by a tall hedge on the northern
side, while at the back a lawn extended as far as the row of
trees on the lip of the bank which fell sharply away to a slug-
gish brown stream. Gerhardt and Scholl had crossed this
brook by way of a footbridge some thirty metres downstream
and had then slipped into the house through the kitchen, the
door to which had been deliberately left open for them.

That no one was there to meet them did not surprise Gerhardt. He guessed that Lammers had told his wife to stay out
of sight in her room upstairs in the naïve belief that this frail
subterfuge would convince the Gestapo that she was not involved in the conspiracy. Although he told himself that it was
only natural for a husband to protect his wife in any way
he could, Gerhardt was still resentful. Compared to the
risks to which Christabel had been exposed all these weeks,
Frau Lammers had little to fear.

Scholl said, 'I wouldn't mind living in a house like this.'

'Who wouldn't?'

'I can hardly remember now what our home in Wuppertal
was really like.' He smiled shyly. 'You see, I wasn't quite
fourteen when we left Germany.'

'The war has a lot to answer for,' Gerhardt said vaguely.

'The war had nothing to do with our leaving Germany—
my mother was a Jewess and we could see the writing on the
wall. Does that surprise you?'

Gerhardt looked at his wristwatch. 'What are you on
about?'

'Nothing really, I just feel nervous.'

'That's only natural.'

'Is it?'

'Oh yes, one is always afraid of the unknown...' Gerhardt paused in mid-sentence and then said, 'I think I can hear the car.'

Scholl crossed the hall and looked through the narrow window. 'There's a Mercedes turning into the drive now,' he said.

'Well, I must say that's a weight off my mind, I was beginning to think that Vietinghoff had let us down. You'd better go outside and meet it.'

Scholl was expecting to see an open tourer but this Mercedes coming towards him at speed was a saloon hard-top and as it drew near and he saw the uniformed SS man, he knew instinctively that everything had gone terribly wrong. He tried to draw the Walther P38 9mm automatic but his fingers were all thumbs and finding that he could not release it from the holster, he turned and ran back into the house.

Gerhardt grabbed him by the shoulders. 'What the hell's the matter with you?' he shouted.

The question was irrelevant. As the car screeched to a halt in front of the open door, a Sturmbannführer and two NCOs piled out, one of whom ran towards the back of the house. Their every move was part of a well-planned drill, yet clearly the fat SS officer did not expect to find himself face to face with a Brigadeführer. His eyes blinked rapidly behind the thick glasses and the Walther in his right hand gradually drooped until it was pointing down at the ground.

Gerhardt released Scholl and stepped forward. 'What is the meaning of this?' he said harshly.

In the presence of a senior officer, Wollweber was usually subservient but this was that one occasion when he was resolved not to be intimidated. There was something vaguely familiar about this particular SS Major-General and he could swear that they'd met before.

Gerhardt said, 'What are you staring at? Do you make a habit of not saluting a senior officer, or is your eyesight so bad that you can't see my badges of rank?'

The NCO at Wollweber's side was like a ramrod as he snapped to attention and for a moment he wavered, and then he noticed that the General's pretty, baby-faced aide was sweating with fear, and suddenly he remembered a photo-

graph in a silver frame standing on a desk in a house at Iserlohn and then everything fell into place.

'Welcome home, Gerhardt,' Wollweber said triumphantly,
'it's good to see you back in Germany. I know the very man
who's dying to meet you, if you'll pardon the pun.'

As Gerhardt's hands slowly rose above his head, Scholl
turned away and moved through the house. The desire to escape was there but although he tried desperately hard to
drive himself forward, his legs would not respond and lacking
co-ordination, he staggered from side to side bumping into
the furniture. Even the most simple task was now almost beyond him and he wrestled frantically with the kitchen door
before he realised that he was turning the key in the lock, and
when at last he did succeed in opening it, Scholl was on the
verge of tears. He blundered out into the garden straight into
the arms of the waiting NCO and, locked together, they fell
heavily. Fear gave him the strength to break free and scramb-
ling to his feet, he started running towards the trees.

The shots came singly, three in number, and in the open
they were no louder than the snapping of a slender, dry
branch, and all were wild except for the one which went
straight through his neck, and the impact sent him cartwheel-
ing down the steep bank into the muddy stream where he lay
on his back staring at the sky above through sightless eyes.

They were dressed for battle now, all six of them alike in
the M44 pattern blouse and trousers with canvas gaiters over
short black boots, and each man had two MP40 ammo
pouches with six spare magazines for his Schmeisser and a
couple of stick grenades stuffed into the leather belt at his
waist. Five men in one Opel 'Blitz' truck anxiously listening
to a starter motor whirring and whirring and whirring were
hoping and praying that the engine would catch before the
battery went flat, while the sixth, Cowper, blasphemed and
mouthed every obscenity known to man because the bloody
thing seemed determined to die on him and there was nothing he could do about it.

Ashby said, 'You've flooded it.'

'I'll wreck the sodding thing before I'm through with it,'
Cowper shouted, 'I swear to Christ I'll smash it with my own
bare hands.'

'Calm down.'

'Calm down? Is that all you can say at a time like this? Christ, I should have known what I was letting myself in for when I joined this bloody shit heap of a unit, I should have known that with a deadbeat like you in charge it was bound to be a disaster.'

Ashby shot out a hand, grabbed hold of Cowper's tunic and slammed him back against the side of the cab. 'That's enough,' he snarled, 'one more word out of you and I'll break your damned neck.' He waited until Cowper had recovered his self-control and then releasing him, he said, 'Switch off.'

'What?' Cowper said in a dazed voice.

'Switch the ignition off and crank it dry and then when the cylinders are cleared, we'll try again.' Ashby got out of the cab and walked round to the back of the truck. 'All right, Quilter,' he said calmly, 'hop out and run to the junction at the top of the lane and flag Gerhardt down. Tell him that on no account is he to move on before we link up with him.' He looked at the other anxious faces in the back and smiled confidently. 'There's nothing to worry about, we'll be a little late but what does that matter, after all Bormann isn't going anywhere in a hurry.'

Quilter vaulted over the tailboard and started running. He moved easily with the grace and economical style of a trained athlete; his thumb, hooked into the sling, held the Schmeisser tight against his back and shoulders so that with each stride it did not thump against his haunches. The lane seemed unending but he remained calm, conserving his energy, and he resisted the temptation to make a futile sprint which would have burned him out before half the distance was covered. Sweat gathered on his forehead and under his arms and ran down his back and his legs felt as if they were made of cotton wool, but he never faltered and he never slacked the pace. None of the others could match him over two thousand metres and he knew it, but he was still some three hundred metres from the junction when the Mercedes flashed past and there was nothing, absolutely nothing he could do to stop it.

He was quite certain that Gerhardt was sitting in the back and, although he only caught a brief glimpse, he assumed that the man sitting beside him must be Scholl. He had been told that they would be riding in an open Mercedes but even though this was a hard-top model, he wasn't all that surprised. Six years of war had taught him that, without exception, every army was capable of making a cock-up and according to his philosophy, the victor was usually the one who made the least.

He looked back at the farm and was relieved to see the truck coming towards him. The time was 1423 hours.

For some time after he had replaced the phone, Kastner studied Lammers in silence. It was part of his technique to arouse the curiosity of a prisoner under interrogation and then to leave him in doubt so that his imagination having free play might conjure up countless fears.

A bleak smile made a brief appearance on his face. 'That was Wollweber,' he said. 'It seems he has just run into an old friend of yours—a Major-General Paul Heinrich Gerhardt. I believe you first met one another when he was stationed in Münster long before the war?' He waited to see if there would be any reaction but Lammers appeared unmoved. 'I'm sure you'll have a lot to talk about; as a matter of fact, he's on the way over here now.'

'He's not really a friend, I look upon him as a casual acquaintance.'

'Really? I find that surprising. Purely for my own interest, perhaps you could explain what he was doing in your house and why his aide tried to escape?'

Kastner took out a notebook and flung it at Lammers striking him in the face. 'Pick it up,' he snarled, 'pick it up and start writing. I think it's time you made a confession.'

Lammers edged the notebook away with his foot. Despite the bloodstained handkerchief which he held to his swollen nose, he managed to look dignified. 'I have nothing to say to you,' he said defiantly.

Kastner said, 'You know something, Doctor? I really don't care. You can save your speech for the People's Court and Judge Roland Freisler.'

Two determined men who were willing to sacrifice their lives might get close enough to Bormann to kill him and perhaps only Gerhardt and this unknown young officer were involved but somehow Kastner rather doubted it. Gerhardt would need help to return to Germany and to stay at large

215

inside the Reich. If that were true, then the conspiracy was on too large a scale for just two men to be its spearhead and perhaps there were other assassins waiting to strike.

A system of check points established on every road could seal and quarantine the city until this possibility had been eliminated. He thought of alerting the local Wehrmacht units for this task but then he remembered that on 20th July, Stauffenberg had counted on the army to arrest Goebbels and seize the main government offices. In the circumstances, he considered it prudent to make do with the special guard company until they could be reinforced by other Waffen SS troops.

To relieve the escort and to disperse the gathering crowds in the Prinzipalmarkt he would first have to persuade Bormann to return to Rastenburg, and once that hurdle had been overcome, he could then announce to the assembled and now restless Gauleiters that their conference had been cancelled.

From the moment he'd started to investigate Gerhardt all the evidence had seemed to indicate that Bormann, possibly with Himmler's tacit approval, was at the centre of a conspiracy to end the war but now suddenly Kastner was forced to abandon all his preconceived ideas about the man. Bormann, in agreeing to address the meeting of Gauleiters which Lammers, using his influential position in the Party had organised, was the victim not the instigator of the plot. He wondered how he could have been so blind and then he remembered that at every critical stage of his inquiry, Kaltenbrunner had pointed him in a different direction. The thought triggered a series of dangerous ideas and he dismissed them hurriedly from his mind for there were more important matters to attend to. Kastner reached for the phone and called the airfield at Loddenheide.

As they moved through the outer suburbs of Münster there was still no sign of the Mercedes staff car which they should have been following. Assuming that Quilter had not been mistaken, it seemed to Ashby that either Gerhardt had deserted them at the last minute which, unless he'd taken leave of his senses, appeared unlikely, or else he'd been picked up by the Gestapo. Like Quilter, he'd been inclined at first to think that the unexpected substitution of an open tourer for a closed saloon was just a simple foul-up, but now he was coming round to the view that there was a more sinister explanation.

He was faced with a simple choice—either he called it off now or else they went ahead regardless of the risks involved—and with the canal bridge in sight, Ashby knew that he only had a couple of minutes left in which to make up his mind. If the alarm was out, it was reasonable to suppose that there would be some outward and visible sign of activity on the part of the police, the SS or the army, but as far as he could see, nothing much was happening. It might be different in the old part of the city but here on the outskirts everything seemed normal enough. To stick to the original plan was asking for trouble but there was another way into the Rathaus.

Ashby said, 'You see that building ahead? That's the offices of the Railway Board; I want you to turn left at that point.'

'Isn't that taking us out of our way?' said Cowper.

'That's right, there's been a change of plan and when you get to the station you'll turn right, go past the "Angel" fortifications and then stop in Klosterstrasse when I tell you to. We're going in through the sewers.'

'How? You said yourself that you needed a key to open one of those inspection shafts.'

Ashby opened a pocket on his blouse and took out a T-shaped key. 'Courtesy of Gerhardt's friends,' he said laconically, 'it came with the map of the drainage system.'

'It's good for any shaft, is it?'

'Yes.'

'So what happens after I've dropped you in Klosterstrasse?'

'You follow the inner ring road past the Hindenburg Platz and then turn on to Route 54. After a kilometre you want to keep your eyes open for a small brook passing under the road because I want you to stop two hundred metres beyond that point and wait for us. We'll be coming out through an inspection shaft in a side street behind you on the left-hand side of the road.'

Cowper said, 'How long do I give you, Colonel?'

'About an hour and a half unless anything goes wrong.'

'And then what?'

'You'd better make it to the Dutch border.'

A tram passed them going in the opposite direction and then the cylindrical tube of the inspection shaft, which looked like a giant toadstool, was in sight. Cowper eased his foot off the accelerator pedal, pulled into the kerb and stopped abreast of it. He sat there behind the wheel, listening to the engine idling and watched a roadsweeper clearing the leaves from the gutter while Ashby climbed out of the cab and crossed the pavement. A minute passed and then another and yet another, and his fingers drummed a nervous tattoo on the spokes of the steering wheel, and then presently he heard a scuffling of feet in the back of the truck, and then someone banged on the door, and with an audible sigh of relief, he shifted the lever into first gear. In his anxiety to get away his foot came off the clutch too fast and the truck, leaping forward like a startled rabbit, suddenly stalled on him. He closed his eyes and turned the starter motor over, hoping against hope that the engine would fire first time, and for once his unspoken prayer was answered.

A voice said, 'What's going on?'

Cowper turned his head. The policeman had one foot balanced on the hub cap and his face was on a level with the open side window. The man was curious but not unfriendly.

'We've been ordered to check the sewers as a precaution,' Cowper said casually.

'I don't envy you.' The man withdrew his foot from the hub cap and stepped back. 'You wouldn't catch me doing it.'

'Nor me,' said Cowper.

He let the clutch in slowly and this time the Opel didn't stall.

Kastner's face was white with anger. He looked from Gerhardt to Wollweber and then back again.

'Why is this criminal not in handcuffs?' he snarled. 'And why is he in SS uniform?'

Gerhardt said, 'Must I remind you that as an officer of...'

'You're a filthy traitor in anybody's language, a disgrace to the German army and you defile that uniform.' He knocked the hat from Gerhardt's head and slapped him across the face. 'You insignificant, conceited little man, what right have you to betray the Führer?'

'What right has he to destroy the German people?'

'A philosopher,' said Kastner, 'we have a philosopher on our hands, Wollweber.'

'And a man of action, Herr Oberführer.'

'Oh yes, there's no doubt about that, and he has friends too who are prepared to help him in this enterprise.' He studied Gerhardt carefully. 'Where are they now,' he said, 'these friends of yours?'

'We came alone.'

'And you failed just as your friends will also fail.'

'I've already told you we were just two in number.'

Kastner glanced at his wristwatch. 'Why persist in lying? In a few minutes Bormann will be on his way back to Rastenburg and this hall will be empty and we shall be waiting for them. They can't possibly escape, so why not make it easy for yourself?'

'I repeat, we came alone.'

'Your wife has been held in the Lehrterstrasse Prison in Berlin for the past week; do you want her to rot there for ever?'

'I have nothing to say.'

Kastner said, 'All right, Wollweber, let's see what you can do with Lammers and this swine Gerhardt. Lodge them in the cells at Aegidii Barracks and then break them.'

'And Frau Lammers?'

'What about her?'

'I left her under guard at the house.'

'Fetch her,' he said crisply, 'and let's see how brave the good Doctor will be when you start questioning her in his presence.'

The Guard of Honour, numbering some forty officers and men who'd been drawn up in the Prinzipalmarkt to await Bormann's arrival, had already dispersed by the time the Gauleiters emerged from the council chambers. Broken down into small groups, they were now moving through the suburbs to establish road blocks on the outer limits of the city. Including the standing patrol in the Syndikatplatz and those sentries still inside the building, there now remained rather less than twenty men in the immediate vicinity of the Rathaus which, in Kastner's view, was more than sufficient since he was labouring under the false impression that Bormann was on his way back to Rastenburg. And this might have been the case had Bormann not been obliged to wait at Loddenheide airfield while his aircraft was refuelled for the return journey. Faced with this delay he became impatient and then as his resentment mounted, he announced that once he'd informed Himmler, he intended to drive into Münster and assume command of the Waffen SS.

The bottle was empty now and Jost was sprawled in the chair, a dead cigar clenched between the fingers of his right hand. This was a day to forget and he'd set out with the intention of drinking himself into a stupor, but somehow the Schnapps had failed him. By rights, he should have been insensible but all he experienced was a feeling of nausea and a splitting headache. The bile rose at the back of his throat and although he fought against it, his stomach began to heave and, rising to his feet, he half ran, half staggered across the kitchen and vomited into the sink. He threw the dead cigar away and holding on to the draining board for support, was sick again. Heartburn seared his throat now and reaching for a chipped cup, he filled it with water from the tap and gulped it down until some of the sour acidic taste left his mouth and he felt a little better.

Jost had spent two and half years in the Airborne Infantry before he was invalided out in the winter of '41 and, although they were still a long way off, to his experienced ears the sound of army vehicles on the move was unmistakable. It was quite illogical of course but he was convinced that they were coming for him, and perhaps as a gesture of defiance, he went out into the yard to meet them.

He could see them clearly now, a Kubelwagen and two Opel trucks, and they were travelling at speed as if their business was urgent and suddenly his nerve failed him and he ran back into the house. Lying somewhere in the kitchen hearth was the death pill which the Englishman had given him for such a moment as this and it had become supremely important that he should find it before they arrived.

And the whine of their propshafts grew louder and he judged that they were only a few hundred metres from him; and then he saw it and scooped it up with a cry of triumph, and for a few passing seconds he stood there before the mantelpiece looking at the photograph of his wife taken a couple of months before she died of cancer in the summer of '43, and then he opened his mouth, inserted the cyanide capsule and bit on it.

The trucks went on past the farm until they reached the Wolbeck road where they stopped to drop off a detail of six men who were to establish the first of Kastner's check points on the outer limits of the city.

They moved in single file on the raised footpath above the sewer and the handkerchiefs which covered mouth and nose offered little protection against the dank and fetid smell. They could hear the quiet urgent pattering of feet and sometimes the beam of light from Ashby's torch would hold a rat transfixed in its glare. They were five hundred metres from the Rathaus at their start point but down there in that dark and foul-smelling world, they were forced to move slowly. halting frequently to check their bearings in case they should take a wrong turning. Ashby was navigating by dead reckoning with Ottaway counting off the paces in a low voice and tapping him on the shoulder whenever they had covered a round hundred.

After one hundred and twenty they met the Ludgeristrasse sewer, turned right and began to walk up a slight gradient. Water cascaded from the outlet pipes which, laid beneath the raised footpath at irregular intervals, drained the side streets and fed the main channel with waste. It was possible, just possible, to divorce the mind from the present but always the odour was there to remind them of the danger; if there was any marsh gas drifting towards them down the tunnel they had no means of detecting its presence and no means of combating its effects.

Ottaway tapped Ashby on the shoulder. 'I make it that we've covered three hundred metres since we entered this section,' he said. 'In another twenty or so we should hit the Klemensstrasse intersection, that is if we are heading in the right direction.'

'We're all right by the compass.'

Ottaway stopped abruptly. 'Okay,' he said, 'we should be over the tunnel now, Colonel.'

Ashby knelt at the edge of the path and flashed the torch up and down the length of the gallery.

Presently he said, 'I think I can see it.' He sat down, twisted the upper part of his body through almost ninety degrees and then gripping the stonework, lowered himself into the channel. He pushed upstream for some twenty metres and then called back, 'I've found it; you'd better come down and join me.'

Contrary to what Ashby had thought when he'd studied the map, there was no footpath in the Klemensstrasse tunnel and, despite keeping to the side, the water level almost reached to the top of their short boots and, if that were possible, the smell of excrement was even stronger. It affected some worse than others and Stack, who was the last man in the file, was constantly retching. The sludge on the cobbled surface was yet another hazard and each man dreaded the thought of slipping beneath the foul water.

Ashby, still in the lead, moved slowly, keeping his torch trained on the wall so that he should not miss the feeder pipe which led into Gruetgasse. It turned out to be set at a higher level and the sound of water trickling into the main channel was the first indication he had that they were almost upon it. The tube was also a damn sight narrower than he had anticipated.

He stopped, signalled them to draw close and then, pointing his torch into the mouth of the tube, said, 'We may have to walk bent double but this passage leads right into the back yard of the Rathaus. We've got about sixty to seventy metres to cover before we reach the shaft which goes up to street level. We'll be coming out in the alley which is just around the corner from the Syndikatplatz where I am told there is a standing patrol of six men. I shall raise the manhole cover, set it to one side and climb out as if it was my business to be there, and I reckon to be able to take them before they know what's happening. Up to that point we should have the advantage of surprise but from then on it's going to be a hard grind. We shall have to move fast and once we're inside the council chambers there'll be no time for any subtleties—we're simply going to bomb everything and shoot everyone who stands in our way. It's going to be Quilter's job to make sure that no one cuts us off from the manhole because it's our only lifeline.' Ashby paused a moment and then said, 'Anybody got any questions?'

Nobody had but he offered them a crumb of comfort. 'Two to one says we can do it and get clear away in the ensuing panic.'

No one seemed inclined to place a bet.

Ashby heaved himself up into the feeder pipe and bent almost double, began to edge his way forward; one by one the rest followed him.

The time was 1548 hours.

With one eye constantly on the rear-view mirror, Cowper hummed a tuneless dirge and tried to ignore the sallow, dark-haired girl of sixteen who kept ogling him as she cycled aimlessly up and down the road. It was very clear from the number of sour looks which came his way that most passers-by thought he was encouraging the girl to flirt with him but nothing could have been further from the truth. She was fast becoming a nuisance as well as an embarrassment which he could well do without. On her present form, he thought it was only a matter of time before she plucked up sufficient courage to accost him, and Cowper wondered how he would then get rid of her without causing a scene. He felt like telling her to go and try her luck outside the Aegidii Barracks where there were any number of men only too happy to oblige.

He lit a cigarette and leaned back in the seat. He spared a thought for the others who were moving through the sewers and wondered how they were taking it. You had to hand it to Ashby, he had all the determination in the world and where most people would have called it off when Gerhardt deserted them, he'd simply changed the plan, and he hadn't been content with a minor adjustment but had introduced a startlingly new concept. And for some reason, people like Quilter and Stack and Frick and even Ottaway had accepted it without a murmur. Perhaps, like Ashby, they really believed that in killing Bormann they would start a revolution that would end the war.

The girl, going through every trick in the book, stopped just in front of the truck and contrived to get her skirt hooked over the saddle as she dismounted, and she made sure that he had the opportunity of seeing a bare expanse of thigh before she adjusted her clothing with an air of false modesty. She looked round to see what effect this exhibition had had but Cowper's eyes were elsewhere. They were locked on the rear-view mirror for, in the distance he thought he could see a number of military vehicles moving towards him at speed.

Two BMW motor-cycle combinations and a Kubelwagen stopped just short of the stream and then manoeuvred in such a fashion that it soon became apparent that they were intending to form a road block. There was no doubt in his mind that before very long they would begin to take an unhealthy interest in the Opel truck which was parked not three hundred metres from their position. Ashby had said that if anything went wrong he should try and make it to the Dutch border and clearly something had gone terribly wrong.

Cowper did not believe in having second thoughts. Without any hesitation, he started up and drove off. Enschede was just eighty kilometres up the road. He planned to abandon the vehicle just this side of the border and he reckoned that with any luck he should be able to reach the Zwinjnenberg Hotel on Molenstraat and make contact with the Dutch Underground by nightfall.

Iron rungs set in the vertical shaft which rose to street level provided easy hand and foot holds and with careful positioning, it was possible to get three men on the ladder at the same time. Using his feet to thrust his back against the wall, Ashby wedged himself in the chimney so that both his hands were free to unlock and raise the manhole cover.

It was heavier than he'd expected and although he tried to place the cover quietly to one side, it made a loud scraping noise on the cobblestones. Two men from the standing patrol who were stationed in the Gruetgasse alley turned and stared in his direction.

Ashby climbed out and sauntered towards them holding the Schmeisser loosely in his right hand. 'Want to swap jobs?' he said. The Germans eyed him suspiciously. 'I tell you, it stinks to high heaven down there.'

The taller of the two men said, 'What have you been doing?'

Ottaway was out of the shaft now and Quilter was just appearing in view and he could see from the expression on their faces that he'd only a few seconds of grace left. 'Well, I'll tell you,' Ashby said casually, 'we certainly weren't having a bloody picnic.'

They were still smiling faintly when he flipped the change lever over and fired two quick bursts. At ten metres he could scarcely miss even though he was still only holding the Schmeisser with one hand.

And now it was simply a race against time and leaping over the dying SS, Ashby, with Ottaway and Quilter hard on his heels, made a frantic dash for the side entrance to the Rathaus. Frick was slow to leave the manhole and by the time he began to follow them up the alleyway towards the Prinzipalmarkt, two more of the standing patrol rounded the corner from the Syndikatplatz and were behind him. There was a brief respite because they were unable to identify friend from foe, and this numbness lasted until the moment when Ashby, finding that the side door was locked, first emptied a magazine into it and then kicked it in, and after that they were no longer in doubt.

The first engagement was brief, wild and bloody. In the initial exchange of fire, Frick had both legs shattered while Quilter, turning swiftly, killed one man and forced the other to dodge back into the Syndikatplatz where the angle of the building protected him. Stack, who until this moment had been sheltering just below the lip of the manhole, now emerged and committed himself to a headlong dash, hoping that Quilter, crouched in the open doorway of the Rathaus, would be able to cover him.

Stack came fast with his legs pumping beneath him and his head thrown back, and he stayed well to the left so that Quilter should have a clear field of fire, and the noise inside that narrow passageway was deafening and he could see tiny moles of dust rising from the brickwork, and Frick was screaming after him, and then Quilter suddenly stopped firing because most of his face had been shot away, and in that instant Stack realised that there was a sniper on the roof directly opposite the entrance and then he knew that he never could, never would cross that open space that lay between him and the objective, and fear gripped hold because he was cut off and, apart from the dying Frick, he was alone in an open-ended alleyway.

And now they were firing into Gruetgasse from the Prinzipalmarkt and he was forced to give ground, moving sideways like a crab with his back to the wall, and firing burst after burst first in one and then in the opposite direction because he had that damned sentry in the Syndikatplatz to contend with. The stick grenade came arching high into the air and, striking the face of the building behind Stack on its downward path, was deflected at the tangent and Frick, unable to move, watched it land and roll towards him, and he closed his eyes and then there was this brilliant flash of orange light which in the end gutted him like a fish.

And now the open manhole was but a few paces away and Stack, firing from the hip, launched himself at it and made it before the sentry in the Syndikatplatz reappeared. There was no time to drag the cover across and he went down the iron rungs one-handed, bruising and skinning his shins and elbows, and then he turned round and scrambled into the feeder moving as fast as he could because he had to reach the first bend in the pipe before they dropped a grenade down the shaft. And then he heard it splash into the water behind him and he lay down in the sewage because there was no other way to avoid the fragmentation pieces, and when the blast came it almost ruptured his eardrums. Covered in filth, vomit spewing from his mouth, he made the first bend before the second grenade arrived.

The mêlée on the ground floor was over in a few seconds. Moving towards the staircase, Ashby glanced to his left and saw that two sentries had been posted in the main entrance and he killed them both. Then, sheltered by the interior wall, he crouched down and continued to fire into the Prinzipalmarkt while Ottaway, working in tandem, slipped past him and began to climb up to the floor above. Based on the information which Gerhardt had supplied, they assumed that they had already accounted for half the force deployed inside the building. But they were wrong for, apart from Kastner and two NCOs waiting in ambush on the landing above, there remained the enlisted men who were guarding the passageways which led to the adjoining Stadtweinhaus.

Ottaway, his back pressed against the wall, maintained a

steady rate of fire as he moved upwards. He had little hope of hitting anything but it did ensure that no one on his right mind would risk exposing himself to get a clear shot. One man did attempt to roll a stick grenade towards him but it lodged against the banisters and, because it had been released too soon, Ottaway had time to pick it up and lob it back.

Kastner survived because the grenade landed between the NCOs and they absorbed most of the blast but one fragment of the outer casing, missing this human shield, virtually severed the calf of his right leg, and staggering forward half crazy with pain, he almost toppled over the banisters. His legs slowly gave way beneath him but as he sank down on to his haunches, he somehow managed to empty the Walther and, although incapable of producing an aimed shot, one round hit Ottaway in the jaw and felled him.

Ashby fired one last burst into the street, changed magazines for the second time and then started to move up to the first landing. He saw Ottaway fall and looking up, noticed Kastner slumped against the banisters and instinctively opened up. Four bullets hit Kastner in the stomach, chest, shoulder and neck and hurled him back against the far wall.

Ottaway raised himself up and started to crawl on hands and knees. The front of his blouse was covered in blood from the shattered jaw and the stairs seemed to sway as he experienced difficulty in focusing on them, and then a hand grabbed hold of his belt and Ashby was carrying him like a suitcase in his left hand and the stair carpet passed in a confusing blur, and the Schmeisser was chattering in Ashby's right hand, and his last recollection before he blacked out was of the floor rising up to meet him.

As he entered the vestibule on the second floor, Ashby noticed that one of the oaken doors which opened into the Hall of Peace was still ajar, and releasing Ottaway, he ran forward, hit it with his shoulder and burst into the room. The Schmeisser in his hands described an inquisitive arc of ninety degrees but remained silent because the prize was no longer there for the taking and instead he saw that some thoughtful person had emptied all the ashtrays, made a neat pile of the scratch paper which had been placed on the table in front of each delegate and had collected the carafes of water together and stacked them on a tray. And as Ashby stood there, bewildered and frozen in apathy, the old man who'd been hiding under one of the tables thought it safe to come out and in so doing, died in a hail of fire which his sudden and unexpected movement in the otherwise deserted Hall had invited.

The sky was beginning to cloud over and a chill breeze had sprung up and, although he was wearing a coat, the Bürgermeister was shivering with cold. Frustrated because he had been unable to contact Himmler and the situation in the town was such that he was reluctant to leave the safety of the airfield, Bormann had turned on the Bürgermeister who'd taken the brunt of his abuse and had been thoroughly humiliated in front of the assembled Luftwaffe and SS officers. He was an old man, gentle in his ways, and never in all his years in office had he been treated so shamefully. It seemed inconceivable that any man of intelligence could blame him for what had happened, but then perhaps he'd expected too much from this boorish lout, Bormann. Without any regret, he watched the Junkers 52/3M climb into the air and turn away from Münster. As he slowly walked back to his chauffeur-driven Wanderer, the SS escort broke ranks and piled into their waiting trucks.

The time was 1624 hours.

Ottaway opened his eyes and for a few moments the haze cleared and he found himself looking at the body of an old man who was nearly bald, and he tried to call out but he could not open his mouth and when he touched it gently with an exploring hand, he found that someone had tied a crude sling over his head to hold his jaw in place. And then before he slipped back into unconsciousness, he heard the sound of heavy firing and he wondered how much longer it would last.

They were trapped and Ashby knew it. From his vantage point on the second floor he could keep them at bay as long as the ammunition held out but it was only a question of time before they finished him one way or the other. To swallow the cyanide pill would be the easy way out but there was Ottaway to consider, and somehow now that he was faced with making the decision, he found the idea of suicide repellent and he knew that he couldn't do it. He felt guilty because, contrary to his own orders, Ashby was still wearing British army identity discs around his neck, and that was almost a tacit admission that he'd never intended to take his own life. Later, he would be surprised to learn that he was not alone in this, for Quilter, Stack, Frick, Scholl and Ottaway had also retained their tags. Hearing movement on the landing below, he lobbed over his last grenade.

Stack was running blind through the sewers and the distorted sound of raised voices came at him from every direction. They were like ferrets after a rabbit and he knew that the end was not far away. He stood there in the middle of the channel with the water tugging at his thighs and the sweat running off his face and his chest heaving, and for the first time since childhood he felt the need to pray.

'Hail Mary, sweet mother of Jesus,' he whispered, 'help me now.'

A dull clanging noise close at hand startled him and glancing to the right, he saw a glimmer of light entering the sewer, and then he heard them climbing down the shaft and filling his lungs with air, he sank beneath the water. He stayed under until the blood pounded in his ears and his lungs felt as if they were going to burst, and then he rose slowly to the surface and, had he managed to control the tickle in his throat, he might have got away with it because the patrol had gone past him, but instead, he broke into a fit of coughing as he struggled towards the vertical shaft and they came hurrying back.

He could see the sky above and he began to claw his way up to the street but his muscles were slow to respond, and although the sound of gunfire was deafening, he did not associate it with the crippling pain which was now shooting through his right leg. And then Stack found that he could no longer bear to put any weight on it and he had to drag himself up hand over hand because most of the heel had been blown off, but somehow he made it and he lay face down while he struggled to regain his breath. And then, when he looked up there was this man smiling wolfishly at him, and the man had a rifle in his hands and still smiling he placed the muzzle against Stack's ear and squeezed the trigger. The noise made by this single shot was almost lost in the open space of the Dom Platz.

It was definitely Wollweber's day for glory. As soon as news of the battle in the Rathaus reached him and learning that Kastner was dead, he broke off his interrogation of Frau Lammers and leaving the Aegidii Barracks, he rushed straight to the Prinzipalmarkt and assumed command. He arrived to find a stalemate, for although the intruders were trapped on the upper floors, three separate attempts to dislodge them had all ended in failure.

The Haupsturmführer had ordered the fire brigade to produce an engine and there was some talk of using the extending ladder to get to the sloping roof where, after removing a number of tiles, it was proposed to break in through the ceiling. The Stadt authorities were, however, anxious to preserve an historic building from further damage and naturally were not in favour of the idea. It was Wollweber who first thought of negotiating a peaceful surrender and he sent for a loud-hailer. While they waited for the tannoy to arrive, the firing gradually died away and an unnatural silence descended on the council chambers.

The amplified voice which came booming up from below startled Ashby and, because the sound was distorted, he failed to understand a word and he waited to see if the message would be repeated.

Wollweber tried again. 'You are completely surrounded; if you surrender now you will be treated in accordance with the Geneva Convention.' He had no idea why he had used that particular phrase but it came rolling off his tongue and it did the trick.

Ashby said, 'We are British Commandos and I have a wounded man up here who is in need of urgent medical attention.'

'The sooner you surrender the sooner he'll be taken to a hospital.'

In his present mood, Wollweber was ready to promise anything if he could be sure of taking them alive. He waited expectantly to see what would happen next and after what seemed an age, a tall fair-haired man appeared at the top of the stairs and began to limp towards them with his hands held high above his head. Something like a collective sigh went up from the waiting storm-troopers and then the Englishman was among them and a rifle butt scythed through the air and smashed into his skull.

Wollweber was very annoyed about that and said so forcibly. As he sarcastically pointed out to the Haupsturmführer, it wasn't easy to question a prisoner while he was unconscious.

Kaltenbrunner had every reason to be satisfied with the way the affair had been settled, but there were still one or two loose ends which required his personal attention. This latest plot against the Reich had been conceived and executed by bungling amateurs, but in the present political climate, it was perhaps wiser to conceal the true nature of the incident. Goebbels would need some guidance, of course, but he was confident that the Minister of Propaganda and Enlightenment could produce an acceptable story which could be fed to the news agencies. It would also be prudent to arrest Osler without further delay, and the Foreign Ministry would have to politely inform Baron Pierre Damon that his presence in Germany was no longer acceptable.

With Kastner dead and the *Münster—Case Black* file quietly buried in the archives, there was no reason why anyone should connect him with the conspiracy. Wollweber would have to be rewarded in some way, but of course a medal was out of the question because the attendant publicity would be undesirable in the circumstances. On the whole, Kaltenbrunner thought it was probably safer to promote him and leave it at that.

The last chance of a negotiated peace had gone for ever and, in a way, they had that quixotic fool Lieutenant-Colonel Hasso Jurgens to thank for that. If he had not chosen to involve himself in the July Bomb Plot the finger of suspicion would never have been pointed at Gerhadt and Kastner's energies could have been directed elsewhere, in which case there was a chance, just a chance, that Lammers and his friends might have succeeded.

The light in his office was beginning to fail in the gathering dusk and he switched on the table lamp. The time was 1815 hours and the charade was almost over.

*

If Wollweber had had all the glory, then Cowper had had all the luck in the world. He'd ditched the truck, the grenades and his Schmeisser in a wood some three kilometres from the border before stealing a bicycle which had been left carelessly unsecured outside a Gasthof, and then, as calm as you please he'd simply ridden it into Enschede. He passed the customs and police post waving cheerfully to the sentry on duty and thirty minutes later he located the Zwinjnenberg Hotel. The Dutch Underground weren't exactly pleased to see him but after an intensive grilling, they accepted him for what he was—an Allied soldier on the run, and because he was hot they rapidly passed him on down the line.

On the night of Friday, 20th October, in a dismal low-lying area between Arnhem and Nijmegen known as the Island, Miles Cowper, in common with one hundred and forty officers and men of the 1st Airborne Division who'd been sheltered by the Dutch Underground following their defeat at Arnhem, was ferried across the Waal in a rescue operation nicknamed Pegasus I. On arrival at the first reception station he was given hot coffee and doughnuts in a field kitchen set up by the 101st United States Airborne Division.

As Stack had once observed, if Cowper happened to fall into a dungheap, he'd still come up smelling like a rose.

His hands were handcuffed behind his back and he sat on a low stool in a bare room, and there was a bandage around his head and a pigeon's egg above his right eye, and his lips were puffy and swollen and two teeth were already missing and Ashby knew that he might well lose some more before the night was out. The light was shining straight into his eyes and he couldn't see Wollweber, but he was there all right.

Wollweber said, 'I'll ask you just once more. I want the names and addresses...'

Ashby raised his head. 'I can give you my number, rank and name,' he said, 'and that's all.'

The length of rubber hose whistled through the air and struck him on the kneecap and the top of his head almost lifted off.

'We can keep this up all night if necessary,' Wollweber said brightly.

'Under the Geneva Convention I'm entitled...'

'You're not entitled to anything. You were captured in German uniform and we therefore have every right to shoot you out of hand.'

'And supposing you do,' said Ashby, 'where does that get you? Nowhere.'

'We might come to some arrangement if you were more co-operative.'

Ashby looked as though he was thinking it over and then he said, 'Can I have a cigarette?'

'A cigarette?'

'Yes, if we're going to talk, it will help me to concentrate.'

Wollweber snapped his fingers and one of the guards stuck a cigarette between Ashby's lips and lit it. 'All right,' he said, 'I'm waiting.'

'Get rid of the guards then.'

'What?'

'I'll talk to you but not with anyone else present.'

'What is this foolishness?'

'I'm not being foolish,' Ashby said obstinately. 'If you're really interested in what I have to say, you'll send the guards out of the room. After all, what have you got to worry about? I'm not likely to run away.'

Wollweber hesitated and then said, 'All right, but just remember this—they'll be waiting outside in the corridor and God help you if you try anything.'

Ashby waited until they were alone. He'd won the first round and it was important that with the opening of the second, he should hit exactly the right note.

'Do you carry any life insurance, Sturmbannführer? I know Kaltenbrunner does.'

Wollweber stood up and rounding the desk, moved into the light where Ashby could see him. 'Don't waste my time,' he said harshly.

'Kaltenbruner knows that Germany has lost the war. He's known it ever since Stalingrad and that's why he's been making overtures to us through people like Baron Pierre Damon.'

'You're lying.'

'You think so? If we didn't have his tacit support we wouldn't have lasted five minutes.'

'Now I know you're lying because it was he who warned

233

Oberführer Kastner that an attempt would be made on Bormann's life today.'

'So he got cold feet at the last minute.'

'I've had enough of this, I'm going to tell my assistants to beat a little sense into you.'

'Damon exists and you know it. Hold on to that.'

'It will give me a great deal of pleasure to have you shot.'

'And after the war you'd hang for it. You'll stand there with a black hood over your head, and your arms and legs will be pinioned and then they'll put a rope around that fat neck of yours. You think about it.'

'Under the Geneva Convention we have every right to ...'

'You won't have any rights, the loser never does, and you're going to lose this war, Sturmbannführer——?'

'Wollweber.' He hadn't meant to give his name but it just slipped out.

Ashby said, 'Do you know what a war criminal is, Wollweber?'

'I think so.'

'Well now, you don't sound very sure. Tell me, how many Jews have you sent to the concentration camps?'

'What?'

'One would be enough to get you hung, unless...'

'Unless what?'

'Unless you had someone like me to speak up for you.' It was out in the open now and he allowed time for Wollweber to digest all the implications. 'Although I can't give you the information you want,' Ashby said slyly, 'it must be quite obvious that Major Ottaway and I can only be of use to you if we're still alive when it's all over.' Ashby spat the cigarette from his mouth. 'You do see that, don't you?' he said.

Night had fallen on the city and the streets were cloaked in darkness. A policeman strolling through the Gruetgasse shone his masked torch into the side entrance of the Rathaus, satisfied himself that the broken door had been secured and then moved on. He stopped at the top of the Prinzipalmarkt and looked back at the council chambers and wondered at the mentality of those RAF terror fliers who had chosen death in preference to a prisoner of war camp. Somehow that story didn't ring true in his ears and he thought it would be interesting to know what really had happened inside that old building.

But he never would know. On Saturday, 28th October the Hall of Peace, in common with over eighty per cent of the old city, would be reduced to a pile of rubble.

Somewhere a clock started chiming the hour of midnight. The long day was over.

GERMANY

April 1945

'Just when we're safest, there's a sunset-touch,
A fancy from a flower-bell, some one's death,
A chorus-ending from Euripides,
And that's enough for fifty hopes and fears—
The grand Perhaps.'

ROBERT BROWNING—*Bishop Blougram's Apology*

20

GERHARDT LAY THERE in the dark listening to the distant rumble of artillery fire and although it was a comforting sound, he knew that by the time they arrived it would be too late. Wollweber had sent him to Berlin where he'd been held in the Prinz Albrechtstrasse while awaiting trial before the People's Court, but on 3rd February, '45, in the heaviest raid of the war, a bomb had struck the courtroom and Judge Roland Freisler had been killed. On the following day, Gerhardt, Lieutenant-General Graf von Macher and Colonel Vietinghoff had been transferred to the Flossenburg concentration camp.

As each day passed without a date for the trial being set, he had begun to hope that they had forgotten all about him. It was an unrealistic attitude to take but he'd heard of at least one case where this had actually happened and he told himself that as the war slowly drew towards its end, the administrative machine was bound to crack and fall apart. This illusion had lasted until 10th April when, in the camp laundry, he'd been hauled before a summary court martial, tried, found guilty and sentenced to death within the space of one hour.

He thought about Christabel and the children and wondered how they had been faring. Wollweber had told him that his wife had been sent to the Lehrterstrasse Prison in Berlin early in October and he knew that the Party had selected foster parents who could be relied upon to see that his children grew up to be good National Socialists. He'd tried to express his sorrow and regret in a letter which he hoped would reach them some day, but his prose had been stilted and he doubted if they would ever understand his motives.

He heard the bolts drawn back on his cell and throwing the blanket to one side, he stood up. There were two of them, hard-looking men who, having supervised a thousand executions, were used to this kind of thing.

Gerhardt said, 'Is it time?'

The Unterscharführer, a wall-eyed man of thirty with bad teeth, said, 'Take your clothes off, you're going to have a bath.'

Gerhardt obediently removed his dungarees and waited for the next order. After six months in the hands of the Gestapo and the SS, his pride and spirit had been completely broken, and when the wall-eyed man indicated that he should cross his hands behind his back, he did so without comment.

The cord bit into his wrists and then, naked, he was led out of the cell and across the yard towards the execution shed, and the first light of day was just beginning to show in the east, and the birds were beginning to chorus, and then he was inside the shed and his eyes strayed to the hooks set in the beam, and he watched the hangman attach a short noose to each one, and then the door opened again and there were von Macher and Vietinghoff marching stiffly between their escorts. And finally they stood there in line beneath the hooks and waited, knowing that at any moment the guards would lift them up one by one and slip a noose around each neck.

Christabel Gerhardt had lost track of time. She was no longer sure of the days but she thought it might be Sunday, 22nd April, and she knew that the end was near. Russian artillery had been systematically pounding the city for the past twenty-four hours and now the screeching banshee howl of the multi-barrelled rocket-firing Katushkas added to the appalling din. The bombardment did, however, have one beneficial effect, for it radically changed the attitude of the guards in the Lehrterstrasse who were now anxious to be on friendly terms with the prisoners with whom they were sheltering in the cellars.

Although she had been held in 'B' Wing with the other political prisoners, Christabel Gerhardt had never been sub-

240

jected to the same rigorous interrogation that she had received from Wollweber and not once during six months had anyone ever intimated that one day she would have to stand trial. It was almost as if they'd forgotten she existed and she was grateful for that small mercy. And now that it was almost over, it seemed there was every chance that she would be killed by a stray shell.

A man's voice said, 'Frau Gerhardt?'

She looked up into the face of an old man. 'Yes?' she said dully.

'You won't know me but my name is Ernst Osler and I was a friend of your husband's. I just wanted to say how sorry I was to hear of his death.'

'Thank you.'

'If there is anything I can do to help?'

'I don't think anyone can help us now.'

'You husband was a very brave man.'

'Yes?'

A hand reached out and patted her wrist. 'You mustn't despair,' Osler said gently. 'One of the guards told me that some of the prisoners were released this morning. Perhaps they will let you go.'

'I think that's rather unlikely, don't you?'

'We can but hope.'

'I try not to think about the children.'

'I know...'

'You see, the terrible thing is that I don't know where they are.'

Osler struggled to find some words which would be of comfort but the phrases sounded banal and meaningless in his ears and, embarrassed by his failure, he got up and moved away. He resolved that somehow he would find a way to help her.

For the first time ever, Johannes Lehr was glad to be a prisoner. If he'd been serving with his Teno battalion there was every chance that he'd now be in battle, crouching behind a street barricade armed with a Panzerfaust with which he would be expected to stop a tank at point-blank range. He'd heard that they'd called up the class of '29 and that even thirteen-year-olds were being pressed into service. Berlin was being defended by old men and children while those heroes

241

in SS uniform were summarily executing anyone who was suspected of being a deserter. It was being said by the guards that if you walked down the Charlottenburger Chausee you'd find a corpse hanging from every other tree. It was probably an exaggeration but he suspected that there was more than a grain of truth in the story.

He nudged Erhard Thierback in the ribs, pointed to Osler and said, 'What do you think that old fool's up to now?'

Thierback said, 'I don't know and I don't care. I regret the day that old goat walked into my shop. If it hadn't been for him, we wouldn't be in this mess.'

Lehr rubbed his chin thoughtfully. 'We had a nice racket going for us while it lasted.'

'You should have stuck to looting,' Thierback said bitterly. 'I said at the time it was a mistake to help someone disappear.'

'And you've been saying it ever since. Sometimes I think you're a bloody gramophone. Look at him, he's talking to another woman now.'

'Who is?'

'Osler. He's a bit long in the tooth for it, isn't he? Must be his second childhood.'

'There's no fool like an old fool,' said Thierback. He leaned back against the wall and closed his eyes.

Osler was back and there was an excited look on his face.

'I have something for you, Frau Gerhardt,' he whispered. He took hold of her right hand and pressed a slip of paper into the palm and closed her fingers around it. 'Don't look at it now, wait until I've gone.'

'What is it?'

'A release slip. When there is a lull in the shelling you can just get up and walk out of here a free woman.'

'Where did you get it?' she said breathlessly.

'From the wife of a Jehovah's Witness. She doesn't want it, her home is in Düsseldorf and she hasn't a hope of reaching it.'

'I must thank her.'

Osler shook his head. 'No,' he said, 'that would be unwise. She knows that you're grateful.'

'I don't know what to say...' Tears began to well in her eyes and she brushed them away.

Osler squeezed her hand again. 'I'm happy for you,' he said simply.

Two hours later, Christabel Gerhardt walked into the guard room on the main floor and took her place in the queue, and the man behind the desk didn't even look up when he stamped her release chit. She walked out into the street and although the immediate area was still being swept by mortar fire, she was deliriously happy.

As night fell on the doomed city, the sky was tinged with a red glow from the fires which were burning in every district, but in the cellar of the Lehrterstrasse Prison there was a feeling of mounting optimism. During the course of the afternoon at least twenty-one men and women had been released and rumour had it that more were to be freed before morning. And then, as if in answer to a prayer, a guard came into the cellar and began to read aloud from the list of names clipped to his millboard.

'Johannes Lehr ... Erhard Thierback ...'

And one by one they got to their feet and stood in line.

'Ernst Osler ... Julius Lammers ... Elena Lammers ...'

Five names and then five more—a communist, a Frenchman, two Ukrainian Poles and a corporal in the Wehrmacht.

Ten singled out from the rest and counted and led up to the security office to receive their personal belongings which had been taken from them when they were arrested—a cigarette case for one—a gold propelling pencil and fountain pen for Lammers—a lighter without a flint for Lehr and the Iron Cross Second Class for the soldier.

And then they were told to pack their things, and one of the guards who was quite drunk was laughing and joking with them and slapping them on the back, and they were like excited children at a birthday party but no one could see that it would end in tears.

And then they were taken out from the cellar into a hall which was in total darkness and presently a flashlight played on their faces and a hard voice said, 'Don't get any wrong ideas, you people are being transferred and we'll have to walk to the Anhalter Terminus.'

And then they were lined up in the street and it was raining hard and Lammers took off his jacket and placed it around his wife's shoulders, and then someone gave an order and the small column flanked by six men of the Waffen SS, set off in the direction of the Invalidenstrasse.

But when they reached the Invalidenstrasse they turned off the road and headed towards the bombed-out Ulap Exhibition Hall because the sergeant in charge said they were taking a short cut, and so they entered the skeleton of this massive building and stumbled over the rubble, and suddenly they were grabbed by the collar and stood apart from each other facing a brick wall, and they heard the bolts rattle and Elena started to cry.

And they died in a crash of gunfire, and then the execution squad marched away into the night and left them lying there in the rain—two Ukrainian Poles, one communist, a Frenchman, a corporal of the Wehrmacht, Ernst Osler, Johannes Lehr, Erhard Thierback, Elena and Julius Lammers.

They were a solid phalanx of between ten and twelve thousand men who, marching on parallel roads, were spread out over eighty square kilometres of the countryside. They were ragged, tired and hungry and they had been on the march for ten days, heading first in one direction and then turning back through almost a hundred and eighty degrees. Each day had brought different and conflicting orders, each day had seen them walking to yet another town as they crisscrossed the map of Germany. They lived off the land because the Wehrmacht was no longer able to feed them and when they passed through a village, it was as if a swarm of locusts had stripped it bare.

Guarded by less than a hundred men under the command of a Lieutenant-Colonel who'd lost an arm and the sight of one eye in the First World War, the POWs had achieved such a moral domination over their keepers that at times it was hard to say who were now the captives. With transport reduced to the absolute minimum, it was impossible to do anything for those who were sick or fell out on the line of march and by common consent they had to be left behind.

Five days previously at Grosse, north of the Elbe, they'd received an issue of Red Cross parcels on the basis of one between two men which they'd held in reserve, knowing that as word of their approach travelled ahead, the local inhabitants would endeavour to make sure that there was nothing left for them to steal. Now that this meagre supply had been exhausted, the distant rumble of gunfire in the west was the only thing that kept them going.

Ottaway marched in silence beside Ashby. That they were still alive on this day late in April was evidence of the miracle which, alone and unaided, Ashby had succeeded in working. He had shown a remarkable talent for blackmail, first with Wollweber and subsequently with the commandant of Sachsenhausen concentration camp who finally had been persuaded to arrange their transfer to a POW camp in exchange for a worthless affidavit which absolved him of all responsibility for the conditions which existed at Sachsenhausen. How any man could fondly imagine that this useless scrap of paper would protect him in the days to come was beyond Ottaway's comprehension, but with the imminent collapse of the Reich staring them in the face, it seemed that there were any number of petty officials only too anxious to obtain some tiny shred of evidence which purported to show that basically they were decent men at heart.

Ottaway said, 'I don't know whether my imagination is playing tricks with me or not but we seem to be moving away from the battle area. The artillery sounds fainter than it did an hour ago.'

'Perhaps it's just as well. I can't help thinking we'd be much safer if we stayed put and let the war come to us.'

'You surprise me, I thought you'd be eager to run into our people.'

Ashby stopped in his tracks and looked up into the sky. 'Listen,' he said, 'can you hear them?'

Ottaway squinted into the sun. 'I can't see them,' he said, 'they must be some way off but you can bet on it—they're ours.'

Ashby said, 'Let's hope they know we're on the same side.'

Before D-Day they'd busted trains, at Falaise it had been the turn of the Tigers, Panthers and SP guns but now with the Wehrmacht on its knees, it was open season for the hunters and provided the target was beyond the bombline laid down by 2nd Tactical Airforce, anything that moved was fair game. From above they saw three orderly columns moving on parallel roads and there was nothing to suggest that the target was other than a formed body of troops on the march. It was one of the fattest, most tempting strikes they'd come across and the squadron leader was in no doubt whatsoever, and he decided to take them from left to right so that the pattern of their attack would resemble a flattened letter S. He spoke tersely and his orders were simple and easily understood, and they came out of the sun losing height rapidly until all nine RAF Typhoon fighters were at tree-top level, and then one after the other they went down the column with machine-guns blazing, and eight made the pass before they discovered their error.

And when Ottaway crawled out of the ditch they were already climbing high into the sky, anxious to leave the scene of their hollow victory and the eighty-five men they had so wantonly killed. And still dazed, he looked round for Ashby and found him lying on his back in the middle of the road, and when he drew close he noticed that Ashby's lips were drawn back over his teeth in a ghastly caricature of a smile as if at the moment of death, he'd appreciated the final ironic twist.

And afterwards, Ottaway remembered searching through his pockets until he found a dog-end and he was still sitting there beside Ashby when the German commandant and the senior British officer arrived.

The Englishman said, 'Now come on, you can't sit there all day, we need your help to bury these men.'

Ottaway looked up. 'Is that a fact,' he said. 'And after we've buried these men, Brigadier, what happens then?'

The German commandant said, 'I have my orders, the march will continue.'

Ottaway stood up, dropped the cigarette-end on to the road and trod on it. 'We're not going anywhere,' he said quietly. 'We're staying here until they find us.'

'I don't think you quite understand the position, Major. As long as I'm in command...'

'There's a village a mile or two back down the road and we're going to relieve them of every white sheet they have...'

'Must I remind you that you are a prisoner ...'

'And then we're going to lay those sheets out on the ground so that if the planes do return they won't make the same mistake again...'

The Brigadier said, 'Now look here, old chap, Colonel Thadden has his orders and you can't expect him to . . .'

'And then we're going to send out recce patrols with orders to find and link up with the nearest Allied unit . . .'

'I am not prepared to put up with your insubordinate manner, Herr . . .'

'Major Ottaway. And you'll just have to get used to my insubordinate manner because you're finished. Do you understand that, Herr Oberstleutnant Thadden?' His voice rose to a shout and he grabbed the German by the lapels of his tunic. 'If, through your stupidity, we lose just one more man. I promise you I'll make it my business to see that you hang for it.' He pushed Thadden back. 'Now just do as I ask,' he said in a quieter tone of voice.

Less than eight hours later they passed into the hands of the 30th Infantry Division, 9th United States Army advancing on Madgeburg.

August 1972

> 'Go, and catch a falling star,
> Get with child a mandrake root,
> Tell me, where all past years are,
> Or who cleft the Devil's foot.'

JOHN DONNE (1571–1631)

21

Epilogue

TRUSCOTT RETIRED FROM the army in 1953 in the rank of Brigadier and emigrated to South Africa where he now lives in a spacious house on the outskirts of Durban. He confesses that he enjoys writing and receiving letters and because of this characteristic, he has stayed in close touch with friends and acquaintances with whom he has served over the years. Without his help it would have been almost impossible to trace many of the people who were involved in this story, and I would like to take this opportunity to express my gratitude for all the advice and assistance he so freely gave to me.

Cowper, too, stayed on in the army after the war and at one stage seemed destined for a brilliant career. The *London Gazette* shows that he was awarded a second bar to his Military Cross for, I quote: 'consistently displaying qualities of the highest leadership and bravery in the face of the enemy'. However, much of the citation deals with the hazardous nature of his escape through Holland, and it remains a curious fact that he was the only member of Force 272 to be decorated. He spent a year at the Staff College, Camberley in 1949 and after a tour of duty as GSO2 (Ops) in HQ BAOR, he served in Korea as a company commander from 1952 to 1953. He was promoted to Brevet Lieutenant-Colonel at the age of thirty-seven and returned to Camberley as an instructor.

Three years later while commanding his battalion in Aden, he was awarded the OBE in the Birthday Honours List and subsequently in 1960 he was made a temporary Brigadier and given a Territorial Army Brigade. Barely twelve months later, having married well, he retired from the army at the age of forty-three. He now runs a property development company which, for tax purposes, is registered in Liechtenstein and spends most of his time abroad in an expensive villa overlooking the sea at Cannes. His wife is the majority shareholder in the business, and they have two girls both of whom are at boarding school in England. Life appears to have been very good to him and he has few problems. He also has very few friends.

Dryland was unable to persuade Truscott that the interests of the army would be better served if he were given an immediate posting to South East Asia Command, in consequence he was still serving in England when Frank Cole returned from the war in May 1945 and found his wife huge with child. There was a rather messy divorce case but after the dust had settled, he and Laura Cole were married. One suspects that Dryland drifted into it and that Laura was the real driving force behind the match. Needless to say, he failed to enter the Diplomatic Service and he was also turned down for a regular commission. After an uncertain start in civilian life, he eventually found a niche in public relations, and was for some years a consultant with Hobkirk, Brewer and Bates until he left them in 1955 when he came into a little money. He and Laura decided to settle in Cyprus and they opened a supper club overlooking the harbour in Kyrenia. They could scarcely have chosen a more inopportune moment for such a venture and the EOKA terrorist campaign all but ruined them and they were extremely lucky to get anything at all for their business. They moved to Kenya where Dryland got a job managing the Reef Hotel at Malindi. One would like to record that he made a success of it, but it seems he started drinking heavily and in 1963, at the age of forty-five, he died of a coronary.

Katherine Ashby did not remarry. She inherited the farm at Market Weighton on the death of her parents and manages to run it successfully without a man about the house. She is still a handsome woman and looks far too young to be a grandmother. Jeffrey did not follow his father into the army but showed a bent towards the law and is now in partnership with two other solicitors whose offices are in Bowlalley Lane and the oddly named Land of Green Ginger in Hull. Elizabeth studied medicine at Guy's, married one year after qualifying and moved to New Zealand in 1969 with her husband and two children. Katherine tells me rather wistfully that they will be coming home again in 1975 for six months' leave.

Of the Germans, Ernst Kaltenbrunner was tried for war crimes at Nuremberg, found guilty and hanged on 16th October, 1946. Detective Emil Maurice survived the Battle of Berlin only to be drowned in the Spree River one night in November 1948 in what, as the police described it, were mysterious circumstances. Ursula Koch, the Gestapo agent who worked with Wollweber, also died violently on the night of 22nd/23rd January, 1951, but in this instance, there was no mystery surrounding her death. She had been living alone in a one-room flat in the basement of a bombed out tenement in Dortmund and had eked out a precarious living as a part-time cleaner. Police records show that between 1945 and 1950 she was convicted for drunken and disorderly behaviour on no less than fifteen separate occasions and on the night of 22nd January she had been drinking heavily in the Gasthof Struber. Although there were no witnesses to the accident, it appears that after leaving the Gasthof she must have staggered out into the main road which was badly lit, and was then knocked down and killed by a hit-and-run driver.

Christabel Gerhardt spent an eventful ten days sheltering in the Anhalter Terminus where she says the conditions were frightful. She admits however, that she was well treated by the Russian soldiers of the 8th Guards Army and she personally was not molested. She remained in the city until October and then managed to make her way to the west. The story of her efforts to find the children is a saga in itself but suffice to say she was reunited with her family on 25th November, 1945. It is somewhat ironic to record that her house in Langestrasse was requisitioned by the British Army and when eventually she returned to Iserlohn, she found that it was occupied by the family of a Major attached to the Allied Control Commission. She made strenuous and repeated efforts to get the requisition order rescinded but to no avail, and it was not until the spring of 1956 that she finally took repossession. Perhaps not unnaturally, she is still somewhat anti-British. On Saturday, 9th April, 1949, she married a widower by the name of August Sachs who has since made a fortune in ceramics. On meeting her for the first time, one is immediately aware of her immaculate appearance and careful grooming but although she is extremely polite, it was impossible for me to get close to her. I felt that, beneath the surface charm, there was a very hard, self-centred woman, and it soon became clear that she was reluctant to talk about her first husband. I was left with the distinct impression that her memories of Gerhardt are tinged with hatred.

Wollweber is still alive but is now almost senile. He was dragged before the de-nazification courts in 1953 and received a nominal prison sentence of two years of which he served eighteen months. He feels extremely bitter about this and blames Ottaway for not appearing in his defence, which is pretty rich when you consider his past conduct. On his release he moved to Thalkirchdorf in Bavaria, and you can find him at any time of the day or night in the Post Gasthof where he loves to watch his friends playing Skat. Occasionally, when he is half drunk, he is quite lucid and likes to boast of the old days, much to the embarrassment of the locals.

Baron Pierre Damon retired from the bank in 1964 at the age of sixty and now lives quietly in his house in Geneva. He is very touchy whenever the subject of his role in Operation Leopard is raised and it is quite apparent that he finds the whole affair exceedingly distasteful and resents the fact that Ashby made him look a fool. His one great passion is the Credit and Merchant Bank and he will talk for hours on that subject if you are foolish enough to listen to him.

Every story should have a happy ending and it is only fitting that Ottaway should supply it. He arrived back in England on 5th May, 1945, and immediately got in touch with Anne Bradley because, as he said later, he'd thought of no one else during his months of captivity. Between VE and VJ Day he first courted her, then married her and finally made her pregnant. They now have four children, all of them girls, two of whom, having married in their teens, have succeeded in making grandparents out of Jack and Anne. Ottaway did not return to teaching after the war but instead became a career diplomat, although to judge from his postings which have included South Vietnam, Cambodia, Laos, Guatemala, Nicaragua and the Dominican Republic, I'm inclined to think he is with the CIA. He is now serving with the United States Embassy in Paris and we often met during the summer of 1972. Both he and Anne look absurdly young for their age and it is quite obvious that they are devoted to each other, which in this day and age is really something.

There remains the mystery of why the Russians saw fit to transmit that fatal message to the 'Choro' Group knowing that it was bound to be intercepted and decoded, and Ottaway has an intriguing theory which is certainly in keeping with the known facts. Throughout the war, the Soviet High Command was informed of any change in the order of battle on the Eastern Front within twenty-four hours of the decision being made in Rastenburg. If Bormann was the spy at Rastenburg, then in the autumn of 1944, it was certainly in the interests of the Russians to ensure that he remained alive and well.

CLIVE EGLETON